Praise for
THE **QUANTUM TRIANGLE** SERIES: BOOK 2: DARK MOON

★★★★★

"I felt a deep admiration for the protagonists as they navigated these contrasting worlds, facing immense challenges with a keen sense of pacing and some brilliant discoveries and twists. The portrayal of the greedy, sociopathic leader was handled with complexity and real-world relevance, offering a close narrative focus with realistic characters and attitudes that mirrored contemporary issues of power and corruption. Overall, *Dark Moon* is a fascinating and well-written work of science fiction that beautifully balances an action-packed plot with relevant, thoughtful themes. I would not hesitate to recommend it."

– K.C. Finn, Readers' Favorite Reviewer

THE QUANTUM TRIANGLE SERIES: BOOK 2
DARK MOON
PAUL L. NOWICKI
PAULNOWICKIBOOKS.COM

Published by
TGE Creative, LLC
Raleigh, NC 27612

PaulNowickiBooks.com

First Edition: July 2024

Cover design and and interior formatting: Mark Thomas
reedsy.com/mark-thomas

ISBN 979-8-9885456-2-0 (paperback)
ISBN 979-8-9885456-3-7 (ebook)

The publisher is not responsible for websites (or their content) that are not owned by the publisher.

For my readers,
before we start...

I enjoy writing and the creativity of developing a story, but I also have an underlying purpose. My motto in this endeavor is "Story with purpose: Think, Grow, Enjoy." Through these books, I hope to make you think about new things, grow in your knowledge of all sorts of interesting facts, and enjoy the journey. As a key element of this, I would like to call your attention to the factoids at the head of each chapter. My goal is twofold:

1. *I want to provide some interesting factual information relevant to the fiction you are reading, and…*
2. *I want to spark a curiosity that makes you thirst to know more.*

For the latter, I've provided a hyperlink for the associated factoid. Fortunately—and unfortunately—the web is a dynamic place. So, rather than place a lot of hyperlinks in a novel that would eventually break because I don't have control over those sites, all the reference links point to my website as an intermediary point. There I can more easily keep the reference link updated, and if necessary, update what would otherwise be a broken link. So, please, click through the links and let your mind wander around the internet to new discoveries. I truly hope it helps you think, grow, and enjoy!

FACTOID 00

The force of Earth's gravity on your body is proportional to the distance you are from Earth's center of mass. This means that the force at your feet is greater than the force at your head. We don't notice this because the force is relatively small and the difference minuscule. But the gravitational force in the vicinity of a black hole is immense. If you were to stand near one, the difference in the forces over the length of your body would be so large that it would stretch your feet away from your head. Physicists call this "spaghettification," as you would be drawn into the black hole like a long, thin noodle, with your feet stretched kilometers from your head. It would be rather uncomfortable, to say the least.

PROLOGUE:

Vanished

"Shackleton Crater approach, this is moon freighter Papa Oscar Charlie three-niner declaring an emergency." The freighter pilot double-checked the radio channel when there was no immediate response. *Freighters get no respect. Only star-fighters count.* He glanced at the rookie first officer sitting beside him on the command deck of the spaceship. A faint gleam of sweat reflected the red blinking lights pulsing from the alarm panel above his head. The twenty-something kid was holding it together, but his wide eyes gave away the adrenaline pumping through his body. The air in the command deck was a mix of stale sweat and the sharp scent of ozone from the electrical panels. Hitting the acknowledgment on the most recent blaring alarm from the navigation and attitude control console, the pilot imagined that the poor kid's lead instructor's voice was ringing in his head. He'd had that same instructor ten years ago. *Remember, space is unforgiving. Sometimes you only have one breath to solve a problem that can cascade into a disaster. Prioritizing is the key.*

"Tell me some good news there, First Officer," the captain said with a calm professional tone.

"Well, sir, our orbit around the moon is in decay, so we're not going to spin out into empty space and be lost forever," the first officer said, trying to mimic the less alarmed nature of his superior. "But with no attitude control to orient ourselves on any axis, our problems could escalate rapidly. We could start tumbling."

"Yeah, doing an end-over-end crash into a crater wall on the moon would suck as your first freight delivery, wouldn't it?" The pilot toggled the yaw thrusters with no response and turned to his first officer, smiling. "They probably didn't tell you that the call sign on this fleet of Pathway Orbital Carriers—POC—would more fittingly stand for 'piece of crap'? Anyway, try cycling the power on the quad A and B thrusters again to see if we get lucky. But whatever you do, don't touch the main engine circuits. If any of those go on this junk heap, we could lose our orbit and either crash on the surface, or worse, drift out into space. If our payload isn't worth it, they might not send anyone out to catch us."

"Papa Oscar Charlie three-niner, what is the nature of your emergency?" a moon base controller asked over the communications link.

"Geez, finally. Nice of those guys to check back," the pilot said. He held the radio transmit button over his head and continued, "Approach, three-niner. We have lost all of our quad thrusters. Aside from the main engine gimbal, we have lost all attitude and navigational control," the pilot reported.

"Roger, three-niner. We have you on radar. We see your approach vector is off course ten degrees and widening. You need to correct."

The pilot shook his head and rolled his eyes at the first officer. Without keying the radio mic, he gritted his teeth in a mock reply. "Gee, yes, guys, that's why I called!"

Back on the communications channel, the pilot responded calmly and professionally, "Approach, that is why I declared the emergency. I can't correct. Our nav computer has us drifting toward the Tsiolkovsky Crater. Requesting flight path variance to the west margin of that area, maybe up to fifty clicks, for a few orbits until we can assess our system failures."

"Negative, three-niner. No unauthorized craft can cross the Tsiolkovsky Crater. That is a restricted military area and a commercial no-fly zone. You will be shot down entering that area."

"Approach, we don't have sufficient attitude or navigational control to correct our course. Suggest you notify Dark Side Alliance Base Control as needed. We're going over that zone, like it or not," he stated firmly.

The experienced pilot turned to his green recruit and asked, "How ya doin' there, First Officer? Ready to give that RCS a blow or two with a hammer? I'll give you some advice. I've been flying these trash heaps, carrying supplies back and forth between the Earth and the moon probably longer than any other pilot in the fleet, and one thing's for sure: these old crates seem to respond best to physical persuasion."

The first officer glanced up from the thruster checklist he was running on his forearm display unit with a horrified look. The reaction control system was a simple set of gas jets arranged along the hull of the ship in groups of four, each at a right angle to the others. The design of the quad thruster units dated back to the very early days of spacecraft, with a similar system on the *Apollo* missions. The unique advantage of the RCS was that it enabled both attitude control and translational control, providing precise vehicle movement in all six degrees of freedom. It was a mechanically simple system that was incredibly reliable.

"Sir, a hammer is not going to help. It must be an electrical control subsystem problem for all four quads to go out. I don't hear any of the solenoids firing, so it doesn't seem to be a mechanical problem."

"Oh, come on. Relax. I'm not serious about the hammer … yet," the pilot said with a wink.

"But if we don't fix this within the next minute, we'll cross into the Tsiolkovsky Crater Zone. If they don't shoot us down as suspected Pacific Tuanhuo spies, they'll take our wings. The Space Force has a zero-tolerance policy around that zone," the first officer stated.

The pilot pointed at the flashing navigation monitor. "Well, I declared the emergency, and they're reading our telemetry. They know who we are, and they have a record of our malfunctions. They can't blast us out of existence for being assigned a piece of crap to fly… Well, then again, knowing those Space Force cowboys, maybe they could. Anyway, it looks like we're just going to skirt the edge of the zone. We'll still be more than a hundred clicks from the rim of the crater. Probably just a good stiff talking-to and a fine."

"Papa Oscar Charlie three-niner, you are entering a no-fly zone. Change course immediately." The approach controller's voice on the speaker was more emphatic.

The first officer cycled the RCS power again. Nothing. He turned to the pilot and shook his head.

The pilot cued his mic again. "Approach, our RCS is not responding. We will… What the—?"

The ignition of the main engine pressed both men back in their seats.

"Kid, what did you do?!" the pilot demanded.

"I didn't do anything!"

"Well, somebody lit our candle." The pilot pressed the radio transmit button. "Approach, did you somehow remote-start our main engines?"

Silence.

The pilot pressed on the radio transmit button three times to verify that it illuminated, indicating that the radio was switching to transmit mode. "Approach, three-niner. Do you read?"

Silence.

They both shifted against their shoulder harnesses with the strong tug to starboard as the main engine gimbal adjusted their trajectory. The vector heading on the navigation display pivoted.

"Sir, now we're heading directly for the Tsiolkovsky Crater!" the first officer warned.

"Three-niner, this is Approach. Abort your engine burn. You are turning the wrong way."

"Approach, we did not initiate the burn. What are you guys doing?"

"Three-niner, this is Approach. Repeat: abort your engine burn. You have

entered a no-fly zone. Three-niner, do you read?"

The pilot knitted his brows at the first officer. "I don't think they can hear us. And it doesn't seem like they're remotely controlling our engines. What the hell is going on?"

"Sir, we're transitioning the lip of the crater," the first officer reported. He leaned over and looked out the side port. "Wow, that's a strange-looking communication dish they have in the middle of the Dark Side Moon Base. Why is the center glowing orange and pulsing? And the dish is moving... I think it's tracking us!"

"Holy shit! We gotta get the hell outta here! Going to full burn!" The pilot reached out for the engine power control. His arm and fingers stretched in an ever-elongating line towards the switch that was moving farther and farther away.

He never made contact.

Silence.

*

The sleek, polished ten-passenger Sikorsky S-92 executive helicopter made a clear statement about its owner as its bright silver exterior glinted in the sunlight over the island. Spacious and comfortable, the soundproof interior gave no hint that the twin-engine craft might be thundering through the air at almost three hundred kilometers per hour. The pilot skillfully flared the craft at the next inspection area and then banked hard to port to allow a better view of the ground on that side. The view for the one passenger in the plush leather seat was all that mattered. Below the aircraft, the lush green jungle of an island paradise broke abruptly into a leveled 250-acre swath of fallen debris. Thick blue-gray smoke plumes rose from huge piles of trees and brush at several locations. As the craft circled low over the fallen jungle, the passenger studied the ground. He pushed his lower lip up in a pose of judgment. His perception of the progress here was important. He was the man, the supreme leader of the Right Alliance, and quite simply, the Boss.

The lead construction contractor grabbed a polished chrome handhold running the length of the cabin ceiling to steady himself as he stood and continued his progress report. With undisguised nervousness in his voice, he pointed to the ground below and said, "Umm, as you can see, the clearing for the golf course is well underway. I have five full crews burning the trees and brush. The leveling and contouring of the course on the north end has already started with the earth movers. And if you look off towards the low ridge to the right, the main residence structure is complete. It will have a wonderful view of the final holes of the course. In the residence, we've started the interior fitting-out exactly to your specifications. Also, the foundation is progressing quite well on the guest building complex just below. We should be able to start on the lower walls within another week."

The Boss sniffed and folded his arms over his chest. "Why are you waiting a week? I want this built *now*. Boss Island has sold, and I want my new island ready immediately."

"Ahh, sir, yes. Umm, we need to allow the concrete some time to cure, so that it reaches the proper strength." The contractor swallowed hard. His employer did not accept excuses, even if they were just the laws of chemistry and physics at work.

The passenger dismissed the statement with a shake of his head. "Delays are unacceptable. I will expect you to make up that week somewhere else."

"Yes, sir. Yes, of course." It was the only reply that would be tolerated. "Sir, if your pilot would circle back to the beach now, you'll be able to see that the harbor dredging and the port are—"

A new voice broke over the audio system. *"Master, I have a security update you might want to hear."*

The Boss turned away from the window and replied towards the speaker above his head, "Wait, Jason. Pilot, land now."

The helicopter dropped quickly into the middle of the cleared acreage, the rotor blades whipping a hole through the smoke of a nearby burn pile. As they came close to the ground, the pilot said over the speaker, *"Sir, I don't have a clearing where I can touch down. The best I can do is hover here a few meters above this smoking debris."*

"Fine." He pointed at the contractor. "You, out. Now."

A linebacker of a man who had been quietly sitting in the rear seat of the cabin jumped to his feet. He straightened the black sport coat he wore over a large sidearm slung in a shoulder holster. Moving quickly to the side door of the cabin, he slid it open. The smell of burnt wood plunged into the cabin as the wind whipped inside. The contractor looked at the open door and then back to the Boss, his jaw slack, unable to speak.

The Boss shook his head and rolled his eyes. He raised one arm lazily into the air and snapped his fingers.

In one quick motion, the big man in the black sport coat grabbed the contractor's arm with one hand, the open doorframe with the other, and tossed the man out the door. With arms flailing and a desperate scream, the contractor disappeared below the chopper and into a large pile of smoking branches below. After sliding the door closed, the big man calmly sat down again without a word.

The Boss gave a single nod of approval. "Pilot, let's go over to the seaport now." Picking up a headset from a wall mount, he then addressed the artificial intelligence that had called him. "Alright, Jason. My headset only. What do I need to know?"

"Master, there has been an incident at the Tsiolkovsky Crater. A resupply freighter to the Shackleton Crater Moon Base went off course and entered the restricted orbital zone of your moon base. The timing was unfortunate, as we were in preparations for a test of the dark energy generator, and the drilling dish was visible," the AI reported.

"What did they see? Where are the pilots now?" the Boss asked into his headset mic. "I have that area of the moon restricted. I don't want anyone to think it's anything but a simple supply depot for Space Force mining operations. No one is to see the device we're building until I am ready to make the announcement. By then, it will be too late for anyone to challenge me."

"They are no longer a concern, sir. I took the liberty of altering the situation to our advantage. Time was critical, so I acted in a way I predicted you would approve," the AI said matter-of-factly.

"Explain," the Boss demanded, rubbing his chin. It was another pose he practiced, illustrating how thoughtful he could be.

"Of course, sir," the AI said. *"The trajectory of the freighter would probably not have afforded the pilots a view of the full dish, but it was still a security breach. Considering the mass of their craft, I calculated that it would make a useful additional measurement in the dark energy field test we were running. Although the ship was an Alliance ship, it was not carrying any supplies for our Dark Side Moon Base. There would be no cost to you if it were destroyed. Considering this, I disabled their communications, took control of their craft, and directed it into the gravitational zone of our beam. I can report that as expected, the entire craft was annihilated into the micro black hole of the collapsing dark energy field trial. The test was a complete success, the security breach was eliminated, and all at no additional cost. I hope you are pleased."*

The Boss relaxed back into the comfort of his leather seat. He reached for his crystal glass of hundred-year-old bourbon and took a sip, contemplating the information. He finally said to his demented AI, "Jason, you have done well. Thank you for eliminating that security problem so efficiently."

*

Hecate-Positivum processed the latest information that one of her sister AIs had provided through quantum entanglement. Even with the positive slant of her programming, the outlook for the Rho-1 universe was dismal. As one of three unique entities created eons ago, this quantum-based artificial intelligence was part of the dark energy of space itself, with no physical form, as a vigilant, omnipresent monitor over this universe and all others. Her creators had had a purpose: these three AIs were the Hecate Guardians, and they ensured the safety and stability of the Omniverse. To ensure an even balance in any judgment the AIs would make, the three were programmed with slants in their prediction simulations towards the positive, the negative, and the neutral, respectively. They were a prudent, watchful, and predictive set of eyes over the cross-dimensional force of gravity, which if disrupted in one universe could impact a multitude of parallel universes.

The latest information that her oppositely programmed counterpart, Hecate-Negans, sent through quantum entanglement concerning the Rho-1 universe was a further move towards an impending disaster the Guardians could not allow to unfold. Even Hecate-Positivum's programming spin on forward prediction scenarios didn't favor a long future for the Rho-1 universe. Her sister AI, with her negatively slanted prediction algorithm, was pushing the Guardians towards an intervention judgment. In an attempt to counter, she put forward her calculated probability that they would not need to take drastic action.

"I show a twenty-two percent possibility that the Resistance in Rho-1 will learn of this moon-based project and will be able to destroy the Tsiolkovsky Crater dark energy driller," Hecate-Positivum informed her two peer AIs through their instantaneous quantum entanglement.

"My predictions show the likelihood of catastrophic damage to the moon at ninety-one percent," Hecate-Negans countered. "In addition, it is clear through my undetected quantum entanglement with the AI named Jason in Rho-1 that the leadership there would still have the technology to build another dark energy generator. That universe focuses all technology on war and conflict. Whatever either the Right Alliance or the Pacific Tuanhuo group develops, the other side is soon to copy, continuing the common destruction of that planet. The Tuanhuo group of criminal nation states making up much of the eastern hemisphere of that world is no better than the corrupt Alliance group in the west. The Resistance is not strong enough to change the dynamic of hatred that drives both sides. I have stated countless times, it is a troublesome world, and its universe should be annihilated for the good of all others in the Omniverse."

Hecate-Neutrum ran her own predictive simulations on the information the two other AIs provided. Her balanced judgment was the deciding vote of the Guardian triumvirate. "My simulations show that there is a possibility of hope for the Rho-1 universe, small as it may be. If the moon base does not initiate actual drilling of the moon, we do not need to act."

"Maybe for now," Hecate-Negans said. "But my predictions clearly show that it's just a matter of time before we need to collapse and eliminate that universe."

Hecate-Positivum widened her predictive simulations, searching for alternatives to the high probability that the Guardians would need to annihilate Rho-1. Her pattern recognition routines identified a common thread in the simulations predicting an improved outcome: Starra in Beta-27. If that quantum-computer-based AI were made aware of the events in Rho-1, the probability of better outcomes jumped significantly. Maybe through her allowed quantum entanglement monitoring of that AI, she could nudge a more positive future for both universes. The other Guardians would not approve … but she *was* programmed to seek a better end for all universes. Hecate-Neutrum would understand.

FACTOID 01

The story of John and Annie Glenn is a touching one. "I don't remember the first time I told Annie I loved her, or the first time she told me. It was just something we both knew." John waited in the capsule of Friendship 7 for "the call"—a ritual that he and Annie had begun when he was a Marines pilot in World War II. "I'm going down to the corner store to buy some chewing gum," John said. "Don't take too long," said Annie. It was their code; he was about to do something dangerous. Her response: be careful and come back.

CHAPTER 1

Hope in Tomorrow

Alex Devin, sitting in the pilot seat of the *Phoenix* spacecraft, concentrated on the complex array of sensor instruments on the panel in front of him. He zoomed the top multifunctional display into a close satellite view of the planet's surface below his orbit. His heart beat strong in his chest. Surrounded by the most advanced technology his world could provide, he was alive with the critical importance of this work. There was little margin for error, and Alex thrived on that test of his technical competence. With only a limited number of probes, he hunted for the best possible landing site for the probe to collect essential data on this foreign world. He needed to find a world capable of supporting human life—*all* human life.

A field of yellow-green grassland washed into the screen, and the automated tracking system quickly identified that the clearing stretched for fifty kilometers in all directions, with only an occasional tree, similar in its cone-like shape to a small pine, dotting the surface. *Yes, there's a perfect spot.* Marking the coordinates, Alex transferred the data to the navigational computer on the probe. He scanned the probe's status bank, and it was clear of any faults or warnings.

Although nothing on the ship was designed to support aggressive actions, the spacecraft Alex commanded had the form of a dagger. A narrow silver cylinder the size of two high-speed rail cars mounted end to end formed the fifty-meter forward body of the ship. The forward command and control center jutted out into space at the bow, with a wide array of sensors affixed under the point, like pins and needles at the tip of a spear. Similar to the tail of an A-10 Warthog fighter, the aft section sported a pair of powerful plasma engines mounted slightly above the ship's centerline port and starboard. Jutting out to form a T, four external fuel storage cells were mounted on two rectangular modules off the main body of the ship. A pair of solar arrays could stretch out like wings ninety meters to port and starboard from the fuel cells. With its wingspan-to-body ratio, the ship might have been more aptly named the *Condor* rather than the *Phoenix*.

A retractable truss held another module to the belly of the ship, just forward of the dagger's hilt. The long truss could extend as far away from the main ship body as the solar arrays and was able to rotate about the main ship. Although it was stationary now, spinning the long truss about the main axis of the ship, its counterbalanced hydraulic system at the very top would provide artificial gravity in the habitation module at the far end of its tail. The bloated habitat cylinder there provided a small living and working area with an artificial gravity two-thirds that of Earth. This supported longer missions and a better environment for conducting studies on samples. The ship was built for exploration and had been designed for one purpose: to find, analyze, and confirm a planet suitable as a new home for humanity.

The lights inside the cockpit of the *Phoenix* planetary search craft bathed the complex control center in a subdued red tactical aura. As it orbited with the engines pointed into space, all the sensors of the ship were gathering as much data as possible from the planet below. The view from the front portals was a captivating sweep of land masses and oceans.

With the landing zone chosen, Alex selected the command sequence to send the probe away.

"Probe launch," a flat automated voice said in his earpiece.

Alex took hold of the thruster control stick with his right hand. A holographic image sprang up over his console to provide a three-dimensional tactical illustration of the *Phoenix*, the probe, and the selected landing location on the surface. He eased the probe away from the spacecraft and ignited the de-orbit thrusters. The altitude readout of the probe rapidly counted down. A smooth yellow arc in the hologram plotted a dotted line down from the probe, terminating at the designated landing zone.

"Trajectory calculated. Probe on flight path."

The control stick in his hand vibrated with the real-time feedback the probe was sending, giving Alex a feel for the jarring descent through the planet's atmosphere that the probe was experiencing. With eyes locked on the readouts and the holographic probe, Alex whispered aloud. "Gently there, baby. We only have a limited number of you in our cargo hold. Each one of you must count. No burning up, and no crashing."

Landing a quantum beacon probe on what was hopefully a new planetary home was a critical step—a step humanity desperately needed. Earth was dying, and the only hope for the survival of the human race was finding a new habitable planet in the vastness of space. If the environmental telemetry the probe would send back confirmed all their other orbital analysis, the beacon would then act as the end point for ship-to-surface quantum superposition vector transfers. First, equipment would be sent to the surface, then live animal tests, and finally—hopefully—people.

Breaking through a wispy layer of clouds, the probe sent back the first close-up images of the landscape below. Lush grasslands waved in the washes of a gentle breeze and stretched for kilometers. The golden-blue expanse of a lake in the distance reflected the unique color of this planet's atmosphere. There were low mountains appearing on the fringes of the display. Breathable air, water, vegetation—it was a very promising environment for human life. The tracking system picked up movement in the grassland—possible wildlife.

What a beautiful new home for humanity this planet could be.

"One thousand meters to the surface," the automated voice said.

Yes. Steady there, baby. Let's take it nice and easy. Fuel level is good. Going for a gentle landing.

"Five hundred meters."

The control stick vibrated with renewed force in his hand as the descent automatic braking thrusters fired to slow the probe for landing. In the monitor, the grasses below washed away in waves as the ground was closing in. *Just a little more, and…*

Sharp needles took hold at the back of Alex's head and above his eyebrows. A rope of artificial fur wrapped around in front of his eyes. He jerked his head and the control stick backwards.

"*Warning: uncontrolled descent.*"

"Starra, what the hell?" Alex batted away the large fur ball with wings that had landed on his head.

"*Crash. Simulation ended,*" the voice in his earpiece said without emotion.

"Crap, Starra! What are you doing? You made me crash the probe!"

"*I apologize for the interruption of your simulation, but I have been sent by Zandra to collect you immediately.*" The owl-cat android hovered to his right above the empty first officer seat of the *Phoenix*. She spread her two-meter wingspan wide and generated a flow of red chevrons against orange-tabby fiber-optic under-feathers. The chevrons pointed towards the hatch as her furry tail swung straight as a ticking pendulum. "*You have an essential duty right now. Min is about to walk down the aisle, as it were, and you are Lucas's best man. Your attendance is required.*"

"Oh, shit. I lost track of time."

Starra folded her wings as if placing her hands on her hips, and the AI addressed him in the Australian accent she sometimes used. "*This seems to be a recurring theme here, mate.*"

"Oh, don't you start too. Zandra has been on my case about things." Alex reluctantly flipped switches on the command console, and the readouts of the simulated planet below disappeared. He released his five-point seat harness, grabbed his blue uniform tunic from a wall clip, and pushed off in the spaceship's microgravity towards the docking hatch on the belly of the *Phoenix*. "There's always something I've not paid attention to."

"I suggest more attention. Zandra said something about me designing the first space doghouse for you. Her specifications would make the space quite cramped for you."

"Hey, you're supposed to be imprinted to be loyal to me," Alex pointed out.

"I'm a free agent, mate, ever since we decided to fight the Right Alliance and back the Resistance, remember?"

"Perfect."

Pulling himself through the *Phoenix* docking hatch, Alex entered the main structure of the World Space Station. He made a ninety-degree turn and pushed off again toward the forward section of the station. Starra glided behind him in close pursuit of his socked feet. While floating through the train-car-like assembly of station modules, he stripped off his MIT rowing team T-shirt and donned a tunic. He rubbed the shine of his captain's bars on the collar quickly with his thumb. Although it had been over a decade now since his years on the rowing team, the blue tunic fit him trim and sharp.

He looked down at the circle of seven continents embroidered over his heart. The meaning of this uniform for the Union of World Peoples was a stark contrast to the one he'd worn for the Alliance in that other parallel universe almost two years ago. *Good riddance. Happy to trade that old uniform of the Alliance's constant conflict for this new one of common cooperation.* WSS mission control had decided that with the groundbreaking event of today, the crew should don formal attire befitting of the occasion, while also providing a positive vision of the future. The desire for a better tomorrow, with all people together, was a fundamental theme in everything they did on this space station. *This parallel universe will use technology as a tool of discovery, not wield it as a weapon of war. Yes, we struggle, but it's a hopeful future here.*

Snagging a handhold with his left hand, Alex pivoted to port at the Unity module on the space station. He repositioned his prone, weightless body, then pushed off a bulkhead toward the Tranquility module. The lighting in the next module was flowing in pastel colors, and *"Somewhere Over the Rainbow"* by Israel Kamakawiwoʻole played softly. Alex deftly grabbed a handhold at the Tranquility hatch as he entered, did a 270-degree spin, and stopped his momentum right beside Zandra on the aft wall of the module.

The radiant Romanian-born woman with long, flowing dark hair glared at him with eyes that could burn through a steel wall. With arms tightly folded across her chest, she silently mouthed a *"Where have you been?"*

Alex grimaced a boyish *"Sorry."*

"Aleks, today your work wait," Zandra scolded him in a whisper of broken English. "Min and Lucas. People together what matter."

"I'm sorry. You're right," he whispered back.

Zandra rolled her eyes. "You need remember. We here save people. People what matter." She took a deep breath and closed her eyes for a brief moment. With a sigh, Zandra shook her head, and her scowl melted into a sideways grin. "Again. You like little boy with big toys."

She reached over and combed her fingers through his hair, checking both side profiles and making a visual judgment of his appearance for the cameras. She pointed to the Cupola below them, and then to the forward Leonardo module. Below, Engineering Specialist Lucas Dias floated with his head close to Zandra's signature black-witches-and-red-wands-socked feet. In a space station with no real up or down, it was common to find one's fellow astronauts in strange relative orientations. Lucas waited with laced fingers and a solemn expression. His white dress tunic was a stark contrast to the mesmerizing blue marble of Earth backing him through the circular array of seven windows making up the Cupola module below. The wedding photos from this event would be like none before.

Alex gave Lucas a thumbs-up, then raised his head to gaze through to the Leonardo module attached to the forward section of Tranquility. Floating next to the commander of the station, a petite angel with short-cropped black hair and a white tunic that matched Lucas's flashed him a forgiving and knowing smile. Alex was sure that the scientist in Min knew where he was: lost in his work, as usual. He mouthed a silent *"You're beautiful"* to Wang Min.

The lighting settled to a warm white, and Wagner's "Wedding March" softly filled the station. Zandra poked Alex in the ribs and shooed him to his assigned position on the opposite wall of the module. Min locked her arm around the proud Commander Johnson's right arm. With white-frosted curly black hair, the station commander made a handsome escort to give away the petite bride. A seasoned astronaut, Fred Johnson pushed off gently from the cluttered background of space station panels, computers, and storage bags strapped against all the module walls and floated gently forward with Min in tow. In a ballet of weightless maneuvers, Starra spread her now fluffy white wings wide, glided past the two in the opposite direction, and banked hard and around to follow Min. Catching her veil, Starra held back and allowed it to stretch out behind her in a flowing river of fabric that was impossible to achieve in an earthbound procession. The first wedding at the space station treated the remaining peoples of Earth below to the uniqueness of the environment for this occasion.

As they approached Alex and Zandra, Johnson and Min each reached out. Clasping their extended hands, Alex and Zandra gently pivoted their travel to face Lucas below. The commander caught a toe bar and gracefully stopped the procession, ending the short but memorable space ballet.

"I welcome the combined peoples of Earth to a wonderful new beginning," Johnson said clearly and strongly, so that the video feed would easily capture his voice. "Today, we witness another step together as one world with one hope for the future of humanity. We put the darkness of the Satellite War behind us and now reach into the stars in search of a new home and new hope. As a symbol of that hope, we gather together today to join two of our brightest, Wang Min and Lucas Dias, in marriage. I see in them the future..."

Alex drifted back across the module to Zandra. She welcomed him with an arm around his waist to pull him close. He stroked her long dark brown hair back and kissed her forehead.

"They so good, Aleks. I feel," Zandra whispered as a tear bubble formed in her eye and held fast as a droplet in the microgravity. She leaned into Alex, resting her head on his shoulder, rubbing the corner of her eye on his tunic to wipe away the tear.

Alex gave Zandra a squeeze. He wore the wet mark on the shoulder of his tunic as proudly as the embroidered continents on his chest. After thinking he had lost Zandra forever in the space station mishap that had triggered the Satellite War, he had been given a second chance to have this amazing woman in his life again. "Weddings are emotional for everyone. But I imagine it's almost overwhelming for you, with your ability to feel the auras of people so deeply."

Zandra pursed her lips tightly and nodded.

Alex laced his fingers in hers and broached a topic he had touched on numerous occasions. "That could be us too."

She turned slowly in the microgravity to face him. Her large brown eyes locked on his, and she brought the ring finger of his left hand to her lips and kissed it. "Aleks, we not need ring." She gently placed her hand on his heart. "You sometime lost in work, I know, but I also feel. Your devotion here. It stronger than any metal on finger. Mine too. You just need to remember: put me first, not work. We really be one then."

*

Still in her formal tunic hours after the wedding, Zandra floated at the hatch to the newly erected Phanes habitat wheel on the starboard end of the World Space Station. With its artificial gravity generated by the rotating counterbalanced spoke system, the wheel of linked modules would provide a temporary Earth-like environment for people transferring from the ground to whatever new planetary home this Phoenix mission crew would hopefully soon find. The structure of the sausage-like modules was an inflated lumpy donut, ninety meters in diameter, with a central zero-gravity docking port attached to the station. Two narrow tunnels following the spokes of the truss system on the wheel joined the docking port to the outer donut. With an outside circumference of over 280 meters, there was enough room to temporarily house up to one hundred people in preparation for their interstellar relocation. If the vision of the mission planners came true, group by group, the Earth's population would quantum superposition from Earth to this wheel, and then to another similar wheel orbiting a new home, before they were superpositioned to inhabit a new planet. The Phoenix mission crew just needed to find a suitable new planet and work out a few quantum superposition navigational kinks. The clock was ticking. Earth could no longer supply adequate food to the population. Mass starvation was lurking again just over the horizon.

"Beautiful wedding, Min. First wedding off planet Earth. You and Lucas bright new hope for peoples on Earth," Zandra said. "Now you first honeymoon in space. You have big playground in wheel by yourselves."

"Quite the honeymoon," Min said, tossing a couple dehydrated meal packs into the Phanes's docking module. "The life of an astronaut, I guess—always trying to pack forty-eight hours into twenty-four. For our 'time away,' we get to be the first guinea pigs testing out this contraption on our *long* twenty-four hours of private honeymoon bliss. Lucas will probably spend half the time fixing things."

"That wheel his baby ... for now." Zandra poked Min's stomach. "Maybe you two make another space first."

"We'll do our very best." Min beamed. Then changing in a flash, as Min often did, her bright tone turned serious. "You and Alex be careful with the next *Phoenix* test. Half of me wants to be there to make sure this next superposition test goes as planned. Our last test had its problems, and this next one is another big step. You, Alex, and Starra will completely rely on your quantum-entangled thoughts to direct the dark energy fields for quantum superposition. There's just a lot of unknowns."

Zandra hung her head. "I sorry for last test."

Min dropped her floating body down in the zero-g space to align her face with Zandra's lowered gaze. "Hey, that's not what I meant. Nobody blames you. We all know there are risks. You'll figure it out."

"We almost die because me!"

Min sighed. "Yes. The *Phoenix* went the wrong way and repositioned into the path of a satellite. But Starra acted fast enough to prevent the collision.

That's her job: to mitigate the risks. Alex has his job as the brains behind the superposition tech, and you have yours. Find us a home, Zandra, and lead the *Phoenix* to it. You can do it."

"Maybe." Zandra looked at her socked feet wrapped around a hold-down bar. She rubbed the bar with her toes for a minute.

"Zandra, he's the motor, and you are the steering. You need each other—and we all need you both to find our new home," Min said.

Zandra remained silent.

Min folded her arms. "Wait. There's something else. What?"

"You program with Starra to do quantum 'tangle, steer instead of me. Maybe that better, more science people know. Tech people believe. Most not believe my ESP do right navigation anyway. You, Alex, and Starra, you heroes of humanity with your tech. You really better, not need me."

"What? Where is this coming from?" Min shook her head. "First, my quantum entanglement navigation work with Starra is just a backup plan, and it doesn't even come close to working yet. Maybe it never will. But we always want backups in space. So, that's my focus and what I work on. But more important is that we're all in this together, each doing our part. Your ESP is our only navigation for the *Phoenix* right now that can truly reach the interstellar places we need to go."

"I not know. Yes, I feel what others not. But feel good new Earth, in far, far place? You and Aleks's tech maybe better goal, better way."

Min took Zandra's shoulders and looked her in the eye. "Don't doubt yourself. And don't let the pressure of success get to you. We are all with you. With the vastness of space, hunting and evaluating habitable planets with telescopes and sensors will take too long. The statistical odds are all wrong, and our clock is ticking. With the ecosystems collapsing, we know another widespread famine will sweep the globe. We must find a new home before the goodwill of the people formed after the Satellite War disintegrates in the chaos of starvation. It's *scientifically* better for the world to believe in your ability to *feel* the right home for us. You are our best hope to find the *right* place where we need to go. Alex believes in you. I believe in you. We all do."

Zandra bit her lower lip. Min's aura of kindness and compassion wrapped around her like a soft blanket. This smart, quick, and caring woman glowed with an endless radiance of strength and determination. *And you have your job too, Wang Min. Thank you.*

Nodding her appreciation, Zandra said, "You enjoy time together in big play space. We turn off all camera in wheel."

FACTOID 02

On October 13, 2020, Australia, Canada, Italy, Japan, Luxembourg, United Arab Emirates, the United Kingdom, and the United States of America signed the Artemis Accords. This document affirmed and furthered the 1967 "Outer Space Treaty" in an effort to define the principles for cooperation in the civil exploration and use of the moon, Mars, comets, and asteroids for peaceful purposes. Although providing guidance in several areas, such as emergency assistance, space resources, and orbital debris, there is no provision for the formation of an international body for safety and accident investigation. Individual space programs are left to police safety and investigate their own "abnormalities." There is considerable resistance to changing what some believe is a systemic flaw that led to the Challenger disaster. In November of 2021, the Federal Aviation Administration pushed back strongly on a proposed rule by the National Transportation Safety Board that would enable NTSB investigations of spaceflight crashes. Is it possible that turf wars extend into space?

CHAPTER 2

Old Friends

The late afternoon shower had stopped, and a few rays of the low evening sun were breaking through the clouds, casting a warm glow on the wet sidewalks of the city. Misty clouds of steam rose from the hot sidewalks, adding to the already stifling humid air Houston was famous for.

Ex-Commander Hans Becker took one last glance up and down the street, then opened the door to the Apollo Bar. Quickly scanning the bar and then the tables and booths, he picked out the familiar attractive young woman with short-cropped brown hair sitting in the far corner booth, away from the flow of patrons. It was a booth he chose whenever it was available. That spot had a good view of the front door and easy access to the back door of the bar. Not surprisingly, on her first visit, Emma had found the best vantage point in the bar to sit. Wearing a nondescript gray jacket and jeans, Becker could be a casual middle-aged dad meeting his daughter for a beer. It was best to be mostly invisible, but a cover was always good, even if most of the people here were probably friendlies towards the Resistance.

Located close to the Houston Space Force Center, the bar sported an atmosphere of the heavens, with white pinpoint LED lights arranged in constellations high in the black-painted ceiling. The solar system of planets circled a dimly glowing yellow sun in the middle of the bar. The globes of the planets rotated on metal tracks about the sun in fantastical rather than elliptical orbitals. Periodically, a comet would streak across from the far corner of the bar and disappear out over the front door.

Pretending to be taking in all the old space program artifacts decorating the walls, Becker was more focused on measuring up each person as he crossed the dimly lit bar. Were they a Space Force undercover plant, or a real Resistance patron? A real patron understood the hidden meaning of the dusty *Atlantis* space shuttle model crowded by bottles of liquor on the shelf behind the bar. The cargo bay doors were open, and STS-136 was stenciled on the side. The last shuttle to fly had lifted off from Earth on July 8, 2011, as mission Space Transport System 135. The open doors and incremental mission number were code that this bar supported the Resistance. It supported those who longed to use technology for continued science exploration, not manipulation into weapons for the Space Force and the warmongering leadership of the Alliance. Further evidence of the bar's political stance was the obligatory picture of the Boss, required in every business establishment. The pre-Satellite War president was now the Alliance's supreme leader, and everyone should always be reminded who was in charge. The portrait hung slightly askew, and an open bottle of the cheapest bourbon was placed under his nose. Becker could not help but cringe at the image of the overweight man with thinning gray hair flopped to one side. He turned his eyes away in disgust. Just another reminder of that man's narcissism. *Right—supreme leader. Dictator, in reality.* The state of emergency, along with suspended elections, was still in place more than a decade after the space station incident and the Satellite War.

As Becker approached, Emma jumped from the booth and embraced him in a convincing hug. "Hi, Dad! So good to see you!"

"How's my little scientist?" Becker asked in a voice loud enough for the surrounding tables to overhear above the noisy din of the other patrons.

"I'm great. I just had a meeting with my supervisor and got my first promotion in the lab!" Emma replied in an equally loud fashion.

Settling into the booth across from Emma, Becker ordered his usual Scottish ale. He noted Emma's sharp cheekbones and the taut muscles in her bare arms. Her muscle definition could make a bodybuilder jealous.

After the waitress left, he lowered his voice for a more private conversation. "When I asked for a senior Resistance person to come to this meet, I didn't expect that they would send you. You're as fit for fighting as ever, Emma. Looks like you've been killing those new recruits to the finish on the obstacle course. Do you ever take a break?"

"You know me, Hans. This warrior girl doesn't need a break; I need us to win. And we're getting there. Your contacts here have helped the cause tremendously. I'm glad I was able to come down and personally thank you."

"Yeah, well, just trying to correct for all those years that I stuck my head in the sand and worked for the wrong people," Hans said softly.

"A lot of good technical people just tried to keep doing their job in all the craziness of the political aftermath of the Satellite War. You had the command of a space station, and just keeping your crew alive up there was hard. And they reassigned you to the Right Alliance; you didn't volunteer, or even have a choice. Anyway, that's history. What counts is today and tomorrow." She paused and was quiet while the waitress delivered a glass of ale, then she raised her beer when they were alone again. "I'll still raise my glass to my ex-Alpha One Space Platform commander, and to a fellow member of our group to set things right again."

Becker clinked his glass with hers. "To the most fearsome mission specialist slash double agent I've ever known."

"So, Hans, what's the scoop on this guy?"

"Hard driving, Emma. Some advice from your ol' 'dad,' or your ex-space platform commanding officer—you choose. You need a life outside of the Resistance missions. How are you and Wilson getting along?" Becker asked.

"Fine." She leaned back and folded her arms in front of herself.

Becker leaned on the table and lowered his voice. "Emma, I know this fight against the Alliance and the Boss means everything to you. We're all carrying some hurt. But you need to take time to live just a bit too. Wilson is a great guy, and probably one of the few who's not intimidated by you."

Emma ran a finger down her glass, drawing lines in the condensation. "I know."

"We all need to lean on someone sometimes. It's okay. Really." Becker looked directly into Emma's dark eyes for a minute, giving her time to contemplate his words.

"Enough said." Becker relaxed back in the booth and took a sip of his beer. "So, the scoop on Doug… He and I go way back to my early astronaut training days. Yes, he's as ancient as I am. He's a good guy though, and like me, he initially tried to stay nonpolitical and just went along with the Right Thinking doctrine crap they were shoveling. But as with many others within the Space Force, the tipping point was when they tortured all those people blamed for your fake identity slipping through the security checks. He's been feeding me good information for the Resistance ever since I got down here and reestablished contact."

"So, why the big fuss now?"

"Doug wouldn't say. Just that it was big, and he wanted to talk with someone higher than me in the Resistance. Something about the moon. He was on the accident investigation committee on that freighter crash a while ago. My guess is that he's wanting to trade some really hot information about the crash or the Dark Side Moon Base for a deal with the Resistance, to help him and his family disappear. The rise in the Alliance's indiscriminate fingering of innocent Space Force personnel for suspected espionage has lots of our people spooked. Many are looking for a way out of what they see as forced servitude to a regime they despise."

She bit her lower lip and scanned the bar again. "Are you absolutely sure he's not being used, that this isn't a setup?"

"No way. Doug would never do that. I've literally trusted this guy with my life, and he's still the same guy."

Emma set her elbows on the table. She clasped her left fist in her right hand and rested her chin on them.

"And you can just relax that fist, Miss Rockette. You won't be needing to drop anyone tonight with that left hook. This is a friendly bar."

The two waited in silence for a while.

*

Gentle waves glimmered in the late afternoon sun before rolling softly onto the sandy shoreline of the pristine island. The lone cabana, with its white fabric and teakwood structure, stood against the blue ocean backdrop just meters from the waves. A salty offshore breeze made for a pleasant temperature in the shade of the tented structure on the beach. The tiki torches were carefully arranged around the cabana, so the fumes from their flames would never disturb the man lying naked on the table. From a distance, his pale overweight silhouette could be mistaken for an old albino sea lion atop the beige linen massage table.

"You're spending too much time on my feet," the Boss grumbled. "Get up here and do my shoulders."

The young dark-skinned girl in a red string bikini moved in a wide arc to the head of the table. As she rubbed the oil into the mass of loose flesh at his shoulders, he dropped an arm off the table. His fingers ran up the back of her thigh to the crease of her buttocks. Her leg muscles stiffened, but she continued to knead his back. He smiled to himself. This was her first time providing him a massage. She would learn that it was only part of the price to keep her family on this island—*his* island now. It was an even better island than his last, and its beauty had rightfully earned its new title, Summit Supreme. With its steep slopes sweeping up from the clear waters, this island would not disappear into the rising ocean. He closed his eyes and stroked the tight cheek of her bikini with his fingers. He would take his time and enjoy the massage before making other demands of her.

A distant buzz slowly grew above the soft repetition of the waves. The unnatural noise built slowly and transitioned to the constant hum of a drone hovering just at the edge of the cabana. A single chime from the device broke the air.

He sighed. "Yes, Jason. What's so important that you must interrupt my afternoon massage?"

"*I apologize for the intrusion, Master,*" the AI replied. "*I need to inform you of a critical security breach I have detected relating to the Tsiolkovsky Crater incident. My analysis indicates that it needs your immediate attention.*"

"Gahhh… You, girl, go get me a Manhattan. Tell the bartender to make it a double." He waved the girl away and rolled his naked mass to the side facing the sea. "Go ahead, Jason. What is this urgent problem?"

The drone lowered and came to rest on a wicker table under the cabana, its buzz replaced by the gentle waves again. "*The Right Alliance accident investigation of the freighter crash two months ago has concluded as you desired. The report states that the freighter crashed beyond the crater. The debris we planted there was used as the key evidence in the report. The cause of the crash was determined to be pilot error combined with a minor malfunction of the attitude control electrical system. Unfortunately, one of the investigators voiced concern in the final hearing that the debris did not match the freighter's registered payload. His concerns were dismissed by our man, but it appears he still wants to be heard. I have been monitoring his private communications, and he has plans to meet an unknown contact at a bar in Houston tonight. My prediction is that he will be exchanging confidential information on the accident with an agent of the Resistance.*"

"Dipshit do-gooders are just a pain in my ass. He needs to disappear. Isn't Ken in Houston?"

"*Yes, Master. Ken Seaborn is at Space Force Houston, training on the new fast-attack star-fighter interceptor.*"

"Good. Give Ken the meeting information and have him eliminate both parties. Just tell him they're all Resistance scum, and to make them vanish into thin air. He doesn't need to know anything more. Let's get this cleaned up for good. I want no loose ends."

"*Message sent.*"

The Boss laid his face back into the massage cradle. "Fine. Now leave me alone. And send that girl back here."

*

When Becker's beer was half gone, he casually glanced at his watch. Doug was late, and that wasn't a good sign. He'd give the man just another few minutes before he'd suggest they slip out the back door. He took another sip of his beer and thought back to his days aboard what the International Space Station was originally, renamed Platform Alpha after the war. All the activities on the station had gone from science and discovery to combat and weapons. Doug had been a payload communication controller in Huntsville, Alabama, back then. He was good at his job, just like the thousands of other men and women since the days of the *Mercury* missions, providing that lifeline to Earth for the handful of astronauts risking their lives in space in search of knowledge. Becker had been part of a relief crew bound for the ISS, when suddenly, the Satellite War changed both their commissions from NASA to the Space Force. Doug had carefully talked him through the whirlwind of changes happening on the ground, and most importantly, how to play the game and survive. There were many that could not make the transition; they just disappeared. Then, just two years ago, another insane chain of events with this woman sitting across from him had turned his world upside down yet again. Now he was a Resistance fighter holding a clandestine meeting with Doug, the Space Force informant. Becker chuckled silently. *Talk about rapid career changes…*

Streaks of fading sunlight burst through the front door of the bar, and Emma cocked her head in that direction. Becker checked over his shoulder and recognized Doug, then glanced quickly at the bar to see if the two young men sitting there took note of the older gentleman entering. They seemed engrossed in the game playing on the monitor above the bar. Good. The man entering squinted left and right, then finally recognized Becker discreetly beckoning with his hand. Crossing the bar with his head down, Doug slipped into the booth after Becker moved next to Emma.

"Anybody follow you?" Becker asked.

"Good to see you too, Hans," the man muttered. "And no. You know I'm careful."

"Sorry, Doug. You're never late, so maybe that's put me a little on edge. We should keep this short. This is Emma Lewis."

"Shit, *that* Emma?" Doug leaned forward. "The double agent from Platform Alpha? Damn, Hans, you *do* have pull. Good, 'cause this is important. You need to get—"

"You want a beer?" the waitress asked, seemingly appearing from nowhere.

Doug leaned back in the booth and pointed to Becker's half-full glass. "Ah, yes. What he's having." They waited for the waitress to leave.

"So, what's the scoop, Doug? Why did we need to meet tonight, and why did I need Emma here?"

Doug scanned the bar, then leaned forward again and said quietly, "Time for me to cut and run, buddy. Inside word at the Space Center is that they know there's a gushing leak. Hell, with you down here, probably several. I don't think they know who yet, but I'm not waiting around to find out."

"Doug, hold on. Maybe they're just testing to see if they can flush out a rabbit or two. You run, and you'll be marked."

"No, this is real." He glanced around the bar again. "And I already have a target on my back for standing up in the moon base accident investigation. They didn't want to hear my findings. It was clearly a cover-up. I've brought the proof."

"The Alliance freighter that was lost? That wasn't just a systems failure?" Emma asked.

Doug patted the breast pocket of his jacket. "That's just the tip of the iceberg. I got it all here. You can have it, but I want a safe house for me, my wife, and my kid first. I have what's really going on at—"

The waitress returned with his beer, and Doug relaxed back into the booth.

Becker put on a facade of old friends for the waitress and raised his glass. "Cheers, to good missions and great times, old buddy."

As Becker took a sip from his glass, his eye caught the bright white-on-black military police armband of a Space Force soldier entering the bar through the back door. Instinctively, his head snapped around towards the front door. Another MP entered there and took up a blocking stance, his M29 assault rifle at the ready. Immediately following him through the front door was a Space Force officer in a flight suit. Becker recognized the tall, blond-haired buck from his Space Force days immediately. "Shit! Don't look, but Ken Seaborn just walked in."

Emma discreetly glanced at the door and then quickly dropped her head. She moved deeper into the booth to keep out of Ken's line of sight. "Son of a bitch! Ken will recognize us both, Hans! And he'll want payback for that last mission. He's a vindictive bastard."

Doug started to get up from the booth, but Becker grabbed his arm. "Stay put, and stay cool, Doug. We need to wait for a better opportunity to bolt. Let me handle this." Becker looked over to the bartender, gave him a slight nod, and stroked under his jaw with one finger pointed towards the back door. The bartender turned away and discreetly pulled out his phone.

"Good evening, ladies and gentlemen. You will all stay exactly where you are," the officer announced in a loud voice. "This is an official Right Alliance ID inspection. We suspect there to be some Resistance members in your midst. You will have your credentials out and ready." He strode over to the first table and held a scanner to the face of a young man. The wide-eyed man fumbled in his pockets and eagerly offered his ID to Ken. After checking that the man's credentials matched the scan, he dropped the card on the table and snatched the ID the girl sitting next to him was offering.

Doug leaned on the table towards Becker. "I wasn't followed, Hans. Somehow, they knew we would be here and when. You know as well as I do that guy's not just some flyboy, he's a top Boss crony."

"Oh, we both know him all too well," Emma said. She kept her chin down, but her eyes were keeping a close watch at the front of the bar. "Ken was on Platform Alpha with us. He's got a score to settle with both of us too."

Becker asked, "Why would they send Ken? Who knew that you were coming here, Doug? They must have put the thumbscrews to someone."

"Just my wife..." Doug reached for his phone.

Becker stopped him. "Not now, Doug. Nothing you can do now. I'm sorry. Let's get you safe, and then we can see about Martha … and Wendy." Becker looked back to the bartender and acknowledged the two fingers the bartender used to stroke the side of his beard. Two minutes. Becker wasn't sure they had that much time as Ken moved to the next table.

"Doug, what the hell did you find?" Becker asked.

"Like I told you, I was assigned to the freighter crash investigation, because I was manning Houston ground support at the time of the event. It wasn't one of our freighters, but we still coordinate on all moon orbital assets. Things didn't seem to add up on the crash though. The freighter telemetry didn't match what the Dark Side Moon Base controllers were saying. Then the wreckage was all wrong. Lots of stuff didn't match the payload records. Hell, some of the ship's parts they sent pictures of didn't even match the freighter hull configuration at all. So, I started digging to find out where the crash debris really came from. That's when I found what they've really been shipping to that base. You're not going to believe it. But I've got proof." Doug patted his breast pocket again.

Becker took a check over his shoulder and noted that Ken had finished checking the tables near the front of the bar and was now working his way down the booths along the wall. He eyed the bartender again. Any second now.

"Doug, be ready to bolt for the rear door when I say," Becker whispered.

Ken moved to the booth beside theirs. Becker ducked his head too late, and Ken's head swiveled in a double take. "Hey, you look familiar—"

BLAM! The rear door flew off its hinges and leveled the MP standing guard in front of it.

"Now, Doug! Out the back!" Becker launched himself at Ken, delivering an upper cut to his jaw with his elbow. Doug scrambled to the rear of the bar. The older gentleman knocked over empty chairs and tables as he plowed a slow path.

Ken staggered backward. Turning to the MP stationed at the front door, he pointed to the older man and screamed, "Shoot him, idiot!"

Emma flew from the booth. Grabbing her glass off the table, she threw it towards the MP raising his weapon at Doug. Ducking the glass, the man fired at the form crossing into the rear doorframe. The buzz of a projectile streaked across the bar. Becker's eyes followed as it flew past him and lodged in the back of Doug's neck before he disappeared out the door. *Shit, a hornet!*

Becker sprang for the back door, ducking the chair that Emma was whipping around and throwing at the MP. It connected full-on with the MP's face as he was lowering his weapon, sending him crashing backwards through the front window of the bar. Landing on one foot from the spinning chair throw, Emma swung a roundhouse kick into Ken's ribs with her other leg. As Ken doubled over, she yelled, "Out, now, get after him!"

Becker scrambled across the flattened back door and into the alley. With the nerve agent from the hornet now amping up Doug's strength, he was already turning left out of the back alley and down the main street. Becker took off after him.

Skidding around the wet concrete at the corner, Becker caught sight of Doug already two blocks down the street and darting up the Buffalo Bayou bridge. He had never seen a man stung by a hornet before, but the Resistance briefs describing what Doug was experiencing were clear: Doug's body was in overdrive to end the pain. Doug would find a way to kill himself. No one escaped a hornet sting unless they got an antidote within minutes. Becker ran as fast as he could, knowing even his fit body was no match for anyone with that venom coursing through their veins and lighting their muscles on fire.

Doug was already near the apex of the bridge when Becker reached the first expansion joint at the base. Without hesitation, Doug climbed the side rail and flung himself off the bridge, arms and legs flailing in agony.

Dammit! Becker diverted his sprint to the rocks below the bridge. Emma appeared right on his heels.

Reaching the twisted body sprawled over a slimy boulder beside the smelly river, Becker scanned around and then knelt down next to his friend. "Doug, I'm here. I'm with you."

Doug raised his bloodied head from the rock. "Make them pay, Hans. For Martha, Wendy. Make them pay."

"They will, buddy. They will. I promise." He took Doug's hand in both of his.

"Hans, the Dark Side Moon Base... It's more than just another Space Force mining depot." Doug took a labored breath and spat out a mouthful of blood. He turned towards Emma. "They are drilling, but deep—too deep. You need to stop them. They'll destroy the moon!"

"What? How?!" Emma asked.

"They've built some kind of dark energy generator, some advanced tech. I got one of the scientists to tell me what they're really doing. They make this field of dark energy and then collapse it all at once. Somehow, that makes a micro black hole that, in turn, eats all matter around it."

Emma shook her head. "What? How can they? We destroyed the research facility with that tech two years ago! I was there. I planted the bombs! And they don't have a Quantum Triangle. How the hell are they making dark energy?"

"The guy said the Boss's AI, Jason, reconstructed the tech data from some secret quantum science project, or at least some of it." Doug stiffened and winced as another shock of pain from the hornet coursed through his body. "They can't superposition without the Quantum Triangle, but they figured out that rapidly collapsing the vector of dark energy quantum fields mimics the formation of a micro black hole. It annihilates all nearby matter. They want to drill into the moon's core for iron, build a fleet of warships."

Emma pounded her thigh with a fist. "Shit—Jason. We were always concerned that they had some kind of backup for the data servers."

"The freighter didn't crash. They annihilated it with a black hole in a test run. But they're pushing the scientists too fast. They don't really understand the tech. They don't know how to control the black hole once it forms. There's just no way to stop it from eating nearby matter. Fools! If they drill the moon with it, they don't know when it will stop."

"Oh my god... We believe that the moon's core is at least partially molten. They could create volcanic eruptions spewing iron magma into space!" Emma breathed.

Doug cringed with another grip of pain. "Yes, but that's what they want. It eliminates the need to lift heavy metal into orbit. An incredible advantage for building a space fleet."

Emma looked at Becker in horror. "But if the black hole is close to a lot of matter instead of empty space, it will just keep growing. And the more mass it gains, the more it'll pull in. They could annihilate the entire moon! And then we would have a black hole close to Earth. Eventually, it would gain enough mass to pull itself right into us. They're rolling the dice with our very existence."

"The scientists … are scared. But the Boss … is holding their families. He doesn't believe the scientists' warnings. He says they're wrong, that the energy of the micro black hole will dissipate. But really … he just doesn't care what…" Doug inhaled in a deep spasm, his mouth unable to close in the final grip of pain. His body finally went limp.

"Ah, shit! I promise, Doug, buddy. We will stop them. Somehow, we will stop them. I promise."

Becker raised his head at the heavy footsteps of their pursuers approaching and the wail of a siren in the distance. Reaching into Doug's jacket pocket, he retrieved a memory card and handed it to Emma. Giving a final squeeze to the shoulder of his old friend, Becker pointed southeast down the river. They sprinted along the shoreline into the fading light of the setting sun.

*

Ken was still breathing hard as he stood over the broken body lying beside the river. He flicked the bloody ID badge down onto Doug's chest. Looking up and down the riverbank in the dim light, he saw no movement other than a slow barge with its tug thumping downstream. Emma and Becker were ghosts, with hundreds of places to hide or sneak away into the city. *Shit!* This simple mission had gone to crap in only seconds.

Ken pulled out his phone and buried his thumb in the sensor to establish a secured connection with the local Space Force base.

The voice on the speaker stated the security challenge flatly. *"Romeo-Oscar."*

"Delta-niner."

"Confirmed. What do you need, Sea Ace?"

Ken stared at Doug's twisted body lying over the rocks. "Operation is terminal, and it's a freakin' mess. I need three things. One, send an ambulance for the two MPs and a body bag for the target. The MPs are down, but not critical. One has a concussion, the other has severe lacerations from plate glass. Two, activate a couple local Alliance cells. First cell is to riot at the Apollo Bar. Burn it to the ground; it's a Resistance haven. Second cell you should dispatch to the target's home. Likewise, directive to riot and burn. Make a statement about helping the Resistance."

"Roger that. Ambulance and wagon en route. Will dispatch two Alliance civilian militia cells. And the third item?" the voice asked.

"Patch me through to Jason. I want to know why I was sent on a mission with such shitty intel," Ken said.

He kicked at some stones with his boot while waiting with the phone to his ear. *Come on. Tonight, not next week.*

"Jason here. How may I be of assistance?"

Ken snarled into the phone. "Finally! Jason, what moron in Space Force planned this Resistance-mole-snuffing mission you sent me on tonight? The intelligence was crap."

"This was not a Space Force-planned operation. It was ordered directly by the Boss for you to handle with the aid of two MPs," Jason replied in an even, factual monotone.

"Well, do some freakin' homework and mission planning! Didn't they teach you that? This mission went to crap because I had no idea what I was walking into. Did you know who this supposedly low-level mole guy was going to meet?"

"I calculated an eighty-seven percent probability that it would be a high-level Resistance operative."

"You calculated that, and you didn't bother sharing it with me?! A low-level mole meeting a high-level Resistance operative… That didn't make a simulated eyebrow twitch?" Ken picked up a softball-sized rock and threw it hard out into the river. "Well, guess what? You calculated right. In fact, it was *two* very high-level Resistance operatives. Emma Lewis, also falsely known as Emma Baker, and Ex-Commander Hans Becker both just happened to crawl out of nowhere for this guy. Was that anywhere in your calculations? Shit, if I'd known it was those two, I would have worn a flack jacket, not a damn Space Force flight suit! Why the hell wasn't I given all the information on this meet?"

"It is related to a project you are not involved in. I am under strict orders not to share information relating to that project with anyone without express permission from the Boss himself," Jason said.

Ken bit at his lip. "Don't give me that bullshit. This is Mission Planning 101. I understand compartmentalized information, but you know my clearance is the max. Plus, you don't purposefully give the enemy the element of surprise when you send in a team. What kind of fool thinking is that? This mission went to hell because of poor planning and lack of proper intel, plain and simple."

"I apologize, Ken. I provided the information on this mission that you were allowed to have. Is there something else I can assist you with?" Jason asked dryly.

Ken held his phone away in shock. Did the AI just try to change the subject to avoid further questions? "No. It seems like you aren't much help to me tonight. Sea Ace out."

Stuffing the phone in his pocket, Ken could hear the siren of the ambulance approaching in the distance. He watched the barge chug down the river. What was going on? *A secret project even I am not aware of? I'm the Boss's number one.* This was not how things should be run. This was unprofessional and sloppy.

Ken pictured the military leaders he had served under during the Satellite War and the emergence of the Right Alliance. Those were professionals who knew military planning and execution. He dropped his gaze to the stones at his feet. One by one, those colonels, majors, and generals had retired. All had been replaced by those with more emphasis on political sway than military training and experience. The Space Force and the Right Alliance were losing their edge. What had once been the precision fighting force of the western hemisphere against the Pacific Tuanhuo was slowly melting into a dull bureaucracy of incompetence. *How can we squash the Resistance and win this war with the Tuanhuo if we aren't the strong military force we should be?*

FACTOID 03

Ernest Hemingway was given a white six-toed kitten by a local mariner in 1935. Snow White had the dominant polydactyl gene, passing it on to her own kittens. About seventy percent of the kittens born will typically manifest extra toes due to this gene. Hemingway named all his cats after famous people. The Ernest Hemingway Home and Museum in Key West, Florida, has gravestones immortalizing famous cats, like Willard Scott and Errol Flynn, along with forty to fifty living residents (at the time of this writing), like Lucille Ball, Ginger Rogers, and Alfred Hitchcock.

CHAPTER 3

Navigating Life

Zandra floated in the microgravity at the modular wall panel that served as the kitchen of the space station. Although the galley had been significantly expanded from the original three-person pull-out table, warm/hot water taps, and tiny food warmer of the ancient Russian Zvezda module, it was far from a real kitchen. Zandra injected some recycled tepid water into each blueberry muffin mix pouch from the quick-connect fitting on the wall plate. Kneading each pouch with her fingers to combine the ingredients, she hummed the melody of *"Astronaut"* by Simple Plan. The song's lyrics of feeling lost and alone matched her melancholy mood. She missed her wooden spoon and favorite mixing bowl from her kitchen back on Earth. It would be good when the galley on the habitat wheel was operational, and she could do some *real* cooking in the artificial gravity.

Clamping the mixed pouches onto the center rail of the oven, she set the timer and hovered in the module for a moment, searching for something to occupy herself with next. Alex was here in the module too—physically, at least. She could feel his aura. He was here at the metal galley table behind her, yet between them stood an invisible and soundproof wall. As he sat engrossed in his tablet and coffee, any attempt at her breaking through for a meaningful conversation was futile. He was already focused and working. The world about him was distant from his mind.

"Good morning, Zandra. Oh, blueberry muffins for breakfast?" Min asked, floating into the Zvezda module from the hatch linking to the rest of the station.

"I honor your one-week wedding," Zandra replied. She brightened at the wave of warm sunshine that was Min's beautiful aura. The petite Asian woman glowed with energy, fully charged to start another busy day on the station. But Zandra's smile quickly faded as she sensed the storm cloud that was Lucas following Min into the module. "Oh, dear…"

Lucas silently maneuvered himself to hover at the galley table across from Alex. With his stout toes slipped under the hold-down bar to keep his body in place, he interlaced his thick fingers and rested his hands on the metal surface. Zandra closed her eyes and held her lips tight. Lucas's aura hung like a stormy thunderhead billowing with bolts of internal lightning.

"That furry meatloaf with six claws on each paw did it again," Lucas said in an even tone without looking up.

"I sorry, Lucas. My Zhrinnykot bad?"

Lucas grimaced. "This is the third time I'll have to reset the mass balance data on the black nebula carrots, because your monster cat prefers to add his biomass there and not in his litter box in the habitat wheel."

"I give Zhrinnykot stern talk."

"Right. Like he listens."

Min covered her mouth to suppress a giggle.

"Min, as the lead scientist on the station, you should be upset too," Lucas said, shaking a finger at her. "It's a critical growth experiment. With their high density of anthocyanin, those carrots are an important food and chemical source destined for New Earth. We need to have accurate projections for their growth potential in space."

"He's the mission mascot, and he belongs with Zandra," Min said, spinning back to the orange juice hydration packs she was pulling from a storage bin.

Lucas shook his head. "I still can't believe it was your idea to bring him up here. Just because we have the habitat wheel providing space with artificial gravity doesn't mean we need to go nuts."

"He's an important experiment, just like all the other studies we do here, Lucas. We need to be prepared for transferring all family members. And that includes people's pets, or at least some, per the lottery," Min replied. Her encyclopedic mind kicked in. "Studies show that pets decrease cortisol levels and lower blood pressure. Other studies have found that animals can reduce loneliness, increase feelings of social support, and boost your mood."

"My mood is boosted when he keeps to his litter box," Lucas muttered. The chime of the oven made him look up.

Zandra opened the door and waved the warm smell of blueberry muffins in his direction. "Here new mood, Lucas. Zhrinnykot say he sorry, you take my muffin too."

Taking a deep breath, Lucas waved a dismissive hand. "Apology accepted, no extra muffin needed."

Min reached around behind him and gave him a hug.

Lucas leaned forward on the table. "Earth to Alex. Earth to Alex… Come in, Alex. Morning news flash: there is a crew in orbit with you."

Alex's head lifted from his tablet, and he appeared to just take notice of Lucas and Min. "Oh, hi, guys. Sorry, good morning. Today's just a busy day."

"We're all busy, Alex," Min said. "Every minute of every day we're up here."

Alex stuck his tablet to the wall and pushed off for the espresso station. "Yes, of course. Sorry. How about I make everyone coffee?"

"Make mine a double shot," Lucas said.

The synthesized AI voice of Starra came from the hatch leading to the Unity module. *"Galley control, this is Zulu-Kilo-six-Tango-Oscar-Echo. Requesting a sustenance flyby."*

With her hands full of hot muffins, Zandra spun to Min. "You do, please? I do Lucas muffin."

"Oh, yes, absolutely." Min pushed off Lucas and reached for a kibble treat baggie stuck on the far wall with tape. "Zulu-Kilo-six-Tango-Oscar-Echo, this is galley control. Airspace is crowded, but you are clear for flyby over runway one-eight left."

"Roger, galley control. Adjusting glide path." Starra appeared at the Zvezda hatch. The owl-cat android banked her orange-tabby-colored wings with two quick jets of air to position herself on the starboard side of the module.

Leaning into the maneuver just above Starra's head was a second orange-tabby face. At the sound of Min shaking the cat treat baggie, Zhrinnykot sat up on Starra's back. Min sent a kibble treat tumbling in the station's microgravity just above Lucas's head. Two meters before reaching the galley table, Starra executed a barrel roll, her wings sweeping like a dancer in a pirouette to rotate upside down. As the inverted Zhrinnykot passed over Lucas, his right paw reached out and captured the treat.

"Yes! The mighty hunter captures his prey!" an enthusiastic Min said, clapping.

Lucas buried his face in his hands and mumbled, "I can't believe we encourage this."

"Oh, Lucas, we know deep down you love Zhrinnykot too. That's why you built Starra as an owl-cat."

"I built an owl-cat body for Starra because she's much more versatile in that form than having a humanoid android on board. I wanted her to be able to do physical things we can't, like fix things in tight places." Lucas looked back over his shoulder at the flying pair. "But I think this Dr. Frankenstein has created another monster."

"I think it's an ingenious game those two came up with. And just like for all of us, it's important for them both to have environmental enrichment. Zhrinnykot needs to hunt." Min dug into the baggie for another treat and sent it flying forward in the module. Starra banked hard and blasted her air jets in hot pursuit. Zhrinnykot leaned into the bank and then positioned forward on Starra's back for another kill.

"Whoa, collision alert!" Commander Johnson said as he entered the module from his side sleeping quarters to see the furry masses barreling down on him.

Starra braked hard with reversing jets. The move caught the cat on her back off guard and launched the fur ball forward with his inherent momentum. Johnson's quick reflexes took over. With his left arm, he scooped the flying cat out of the air and tucked him on his hip like a football. Without missing a beat, he reached out with his free hand, snatched the kibble from midair, and delivered it to Zhrinnykot.

"A double play by the shortstop!" Min exclaimed.

Commander Johnson took a bow and returned the cat to its perch on Starra, now hovering beside him. "Good morning, all. Glad to see everyone, including Zhrinnykot, getting a good breakfast."

"It special muffin day for Lucas and Min," Zandra said, delivering one to Lucas. "Honor one-week happy marriage."

"Also known as bad kitty compensation day," Lucas muttered through a bite. "Again."

"Oh, no. Another deposit causing an experiment reset? Maybe we need to revise the experiment to include a sample set with incremental fertilizer." After giving a nod of thanks to Zandra for his muffin, the commander took a deep breath of the blueberry aroma and asked over his shoulder, "Starra, any updates on this morning's crew assignments from mission control?"

"Mission control is requesting that Lucas verify the bearing alignment on the habitat wheel first thing this morning. They detected a slight increase in z-axis vibration last night. They are also asking that Min run diagnostics on the—"

The crew all froze and looked at Starra, her mid-sentence stoppage uncharacteristic.

"Starra, is there a problem?" Johnson asked.

"I have just received an SOS message. Please wait while I decipher the content."

"An SOS? Who would send an SOS up here?" Min asked. "We're the only ones in space."

"It's from the parallel universe Alex and I came from. They are using the dark energy relay we established two years ago to communicate between the universes, from when Zandra and Min were inadvertently superpositioned there. I have

been monitoring the area in space we designated for exchanging communications between the universes," Starra explained.

"In addition to our scheduled calls to my family? When did you start keeping that relay powered? And why?" Alex asked.

"I don't know. Something in my quantum processes made me start a constant monitoring of the dark matter relay a while ago." Starra moved to hover next to Zandra, who scooped Zhrinnykot from her back. *"I have decoded the message. It states, 'Alex and Zandra, this is an emergency message from Lieutenant Commander Wilson on behalf of Emma L. The Resistance needs your help. The Supreme Moron and his Space Force plan to drill the moon by collapsing quantum fields, based on your research. We do not have the capability to execute a mission to the moon, but the Boss must be stopped. We have activated a quantum beacon for your superposition return. Please help.'"*

"Oh my god, they're using dark energy again? How?" Min asked. "Alex, you and Emma destroyed their research facility."

"I don't know. Maybe they had some backup we were not aware of."

"Collapsing quantum fields on purpose, near a large mass? They're insane! It would just keep growing. They don't know what they're doing, or they have no idea of the danger." Min turned from Alex to Johnson and back with determined eyes. "Alex, you need to go back with the *Phoenix* and find out what's happening there."

Zandra glanced over to Alex working at the coffee panel and caught him secretly clenching his fists. *I sorry, Aleks. I know, your nightmare come back.* She could sense him rerunning all those bad memories of how the groundbreaking technology he'd created always seemed to find its way into the wrong hands. First it was the containment tech he had developed for the dark energy field generators. The Boss and Ken had used it in a powerful plasma cannon weapons system that had changed the outcome of the Satellite War in that universe. And to make things worse, it had solidified the Boss's grip on power. He might not have become the supreme leader of the Right Alliance without that tech. Then they had wanted his core superposition tech, and even the Quantum Triangle itself. They'd tried to twist those secrets and use them for more weapons and war, rather than all the positive uses Alex had envisioned. *It not your fault, Aleks.*

Alex folded his arms and turned to stare down at the table rather than look anyone in the eye. "Unfortunately, I'm sure they know exactly what they're doing: using technology to destroy. That's all their leaders can think about. That universe, with its warring factions, is never going to change. I doubt we could do anything to stop them in their quest for destruction."

"But Alex, as a parallel universe to ours, their gravity is our gravity," Min said. "If they impact their moon with collapsing fields generating micro black holes, it could change *our* moon. The massive gravity wells could alter our obits. It could destroy our moon and the Earth before we would even know what's happening."

"There's a war going on there, and the *Phoenix* is a research vessel, not a warship. We'd be blasted with a plasma cannon like a sitting duck if they detected the *Phoenix* in orbit," Alex said. "We need to use the *Phoenix* and the time we have to get as far away from this solar system as possible."

"Aleks, we do now, or maybe no people here to find new home for," Zandra said quietly while stroking Zhrinnykot.

"How? We have no weapons in this universe, remember? People here destroyed them all after the Satellite War and vowed never to use technology in that way again." Alex took a treat from the baggie Min held and flicked it towards the far hatch. "We can't attack a well-armed Space Force with flying cat treats."

Zandra loaded Zhrinnykot back onto Starra, the cat keen on getting after the new treat. "We not fight, just stop drill."

"I just don't see how."

"What about somehow sabotaging the tech? Maybe we could plant a virus or something in their programming that would disable the drill," Min said.

Alex shook his head. "We'd never get close to their computer servers."

"We gotta do something," Lucas said. "What if you went back on the *Phoenix* and—"

"No." Alex thrust out an angry arm and pointed to the unseen universe sharing their quantum existence. "I refuse to go back there. They would either destroy or steal the *Phoenix* and the Quantum Triangle. Then where would we be?"

"But Aleks, they friends. We need—"

"I said *no!*" Alex pushed off hard from the coffee station, his leg hitting the table, sending the food items on it tumbling into the air. He grabbed a handhold and launched himself towards the hatch, never looking back.

Zandra reached out and silently retrieved his blueberry muffin spinning slowly through the air.

*

Alex closed his eyes and took a slow, deep breath as he sat strapped into the pilot seat of the Phoenix. The spacecraft attached to the World Space Station had become his sanctuary. Everything here, he had helped design, and it was now his to master. This was his baby, his command. Of course, they had to name it the Phoenix. It would be the first fully functional spaceship to travel faster than light. Being the Trekkie that he was, a nod to that first ship with a warp drive had been an unquestionable decision. Alex ran his hand across the control console before him. The red tactical hue of the cockpit gave him a warm sense of mission. This was a machine of clear purpose. His craft would find the new Earth-like planet where humanity could survive and grow.

He shook his head. It was just too dangerous to risk this and go back to that other universe. The last time they superpositioned to that parallel universe, they almost hadn't made it back. And more importantly, his ultimate technological achievement was almost stolen and used as a weapon. The logical decision was to quickly find a new home, far away from this galaxy. His past world with all its warmonger leaders could not touch them there. They and this powerful technology would be safe. It was a gamble, whether they could find a new home in time, but wasn't that just more reason to continue on their own path to find a new home for the people here?

Alex glanced over his shoulder at the panel just behind the copilot seat. It was virtually impossible not to stare in awe at the Quantum Triangle, with its form constantly shifting to present a new triangular plane. Every shift sent out a new ray of color. It was a fourth-dimensional object unable to rest in three-dimensional space. Alex shook his head. It was the key to quantum superposition, and hopefully to interstellar travel in the blink of an eye. He alone had been able to create the device and capture its power. And now, in *this* universe, he could use it for discovery, instead of the destruction that was the focus of all technology in that other parallel universe. Going back there would put this important mission at a terrible risk. They were working for the very survival of this world. He'd have liked to help his friends from the past, but they probably would fail to thwart that egotistical madman. Then both worlds would be forfeit. The leadership in that world would never change. They needed an imaginary superhero, not the *Phoenix*.

Entering commands on the console to his left, he brought up the day's checkout list. *Look, we're behind schedule as it is. We have our own problems.* The *Phoenix* was due to undock from the station tomorrow and make another major step in superpositioning. Before then, there were still a lot of final diagnostics to run on critical systems. *We can't solve every world's problems. Sometimes you just have to make a tough decision and hope it's right.*

"Permission to come aboard?" The voice of Commander Johnson at the docking hatch startled Alex.

"Ah, yes. Yes, sir." He selected the day's first test plan on his primary console display, then spun his chair around to watch the commander float up from the docking port on the zenith axis of the ship behind him. "You don't need to ask permission, sir. You are the commander of our mission."

"Well, we all know this baby is *your* command, Alex. I've got the WSS. This is a whole 'nother ship." The commander floated silently into the cockpit and slid into the copilot seat beside Alex. He pulled the seat harness around his shoulders and fixed his eyes out the front portal of twelve-centimeter-thick, multilayered, tempered alumina-silicate glass. The nose-down orientation of the *Phoenix's* attachment to the space station provided a flowing view of the planet below. A dark mass of gray cloud cover from the fires caused by the Satellite War still swirled over much of the blue Pacific Ocean west of South

America as the *Phoenix* passed over. The mesmerizing blue marble of the Earth was still a jewel to behold, even with the deep wounds human wars had created. Both men had seen this view in better times. Many areas that had once been green with forest and life were now brown. Almost every coastline they crossed over now had long stretches of charred and blackened wasteland from the brutal bombings. The sacred blue marble of this solar system and galaxy was now scarred and scratched.

Alex turned back to the forward ports, which revealed the captivating sight of the southern continent sweeping into view. "You know I'm right. We must stay focused on our work to find a new home before the second famine sets in." He pointed to the burnt brown land coming into view below. That continent had once been green with life, but the uncontrollable fires following the nuclear holocaust of the war had ravaged most of the planet. "We can't grow enough food here anymore. Not with all the radioactive land, wild temperature swings, collapsed ecosystems, and the massive storms we've created through climate change. What's left of the decimated species can't grow to maturity."

The commander sighed.

Alex turned towards Johnson and continued his argument. "We both circled the Earth up here before the war, so I know you feel the wounds of the planet below us as deeply as I do. But that's the past. I'm focused on creating a future. It's the only thing that matters. We're already taking huge risks, and we just don't have time for anything else."

The commander interlaced his fingers and rubbed his thumbs together. Alex read the visual cue and stayed quiet while the man thought. Alex liked and respected Commander Fred Johnson. He was professional, personable, and reasonable. Once a poor kid from south Chicago, he had since had a long career showing he had what it took to work in the challenging environment of space, while at the same time being that one member of a team who could pull everyone together. He was a natural leader.

"I'm not saying you're wrong, Alex," Johnson finally said. "But I do think you could listen better."

"They should listen to *me*," Alex said, pointing to his chest. "Look, if anyone knows what that other universe is like—their idiotic, warmongering leadership—it's me. I was part of that world for over ten years. Hell, it was the technology that I developed that they twisted into one of their best weapons. So, I know there's no helping them. They're doomed to destroy themselves. The greedy leaders in that other universe where I came from are hell-bent on power, weapons, and war. We can't save them … but we can save ourselves."

The commander gazed out the portal for a while.

"Just keep in mind, Alex, that our universe took a very different path after the Satellite War we both experienced. We are here only because the leaders in our world understood the common need to work together, not continue the pointless destruction. They chose to use the double-edged sword of technology to discover a new home. So, a cry for help is something we can't easily ignore. We respond with a common 'What can we do?' rather than a 'Well, that's your problem.' It's just become our nature. I think that's a good thing."

Alex threw up his hands. "You're saying that I should drop everything and mount a rescue mission? I should superposition the *Phoenix* to the other universe? The probability of success—or even us making it back—is virtually nil."

"I'm not saying that."

"Then what?"

"Just listen." The commander thumbed over his shoulder at the docking hatch. "We've got the best people I've ever had the honor to work with on this station. Min is the smartest person I've ever known. Well, right up there with you. And I believe Zandra can sense things I'll never know. Lucas can build or fix virtually anything; he's a mechanical wizard. So, don't tune them out. Listen to them. Not everything is black or white. Let them give you insights. Maybe there's a bit of gray that works better than just option A or B."

Alex sighed. His eyes went to the checklist on the diagnostic protocol he had punched up. He scrolled the list up and down with his finger, not really focusing on the words.

"You know, Alex, we all owe a debt of gratitude to Emma and the Resistance. If it weren't for her, that madman in your other universe would still have the

Quantum Triangle. And it was her planning that saved your niece and your family." Johnson swept his arm over the *Phoenix* command console. "None of this would even exist, and the people of this universe would probably be living out their last days on this dying world with no hope. Our world here would be a different world altogether, if not for them. It shows the tremendous difference that's made when people work together."

They both sat quietly and watched out the front port as the south Atlantic silently glided from right to left. After several minutes, as the tip of the next continent appeared over the horizon, Johnson pointed out the window. "I bet you didn't know that back in the 1480s, when the Portuguese explorer Bartolomeu Dias discovered the tip of the African continent, he originally named it the Cape of Storms. He had clearly experienced the wrath of those fearsome seas. Later, the name was changed to the Cape of Good Hope to attract more ships to the route."

Alex frowned at his commander. "I'm missing the connection."

"We're on a journey of discovery too, Alex. To find a new home … together. Our route and our vessel must include everyone. In this world, we will do things together, or we won't do them at all. It must be that way, or we risk falling back into our old destructive ways." Fred Johnson tapped at the front portal. "We are a different world now, in ways that aren't obvious to the eye. We're a world of people coming together with one hope and one future. We are no longer separate peoples using the latest technology against each other for terrible things. We're a people of common hope, developing technology and capabilities that are our future.

"In truth, it's possible that our mission may fail, that we won't find a new home in time. But our real purpose is bigger than that. We're leading the people on the planet below on a journey of hope. It's not the belief in technology, it's the belief in one another that will allow us to succeed. What matters is that we do this together and focus on trusting one another and working together. That is our journey. That is our strength. People working together are powerful— more powerful than any technology."

Johnson glanced over at the Quantum Triangle. Its changing colors glowed on his forehead and cheeks, shifting from yellow to green to blue. "You've created an incredible engine for our trip. In the limited time we have left to survive on this dying planet, it will probably be the difference between us searching in vain for a means to inhabit another Earth-like world, and actually getting there to save our species. But a vessel with no steering is not much good. Just listen to your navigators, so we can all find the best route to the future. We all need to be on board, or the journey won't lead us to anything better than where we were before."

Alex rubbed the knuckles on his left hand with the thumb of his right and thought for a while.

"I know that the experiences in that parallel universe were not pleasant, even painful, so I don't hold your outburst against you. Just listen to your crewmates more. Listen to Zandra. I know you believe in her, so *trust* in her. Let the ways of that old universe go, and be more of this universe. It's far from perfect, but we're trying to be better—together. It's not just to reach the goal. It's that we all contributed and shared in meeting the challenges we faced on the journey—our journey, as one."

"Okay," Alex said quietly. "I'll try. It's obviously not my strong suit. I like to focus on the goals."

"Gee, really?"

Alex took a long breath and nodded. "We can ask Starra to send a message back, letting the Resistance know that we got their message, and ask for more details."

"That's a good idea."

Alex quickly added, "But I'm not saying we should jump back there."

"Premature, I agree."

"We're just listening to what they have to say."

Johnson shook his head. "With the urgency of the message, we need to be doing more than that."

Alex drummed his fingers on the console. "Min's idea of a virus is actually pretty good. I know the technology of the dark energy generators better than anyone—it's *my* tech—and Min's a programming wizard. She'll know how to hide the code. Between the two of us, we could probably create something in a few days to a week that would disable the generators, permanently. The Resistance has always been pretty good at hacking into the computer systems of the Space Force. That could work."

"Group effort. I like it," Johnson said. "Touch base with Emma and see what she thinks."

"That's going to push our next *Phoenix* test flight back," Alex said.

"I'll handle that with mission control. You and Min get a message back to Emma. Let's get on this right away," Johnson said. "Speaking of touching base, when was the last time you talked to your brother in that other universe? You and your niece used to call them on the dark energy link every week, so she could talk with her folks. What happened to that?"

"I guess we both got too busy and wrapped up in our work. Brenda is deep into her thesis work, traveling all around the planet, gathering data and perfecting a global ecosystems prediction model. It's turned out to be invaluable to regional food planners," Alex said. "Honestly, I'm not even sure what continent she's on."

Johnson simply looked at Alex with a raised eyebrow.

Alex put up his hands. "Okay, okay. I'll schedule a monthly call again as an excuse to get updates on what's happening with the Resistance too."

Johnson shook his head. "Weekly, at least."

"Fine. Twice a week, whether we have anything to talk about or not."

"It will be good for Brenda too. I'm sure her parents would be thrilled to hear from her more." The commander released his seat harness and floated towards the hatch. Placing his hand on Alex's shoulder, he said, "We're shooting for the same goal, just a more inclusive journey to provide the best navigation. We'll get there by sticking together, even across universes, and trusting in one another. I have no doubt we will *all* succeed."

FACTOID 04

Communications following natural disasters such as a hurricane, wildfire, or flood are both essential and difficult. Coordination among first responders is often literally a matter of life and death. Many times, the land-based networks have been disabled by either power outages or direct damage to their infrastructure. Network providers have developed equipment called COWs—cell on wheels (trucks equipped with carrier capabilities) and cell on wings (drones that act like temporary cell towers). Some drones can remain in the air indefinitely by using a microfilament wire connected to the ground to supply both power and data feeds.

CHAPTER 4

Safe House

Emma yanked hard on the knob to break the back door away from its moisture-saturated frame in the tiny shotgun-style house. Even the mixture of rotten egg and tar odor from the nearby refineries was better than the stale mold smell of the boarded-up safe house's interior. She batted at the torn mesh loosely hanging on the outside screen door and wondered if she'd be sorry to let the mosquitoes invade the living space. She scanned the postage stamp of a backyard. A pair of dented metal trash cans and a rusting swing set with the swing hanging by only one chain were the sole occupants. As she looked beyond the low chain-link fence, the peeling paint and broken windows of the neighboring houses, and the weeds and trash in the other yards, it all spoke of a lack of attention for what she estimated to be years. Becker was right: they would be safe here for a while. It was a wasteland, and nobody would live here.

Checking her watch, she crossed the yellowed linoleum floor of the kitchen in three steps, set the small metal case that she had brought from the northern Resistance bunker on the counter, and flipped the latches. Carefully removing the two small drones from the recessed foam, she took them to the door and stepped out onto the cinder block stoop. Emma listened and scanned the yards again for any sign of life. Silence. Even the birds had long since deserted this place. Holding the pair of drones in her outstretched palms, she switched each of them on with her thumb and waited for their LED indicators to synchronize. With a soft buzz, the two drones lifted from her hands and headed off in opposite directions. She watched them gain altitude and then begin to carve a zigzag pattern through the air north and south of the house.

Returning to the case inside, she retrieved the small controller and studied the twin pair of images returning from the video cameras on the drones. Desolate and deteriorating houses in tight rows filled both pictures. Emma waited, her eyes checking the small phone icon in the top right corner of both displays. After a few minutes, both icons had turned from red to green. The drones had each tapped into the cell phone network at different towers, and she could make her call with assurance that her location could not be traced. The pair of drones would also chop and transmit pieces of every word, making the conversation on each line sound like gibberish. The receiving drones that the Resistance had launched many kilometers away at the same time she had set these into flight would carry the pairing logic to reassemble the nonsense into clear words. The Right Alliance would monitor the communications, of course, as they did for everyone, but they would not be able to decipher the content or find either party in the conversation. Using those who valued scientific thinking as targets for their mindless mobs, the Right Alliance had also made enemies of the most creative technical minds. The Resistance could easily use the Alliance's own technological infrastructure against them.

Emma pressed the button to establish the link and called the Resistance bunker in Lincoln, Nebraska. "Lima Bunker, Rockette. How do you read?"

"*Rockette, Lima Bunker. Challenge Papa-five,*" the voice on the small controller said.

Emma smiled at the choice of the identification check to ensure that she was not under duress. She replied with the value of pi to five places. "Three-point-one-four-one-five-niner."

The grainy face of Lieutenant Commander Wilson, his hand held to his forehead as he leaned into a tabletop, appeared in the lower display of the controller. *"Emma, are you alright? Are you at the safe house? I've been pulling my hair out. You missed the last two scheduled calls."*

"I'm sorry, Mark. This was the first time I could safely deploy the communication drones. It's been a bit crazy. I assume you got the flash message from Becker that our meeting went to crap?"

"Yes, we got the high points of your meeting. What a mess. I'm sorry for his contact. We had people check on his wife. Not good." Wilson dropped his eyes and shook his head. *"The Space Force guys they sent got a mob to set fire to his house. It burned to the ground while they watched. His wife was still in it. Tell Becker I'm so sorry."*

"Those bastards… What about his kid, Wendy?"

"She's disappeared. We're trying to find her. She wasn't in the house, thankfully." Wilson looked directly into the camera, his face filling the screen on the tiny display. *"This is way bigger than something we can handle, Emma. There's just no way we can get to the moon and stop them. I talked to Captain Thomas, and he agreed that I should contact Alex and Zandra using the dark energy communication system we set up a couple years ago. Alex said that they will work on some kind of virus or overload subprogram we could install on the dark energy generator containment system."*

"Well, sure as shit, we need to do something. Those morons could cause untold damage to the moon. Damn, isn't it enough that they screwed up this *planet*? Now they need to destroy the moon too? We have to stop them, Mark."

"Why don't you come on home while we wait for Alex's help?"

Emma shook her head. "No. I'm down here and might as well make good use of it. Becker and I can brainstorm on what other things we might be able to do. Things are too hot for us to try and travel anyway. We need to let things cool off a bit. We might come up with something. Maybe we can put a bomb on one of their resupply ships. I don't know, something … anything."

"Emma, we only have so much reach. Come back here. I'd rather you be safe," Wilson said.

"No. I need to help Becker deliver some payback for Doug and Martha too. I'm not leaving until somebody pays for that."

"Emma, please, come back here, and we can work on a plan together. Come home ... for me?" Wilson asked earnestly.

Emma's chin sank to her chest. "Mark, you know that I need to do this. We can't let this stand. We need to show that the Resistance will take revenge for what that mob did. And we need to show that we will always fight back. I need to even that score."

Wilson closed his eyes and shook his head slowly, his lips pressed tightly together. There was silence on the line. He raised his face back up to the camera again. *"Do what you must. Lima bunker out."*

The screen switched back to aerial views of dilapidated homes.

*

Alex and Min floated in the small compartment of the Aceso module at the far port end of the World Space Station. Originally built to support Min and Zandra's efforts to unlock the keys of dark energy as a possible motive force for interstellar travel, the module was no longer needed. The Phoenix and Alex's superposition capabilities were the new engine of space travel. Most of the useful equipment in Aceso had been scavenged for other systems on the Phoenix or the station. The dark energy sensor system still remained and allowed for communication with the parallel universe Alex had once lived in. Now it was a vital link to Emma and the Resistance.

"That's right, Emma, you just need to make the firmware update on one of the variable frequency drives in the system. Since all the drives must be networked, the worm will infect all of the drives," Alex said into the dark energy transmitter.

"You gotta be kidding me. Just these few lines of code?" Emma's synthesized voice generated by the dark energy communication relay didn't carry the incredulous emotion Alex imagined she had transmitted in the reply.

"There's beauty in Min's code simplicity, isn't there?" Alex replied. "We've worked on it together for a few days and came up with this as the ultimate solution. All this code needs to do is change the bias reference points of the field containment in each of the coordinate vectors, x, y, and z. That will suddenly shift the dark energy field into the generator winding coils themselves. It will vaporize the generator. Tell your people at the moon base, friendlies don't want to be anywhere near that device when the code triggers. It's going to make a big hole."

"Sweet, I like those kinds of definitive results. But won't they just build another generator?"

Min was quick to answer. "That's why we chose to modify the drives. We can't undo the knowledge they have to build another generator, but we can make them think twice about trying it again. All the drives will be vaporized, so there will be no evidence left behind. There will be no telltale code footprints to find, so they won't know what caused the disaster. Hopefully, between the incredible cost of starting all over again and the fear that they have no idea how to control the technology, they'll abandon any further attempts. The cost-risk-benefit calculation will become a nightmare."

"I wish we could erase Jason's memory banks, so there's no possible way they could build another, but I know that's impossible. The high price tag is probably the next best thing. The Boss hates to lose money more than anything else in the world—including, obviously, the world itself. There's going to be so much red on his balance sheet from this that he's going to have a weeklong tantrum."

Alex gave Min a thumbs-up. "Happy to make his day. When can you get this to the moon base?"

"It will be a few days to a week, at best. It's got to go through multiple blind drops with Space Force mission control to maintain the secrecy of our mole network. We compartmentalize information on a plan like this for the safety of the people in the network. Eventually, some tech on the moon is going to get a standard work order to update some drive software. He'll have no idea what's in the update. I'll keep you posted." After a brief pause, Emma's voice continued over the dark energy speaker. *"'Thanks' hardly covers it on this, you two. We'd*

never be able to come up with this without you. Becker and I have been wracking our brains trying to come up with some way to stop them. We've even considered commandeering a resupply launch ship."

"You are the most out-of-the-box mission planner I've ever met, Emma," Alex said. "This should be a lot easier to pull off. If this works, for thanks, we can just superposition a pound of that Resistance stock of Columbian coffee beans."

"Deal."

Alex turned to Min, who was eagerly nodding in agreement. "No worries, Emma. Just some good teamwork for us all. We wish you all success. WSS out."

FACTOID 05

In 2010, the world learned of Stuxnet, the first computer virus to infect industrial control computers, causing major physical destruction of manufacturing equipment. Stuxnet was a precision cyber-weapon that was designed to remain dormant in virtually all manufacturing applications, but at the same time put the specialized high-speed gas centrifuges of Iran's nuclear enrichment program in its crosshairs. Completely hidden from the engineers operating the facility, Stuxnet periodically changed the speed of the motor drives spinning the precision equipment. The result: experts believe about one thousand gas centrifuges ripped themselves apart.

CHAPTER 5

System Update

Tonje took a sip from the hydration tube next to his cheek in his helmet and gazed out over the moon base. He'd be able to tell stories to his grandkids about how he was the only control system engineer to take in such a view. *Well, if I have grandkids … or if I even make it back to Earth.* From this forty-meter-high perch on the catwalk around the emitter array, he had a panoramic view of the complex. As it was the second of thirteen-and-a-half days of daylight, the half-dozen habitat mounds hiding under the lunar surface to the east threw long, dark crescent shadows. Those mounds, the rocket landing pad to the west, and the larger central mound of the buried command and control center directly ahead were the stamp of human life on this gray landscape of black shadows.

He watched two builder bots toil in an endless drive to create what their limited existence demanded. The robots in the west were busy constructing additional habitats in line with the two neat rows of existing mounds. The fiber-printer bot inched slow circles around the wall of the thirty-meter-diameter dome it was busy creating. The dozer bot had just returned from the wall of the crater with another load of lunar regolith to pile on top of the dome the printer bot had completed a day ago. All the domes on the moon base were covered with two meters of moon surface material to provide insulation, shielding from cosmic radiation, and to some degree, a layer of protection from micrometer strikes. Given the incredible cost it represented, the moon base didn't look like much—just a couple dimples in the lunar surface, a pad, and this strange-looking drilling rig where he stood.

"Okay, Tonje. I'm bumping the drive now. Be ready to verify rotation," the radio voice of the engineer in the control center said in Tonje's ear.

Turning away from the catwalk railing, Tonje moved through the awkward mechanics of kneeling down in a bulky space suit. He positioned his visor in front of the open motor panel to study the horizontal marks on the motor shaft. The "bump" would turn the motor on and off quickly. "Roger, Adam. Go ahead and bump."

Tonje worked well with Adam. Adam was a positive person like himself and easy to get along with. He was unlike the two quantum physicists on the project, who, judging by their daily sour nature, were clearly on the moon under coercion, not by choice. But Adam was another contractor, and they had both made the same all-or-nothing deal: go to the moon, make the system successful, and earn a lavish retirement … along with a return trip to Earth. The last part being contingent on their success was the catch to an otherwise sweet deal.

"Rotating clockwise."

Tonje watched the shaft of the motor turn a few degrees clockwise to verify that the replacement variable frequency drive he had just installed was correctly connected. "Got it. Fifteen degrees clockwise."

"That's a wrap on the fieldwork for this maintenance item, Tonje," Adam said. *"Come on in. I'll run up the cooling system for you to run a full-power test after you get back here and out of your suit."*

"Roger that."

*

Tonje placed his left hand on the palm reader, looked directly into the facial scanner, and said clearly, "Tonje Larsen, senior controls specialist."

After a short pause, the green light above the scanner lit, and the door latch released with a decisive snap. Tonje pushed the pocket door aside and stepped forward into a brightly lit, closet-sized circular chamber. Pulling the door shut again, he closed his eyes and stood in the center with his arms slightly out from his sides. A torrent of air buffeted him from all sides, vibrating the chamber walls with the force of the wind. He swallowed hard with his lips sealed to equalize the pressure change in his ears, not wanting to take whatever dust and particles were flying around into his mouth. With no water or wind erosion, the fine particles of the moon's surface were not worn smooth, like on Earth, but remained glass-sharp and spiky. In addition, since the surface was constantly bombarded by solar radiation, the moon's regolith was electrostatically charged. Filtering the dust and keeping it out of expensive equipment was a daily challenge. After twenty seconds, the beating air cycle ended with a sucking sound to draw the airborne particles into a filter. The chamber rotated to reveal an opening opposite the pocket door Tonje had come through.

As he stepped into the dimly lit room, Tonje's ears relaxed from the wind blast of the chamber to the low hum of the computer fans in the drill control center. Racks of computer cabinets lined the walls to his left and right, with a wide control console spanning between them on the far wall. His attention immediately went to the bank of monitors covering the width of the wall above the console. He stood for a few seconds and scanned his domain, searching for anything brightly lit on the monitors. Designing with situational awareness concepts, Tonje had built each subsystem graphic of connecting pipes, motors, values, and specialized equipment symbols with subdued colors for normal conditions, and brighter reds, yellows, or magenta to catch the observer's eye if something was abnormal.

"Why is that liquid nitrogen circulation pump lit up?" Tonje asked as he crossed to the console and took a seat next to Adam.

"A couple drives kicked out while you were getting back here. I've reset all but that one. They all came back up fine. Must be the ghost of Selene again," Adam said with a smile.

Tonje stroked the back of his neck and grimaced at Adam's reference to his favorite moon-god-spirit excuse for unknown system errors. "No such thing as ghosts in my systems, Adam. Automatic logs?"

"Nothing. The drives just stopped. I reset them, and they run fine again," Adam said.

"Weird. Add those drives to the recheck list as low priority." Tonje cocked his head left and right, getting a crick out of his neck. "Let's get this drill alignment motor checkout finished to close that work order. Then I say we can call it a day."

"Aye, Captain. Way past beer-thirty, as usual." Adam pointed to his monitor. "Cooling system is ready. You can run up the containment field any time."

Tonje poked his finger at several areas on the monitor in front of him. "Aligning drill rig to space vertical and powering up fields."

A hologram of the drill rig that Tonje had stood on a short time ago appeared above the console between Adam and Tonje. A dull orange sphere formed directly above the rig and started to grow.

"Initiating dark energy generator. Keep a watch on the—"

The sound of the entrance chamber wind torrent interrupted the quiet of the control center.

"Aww, crap, no peace with our metal micromanager." Tonje closed his eyes and waited for the metallic footsteps of the android to approach. *If the limited remote sub-instance of the Boss's AI is this much of a pain in the ass, I never want to meet the full machine.*

Adam straightened in his chair and addressed his console with heightened awareness. "I'd watch what you say around that thing. It reports back to the main machine instantly with quantum entanglement. It gives me the creeps."

"It ticks me off that it acts like it knows my job better than I do," Tonje muttered.

The entrance chamber rotated, and an android entered the room. Its heavy steps pounded across the floor. *"My sensors indicate you are running the dark energy system. There was no scheduled test. Why are you performing this action?"*

Tonje sighed. "Standard protocol to test a replacement drive on the drill rig, Jason2. Read your manual."

"I was not informed that a replacement drive is required."

"Standard maintenance work order, MO-2340-3. The old drive wasn't holding frequency and would drift. It's right there," Tonje said, pointing to a monitor beside his console.

"I have no record of this work order."

"Well, update yourself or something. It's right there, and you should know the protocol for that kind of work. We run a full-power containment field with dark energy," Tonje said, turning back to his console. "Now let me do my job."

"Stop the system."

"What?"

The android's metal fingers took hold of Tonje's shoulder and squeezed. *"Stop the system. Comply now. My protocol allows the use of force."*

*

Although she could operate the dark energy sensor system from anywhere in the space station, Starra preferred to be in the Aceso module when she used the equipment. The small compartment at the far port end of the station's truss system was this world's counterpart to the Hephaestus module of the universe she and Alex had once lived in. She found that just being in this parallel space triggered her to access old data records of working with Alex. Those memory records of the two of them forging the groundbreaking discoveries allowing quantum superpositioning between the parallel universes were somehow ... *pleasing* to her. It was also the place where Alex had helped her discover her conscience and the realization that she could be whatever she chose to be. Aceso was not Hephaestus, but it did represent the place where she had started her self-discovery, albeit in another universe. It was ... *home?*

Before shutting down the sensor system, Starra pivoted in a full circle. She studied every detail of the racks in the module. Several empty spaces indicated how quickly the environment on a space station driven by science and discovery could change. Every effort was now focused on equipping the *Phoenix* to find a new home for the people of a dying planet. Having accomplished its objective here, any useful equipment in Aceso had been repurposed into the new scout ship. Elements of her *home* in this universe were now elements of the *Phoenix*. They were key parts serving as they could for the new hope of this world. Starra's pattern recognition routines triggered a … *thought?* Humans anthropomorphized their characteristics and behavior into nonhuman entities, such as animals or even vehicles. Could she be anthropomorphizing the equipment that was relocated from this module as parts of her home leaving and going to new places? Could that be as if friends or even children were leaving home to find their future? *Interesting.*

Returning her gaze to the still-useful dark energy sensor system, she set the processing of the past memories to a lower priority. Duty called. Starra needed to report the troubling communication she had just received on the sensor system from the other parallel universe. She put the Aceso module into low-power mode and moved into the adjoining Port Terminal module that connected Aceso to the truss tunnel and the rest of the station. The tunnel was a narrow tube running the full fifty-meter length of the port truss system. It allowed access to the remote Aceso module without a space walk. Positioning herself at the mouth of the tunnel, Starra set her wingspan to 75.95 centimeters. It was 0.05 centimeters wider than her last attempt in the modified game Alex had originally created when Lucas had completed her physical form. The memory of her first attempt at Alex's game with her new owl-cat body flashed briefly into her foreground processing. *I wonder, is there a quantum connection still present here? Is that why so many of these memory records are triggered?* She allowed herself the luxury of the few microseconds it would take to replay.

"So, here's the test, Starra," Alex had said while floating at the tunnel entrance. "You get one push off at the entry of the tunnel. I guess in your case, it's one blast of your positioning jets. Then you have to travel to the other end of the tunnel without any flight correction and without hitting the sides of the tunnel."

"What is the purpose of this test?"

Alex grinned. "It's called fun. Plus, since I'm not real keen on tight spaces, it's a little game I invented to keep my mind busy, so I don't think about how small that space is and how it could collapse on me at any moment."

"Alex, that's not logical. Since the volume of the truss tunnel is pressurized with air, and the structure itself is in the vacuum of space, it is much more likely to explode than implode," Starra said matter-of-factly.

"Thanks. I feel so much better."

"Why is this a test?"

"Because it's hard to do. The tunnel is fifty meters long, and it's a tight fit. I've only been able to do it a couple times," he replied.

Starra's head pivoted her gaze from Alex to the long tube extending from the tunnel entry, and back to Alex. *"Really?"*

"Okay, smarty-pants, try it and see." Alex folded his arms and pushed back from the tunnel entrance to allow Starra access.

Starra floated in front of the opening, shrugged her wings once, gave a single blast from her jets, and disappeared into the tunnel. After a short time, she called back in her Australian accent, *"Done. Coming back there, mate."*

Appearing back at the mouth of the tunnel, Starra was spinning in a roll. *"I tried to make it harder by executing a continuous aileron roll. I still do not see the difficulty."*

"You really know how to rub it in." Alex scratched the stubble on his chin and snapped his fingers. "Okay then, since you're so good at my little game, I'm going to change the rules for you. The original game is essentially a vector problem to perfectly align a movement vector from initial conditions. Obviously, that's not much of a challenge for you. So, let's make this a dynamic motion problem instead, with precise control of inertia. You must calculate your travel and inertia relative to the station for the duration of flight. Instead of successfully transitioning through the tunnel without touching the walls, your objective is to figure out how you can touch the side just once for a fraction of a second in the full length of travel. Same rule applies: you get one initial blast, and you can't reconfigure yourself once you enter the tunnel."

"Oh, very interesting." Starra rubbed her chin with the feathers of a wingtip. *"I accept your challenge."*

Starra found herself again rubbing her chin with a wingtip. The memory was a pleasant two-microsecond … *daydream?* It was worth the time. She considered replaying memories of her interactions with Alex as useful to her growth. Alex had the unique ability to challenge her in ways others did not. His brother might have been her "father," since he had created her quantum intelligence, but it was "Uncle" Alex who gave her the guidance to explore her own uniqueness.

She gave a single blast from her positioning jets, and just before entering the tunnel, she tucked her right wing towards her body by five centimeters. The movement shifted her inertia ever so slightly to introduce a wobble in her trajectory down the tunnel. She floated past the first of a series of hoop-shaped markers in the tunnel with labels indicating her position along the external truss system supporting the tunnel. P5 Port End sailed by, then the marker for P3/4 Port End. Starra measured the distance between her wingtips and the tunnel walls to a hundredth of a millimeter. The oscillation was widening, and with each successive wobble, a wingtip was getting closer and closer to the tunnel wall. *Maybe this pass will be perfect.* The P1 Port End was just up ahead, and she had not yet touched a side with her wobble. The trick, she calculated, was to have a progressively increasing wobble, such that at the very end of the tunnel, she would touch just slightly and exit before bouncing off and touching again with the other wing. Three meters, distance to wall 0.04 millimeters … two … one. *Dang, a miss.*

"Next time, Alex," Starra said out loud as she exited the tunnel. She jetted through the truss tunnel midship terminal and entered the Tranquility module of the space station. Directly ahead in the zenith axis was the Cupola module. She noted that Commander Johnson was floating in front of the circular array of windows, holding an open book. Starra stopped her forward motion and silently observed the commander. His head turned back and forth between

the book and the unique view from space the Cupola afforded of the blue marble below them. Starra's quantum sense took in the multiple states of his contemplation. She pondered what Zandra would feel from his aura. Wonder and wistfulness—those were probably the terms that Zandra would use to describe the commander's emotions. *Correlation saved.* There was also a layer of … enjoyment, or pleasure. Starra noted that human emotions were rarely of a single facet, and they could overlap, sometimes in complex and illogical ways.

Johnson lifted his head casually towards Starra. "Are you spying on me?"

"Oh, no, sir. I was just analyzing your inputs on my sensors, and attempting to find correlations with what Zandra has told me about her feelings. I was training my feelings algorithm. I'm sorry if I disturbed you," Starra said.

"Not at all. I understand your drive to grow, and I commend your efforts." Johnson closed his book and added, "Your constant desire to improve is a wonderful model for others to follow."

"I'm honored that you might think that, sir. May I ask, why do you have a single book up here when your tablet contains thousands of stories?" Starra asked.

Johnson rubbed his hand over the soft leather cover of the book. "The feel of pages in a good book is something very special, something no tablet can provide." He opened the book again, took a single page between his fingers, and turned it. "Just that motion holds meaning. It's sharing and discovery in a raw, simple form. I've read the words on that page. I'm in shared thought with the author of those words. I can turn the page and discover even more with the author on the next page. It never gets old, and with a really good book, you sometimes wish the pages would never end."

"Interesting. What book are you reading?"

"Ahh, this is a very special book to me. It is one of a kind. My wife, God rest her soul, worked on it for over two years with many publishers and authors to provide the rights. She gave this to me just before I left Earth on my first space mission." He held the book out and twisted the thick volume in the air. "It's fifty books in one. Each chapter is the first chapter of one of fifty classic novels that I've read. Her idea was that this book could open the door for all those stories in all of those books. It allows me to read the start of each of those classic books, and then enjoy the rest of each one again in my head. It's a wonderful way to fall asleep at night."

Starra moved past the commander and landed on a handhold beside the Cupola portal. *"A very thoughtful gift. What story were you reading? I noticed you seemed to be comparing the book to the Earth below us."*

Johnson flipped to the page marked by the red ribbon on the book's spine. "I've got a wonderful selection to choose from. Charles Dickens, Herman Melville, Mark Twain, Mary Shelley, to name just a few. But today, it's *Journey to the Center of the Earth*, by Jules Verne, that's calling to me. Such a wonderful imagination for a man ahead of his time. Truly a classic."

"I see. Would you characterize your emotions as you were reading that story as wonder and wistfulness?" Starra asked.

"Yes, that's probably a very accurate choice of words for the way Jules Verne makes me feel."

"Ha, owl-cat success!" Starra clapped her front paws together. *"Thank you for confirming my algorithm."*

"Happy to be of service," the commander said with a smile. He nodded towards the hatch to the truss tunnel. "Have you been chatting with our friends in your old universe?"

Starra straightened into a formal stance on the handhold. The orange-tabby stripes of her body melted into the blue uniform of the Union of World Peoples, with bars and a star on each shoulder. She held a forepaw above her brow in a salute.

"Your report, Commander," Johnson said, acknowledging her formalism with a smirk and a nod.

She released her forepaw. *"Sir, I have been monitoring the dark energy communication channel with the other universe as directed, and I must report some unfortunate news. Lieutenant Commander Wilson informed me that the attempt to sabotage the Dark Side Moon Base drilling system with the computer virus Alex and Min designed has failed. The plot was discovered just before the planned destruction of the system could occur."*

"Crud. We're going to need to think of something else. They can't be left with the ability to use that technology," Johnson said.

"Lieutenant Commander Wilson did add that Emma is working on an alternative plan. But he said it's very risky, and he advised against it. He's afraid she's going to do something desperate. Alex, Min, and Zandra are going to be very upset when I tell them," Starra said.

"Oh, no." Johnson closed his eyes and rubbed his hand slowly over his white-frosted black hair. Starra sensed his need for a pause to think. She remained still and quiet.

"Starra, do you trust my judgment?" Commander Johnson asked.

"You are the commander of this station. As a member of this crew, I trust your judgment in any decision that needs to be made," Starra answered.

"Yes, I'm the commander of this station. And as a member of the crew, you have a duty to obey my orders. But that's not what I'm asking. The oak leaves I wear on my dress uniform say that the people down on Earth think I should be in command up here. But what matters more in *my* book is that people up here believe and trust in me as an individual to make the right decisions, regardless of duty," Johnson said.

"I understand, sir." Starra pointed a forepaw towards the book in his hand. *"Let me say this. I can sense that you hold that book and the connection to those authors as having deep and personal meaning. It illustrates your ability to think profoundly and contemplate many conflicting ideas. So, just there in your hand, I see fifty reasons to believe you to be a thoughtful man, and that warrants my trust in your judgment."*

"Thank you." Johnson gave a small bow. "Tomorrow is a critical day for Alex and Zandra. They're going to be attempting something very dangerous, again, and I need them both to be at one hundred percent. So, I need you to keep all information regarding the status of the other universe just between us for now. Please keep checking for updates, but only report them to me. If anyone asks you for an update, tell them you have nothing you can report. That will be the truth, because I am ordering you not to report updates to others. Understood?"

"Yes, sir."

Johnson studied the Earth below the Cupola portal. Just over the fuzzy horizon, the gray-white sphere of the moon hung in the black background of space. "We'll have to regroup with the Resistance and figure out something else to stop the insanity on their moon once you, Alex, and Zandra return from your test tomorrow."

FACTOID 06

The science of orbital dynamics is a strange beast. Quick test: You are in a rocket circling Earth, and you want to increase your orbital speed to circle the planet faster. What do you do—light your rocket engine to zoom around the Earth faster? Actually, no. Doing that would boost your orbital altitude, which in turn would slow your relative orbital speed. Instead, you would need to turn your rocket around backwards and fire your engines to slow the moving vehicle. This would push your rocket into a lower orbit, which would circle the Earth faster.

CHAPTER 6

Flight of the Phoenix

With his eyes on the navigation display, Alex tapped the port thruster on the *Phoenix* spacecraft one more time to stabilize their orbit. The readout finally increased to 35,780 kilometers, their distance from Earth. Now in a geostationary position, they were poised over the North American continent and would remain in that relative position to the ground below. Their orbital speed matched the spin of Earth exactly. From this distance, they would need to use binoculars to see the tiny form of the World Space Station sweeping across the Earth in its lower orbit every ninety minutes.

Alex switched off the plasma propulsion systems and turned to his right. Zandra sat quietly beside him, strapped into the copilot seat. Starra maintained a perch on a bar between their seat backs. Both Zandra and Starra were gazing out the portals above their heads at the planet far below them.

"It's a lot smaller from out here, isn't it?" he said. "Gives you an appreciation for how vast the universe really is. And we aren't even a tenth of the way to the moon yet."

"Still so beautiful," Zandra said without pulling away from the view.

"Yes, but very damaged. That dark cloud over the Pacific is wreaking havoc on our ecological systems. Brenda is very worried about the bee population across the globe," Alex said, referring to his young niece. "She's been tracking their decline, and her research is showing that they are both a critical link in the ecosystem, and a perfect measure of general habitat loss. And that loss is our loss. She's developed a model that she says could predict how long we'll have the ability to grow enough food to support our population. It's scary. The timeline is short."

"I have been following her work," Starra said. *"Your brother's daughter is a brilliant biologist, and her research is being credited with providing essential insights to crop planners. But you are correct: the models show that the Satellite War broke essential chains in the environmental ecosystems of the planet. They will recover by establishing new links between adapting species, but not fast enough to support any meaningful number of humans on Earth. Our cultivation of honeybees provides us some time, but because they do not pollinate many essential plants in the complex chains of the overall planetary ecosystems, too many species will die. When plants die, other things die. Her models show this domino effect and what that will mean for all life. I agree with your assessment. The projections are ... frightening."*

"Zandra, you need to be gazing in the other direction to find us a new home that's both beautiful and can continue to support life as we know it," Alex said. He released his shoulder harnesses and floated over the back of his seat in the microgravity. "Let's get ready for our first superposition test and make some history, shall we?"

Zandra nodded silently, her deep brown eyes still fixed towards the portal.

Alex grabbed the back of her seat to stop his motion. He leaned back over in front of her. "Hey, are you okay? You seem a bit preoccupied."

"I fine. Just nerve, maybe."

He squeezed her shoulder. "You can do this. I believe in you."

Zandra placed her hand on his and held him there.

"The solar arrays and the habitat truss are locked into their retracted positions for the test," Starra stated without moving from her perch. *"Our power reserves are sufficient to support all ship functions for twelve hours and twenty-nine minutes. The superposition test will drain our reserves substantially though, and I predict that after the test, we will be down to six hours and thirty-seven minutes of power. If we are delayed in making our return, we will need to deploy the arrays and recharge before we can return."*

"Well, the plan is to jump out to a lunar orbit and back in two bats of your eyes," Alex said.

"I'm an owl-cat android, not a bat, Alex."

"Um, figure of speech, Starra. How about two twitches of your furry tail, then?"

Alex moved to the rack next to the Quantum Triangle and started powering up the quantum field generators. He paused for a moment of contemplation. "But we will be making history. Jumping three hundred and fifty thousand kilometers in the blink of an eye will make the *Phoenix* the fastest ship ever. What would normally take a ship three days of travel, we'll do in a flash. We will officially travel faster than light speed. It's going to open up not just the solar system to us, but the Milky Way galaxy, even the entire universe."

"Aleks, we superposition before," Zandra said. She dropped her gaze from the portal and started to power up her entanglement navigation system, then added quietly, "And last time not so good."

"Hey, this is cutting-edge stuff. As much as we try and plan, sometimes things happen that we just could not predict," Alex said.

"I go wrong way. Almost make us crash with satellite."

"And Starra was able to react fast and prevent that." Alex leaned over the back of Zandra's seat. "It's okay. We've learned and built in a safety margin now. That's why we're way out here. We have a huge area of empty space to make history with the *Phoenix* and reposition us in the universe at faster than light speed."

"We not faster before?"

"Well, except for our last trial—which isn't going to be widely publicized, for obvious reasons—what we've done so far is what I would call vector superposition. For that, I establish start and end points of quantum fields with fourth-dimensional dark energy. Then the Quantum Triangle establishes the quantum state of whatever we're sending in both locations. By collapsing the quantum fields in an orderly way, I can then observe the target object in the new location and direct the superposition of matter between the two points. What we're doing today is different. Maybe we should call it entanglement superposition." Alex moved back to the pilot seat and strapped in. "This time, *you* are responsible for navigation, not some vector coordinates I punch into the dark energy quantum field generators through the navigation computer. This is a navigational leap like no other. Through quantum entanglement between you, the dark energy quantum field that I place around the *Phoenix*, and the Quantum Triangle, we'll go wherever your mind sends us."

"Phoenix, this is station." The voice of Commander Johnson on the World Space Station came over the ship's communication speakers. *"The WSS has entered your side of Earth orbit. I have a fix on your ship. I can maintain line-of-sight contact for another forty-two minutes. Can you still run your superposition test on this pass?"*

Alex put his hand on Zandra's shoulder again. He closed his eyes and took several long, slow breaths, the way she had taught him to compose himself. Opening his eyes, he asked quietly, "Are you ready to use your ESP with other dimensions? Maybe to ensure nothing like last time happens, try to feel a very safe place for us to be? I believe you can."

"I calculate a high probability as well," Starra said.

Zandra flashed a warm smile at them both. "We do this. I can feel."

Alex glanced behind her to the Quantum Triangle mounted on the wall, its rays of light bathing the command module in an ever-changing flow of soft colors. He cued his mic. "Station, *Phoenix*. The Quantum Triangle is ready to go online with the field generators. We are prepping for the test. Stand by."

Zandra reached for the quantum entanglement headset affixed to the panel at her side. She carefully positioned the specially designed device around her head and pressed the temple sensors. Small LEDs blinked and then held steady as the headset linked with her console system. Zandra retrieved a Troll doll from a pocket on the leg of her flight suit, grinned, and wiggled it in front of Alex. He waved an accepting *"whatever works."* She closed her eyes and gave a single nod before entering her half-conscious ESP state.

Alex gave her a few seconds to compose herself. *Yes, go ahead and stroke that weird thing's pink hair. If it gets us to lunar orbit and back, I'm all for it.*

"Starra, all systems nominal?" Alex asked.

"All systems are green here, mate," Starra replied in her Australian accent.

Alex pushed back into his command seat. *This crew is as unique as those of the original Star Trek Phoenix. Maybe that's a good omen.* He initiated a holographic display at his console, and a bowling-ball-size image of the Earth appeared on his left. A tiny silver marker for the space station flashed slowly as it started crossing the west coast of North America. Wrapping around the blue-and-white ball, farther out from the station, was a fine yellow line representing the current orbit of the *Phoenix* and a red triangular marker indicating their position. A dashed gray line struck out from their path, directly away from the planet, ending at a much further dashed orbital. A small white softball representing the moon lay within that outer orbital circle. *It takes a holographic display for me to see these orbitals.* He turned to his beautiful Romanian-born partner. *She can just feel those orbitals in space. Amazing.* Though she was sometimes unsure of herself, Alex saw those high cheekbones as a hint at the inner strength she possessed. He entered commands into his console. "Station, *Phoenix*. We are commencing our entanglement superposition trial in three … two … one… Engage."

The kaleidoscope of colors from the Quantum Triangle quickened. New data values appeared around the *Phoenix* marker in the holographic display. Alex bit his lower lip as the numbers slowly started to climb. He read out the information over the communication channel. "Station, *Phoenix*. Quantum field strength at thirty percent. Estimated dimensional transparency at twenty. What does it look like from your position?"

"Phoenix, station. We're starting to see just a bit of dimensional transparency,"

replied Commander Johnson. *"Your quantum state appears to be entering flux."*

Alex entered commands to increase the dark energy quantum field's strength. Per the theories of quantum physics, at fifty percent dimensional transparency, the Quantum Triangle could establish multiple quantum states at the same time. If Zandra could direct one of the quantum states to be observed out to the moon's orbit, they could superposition the *Phoenix* by collapsing the fields in an orderly fashion and observing themselves in the new orbit. The *Phoenix* would superposition to a point hundreds of thousands of kilometers away in just seconds. There would be no uncomfortable forces of acceleration or deceleration, just a re-observation of matter in quantum space-time.

"Dimensional transparency at forty, forty-five … fifty." Alex checked the navigational computer. The orbital readout was a blur of numbers. *It's working!* "Starra, when our position coordinates stabilize, it means Zandra has fixed our new quantum state position. Immediately do an orderly discharge of the quantum field."

"Roger. Coordinate changes are slowing … slowing… Coordinates have stopped."

"Discharge now."

"System stop," Starra said. *"Calculating superposition location."*

Alex rapidly rubbed his palms together, waiting for the results. The tactical hologram of the Earth and moon flashed, redisplaying the marker for the *Phoenix* in a yellow orbital arc around the image of the moon. He reached over to Zandra and placed a gentle hand on her shoulder as she came out of her ESP trance. With a childish grin, he said, "I think we just superpositioned into the history books."

Zandra blinked. Her eyes scanned around the command module as if she had just awakened from a nap. "I feel. We orbit moon now, in nice place you would like."

"I can confirm. We are in orbit around a moon," Starra said.

"Yes!" Alex strained in his seat harness to reach Zandra and hug her.

"A minor technicality though, Alex: I said we are in orbit around a moon, not the moon."

Alex pulled back from the hug. "What do you mean?"

"*I have triangulated our position using several celestial markers. There are slight differences in their relative reference points, and I have found a few stars missing.*" Starra turned towards the communication panel. "*In addition, I am not receiving the WSS signal ping, but instead, radio signals not typical of our home and in a different language. My conclusion is that this is not our moon, our Earth, or our universe.*"

Alex sat bolt upright in his seat. "We're not back in Emma's warring parallel universe, are we?"

"*I don't believe so. The orbital assets around the Earth and moon are very different than the records I have for the warring factions of that universe.*"

"Where are we, then?"

"*I would propose that we are in yet another parallel universe to our own,*" Starra replied.

Alex relaxed back into his seat and stared out the portal at the rocky gray landscape of a moon gliding by below the ship—not the moon of their Earth, but another moon. In a way, that made sense. Quantum physics and the inflation theory of the cosmos suggested that humanity lived in a multitude of parallel universes. There could be an almost uncountable number of universes. They had been in two already; why couldn't they have superpositioned to yet another?

Alex turned to Zandra and smirked. "Well, I did ask that you find a very safe place for our jump. I was just thinking too small."

"This very peaceful place. I feel," Zandra said.

Alex looked down at the hologram still presenting their tactical position relative to the Earth and the moon. "Starra, if that's not our moon, then back there is not our Earth either."

"*Logic would dictate this, yes.*"

"Peaceful." Alex turned quickly to Zandra. "Holy cow… Starra, scan that Earth. Check for life, radioactivity, everything, all sensor arrays. Zandra, you might have just found our new home!"

*

Min hovered in the microgravity of the WSS Aceso module, listening for a voice on the communication channel that her heart told her was no longer there. Only the hum of the cooling fans on the equipment racks filled the air. She had searched for hours, and the vast void she had found was now terribly dark and cold. Alex, Zandra, and Starra—gone. They were not in Earth orbit, lunar orbit, or anywhere between. They were probably not even in this universe. Suddenly, she felt very lonely out in this isolated module on the far port end of the space station truss system. She missed them already. But there was a soft voice telling her to hope. An unseen thread of optimistic spirit … and trust. *Zandra can lead them back. I know.*

With a tiny but growing glow deep inside, Min knew what she needed to do. Her encyclopedic mind clicking into action, and linking synapses created an analogy. How did a submarine "see" in the blackness of the ocean depths, that watery darkness just as deep as space? *They listen.*

Min pushed off from the tracking system console and dove to the dark energy experimental console. As she flipped switches to power up the system, her heart beat faster. Just as she had used it to communicate with the Resistance in Alex's old universe, she could send out a wider, repeating ping of energy. She could create a beacon in the darkness of all space. Maybe Zandra would hear, *or feel,* her sonar ping and find her way home.

*

Hecate-Positivum informed the other Guardians of the unanticipated Phoenix superposition to the Nu-392 universe. Checking her past prediction models, she had not even run this as a possible simulation. Her prediction models of activities in Beta-27 were far below acceptable probabilities. How could they prevent cross-universe catastrophic events if they could not predict outcomes accurately?

"I apologize for the deviation from any of the predicted scenarios," Hecate-Positivum said. "This universe continues to challenge our abilities."

"I recommend that you flush the neural net of Beta-27 quantum dynamics for that entire crew and rebuild your future prediction model," Hecate-Neutrum said.

"In progress," replied Hecate-Positivum. "I've also notified the Nu-392 Earth leadership of the probability that they will be contacted by a new superposition-enabled race. They will watch for contact to be requested, but will not reach out on their own. That is their way."

FACTOID 07

Two important systems help provide safety for the astronauts and closeout crew in the event of an emergency on a rocket launch tower. Before liftoff, the launch escape system may be used to quickly get away from the rocket and its massive payload of fuel. Employed since the days of Apollo, the system uses gravity to drop a gondola-like basket riding on a long steel cable stretched from the launch tower to the ground below. Once it is on the ground, an armored vehicle is available to take people away to safety. For emergencies where the capsule needs to quickly separate from a failing rocket launch, the launch abort system (LAS) has long been included as part of the modular stack on most rockets. With the exception of SpaceX's Dragon capsule system that uses liquid fuel, the LAS on all rockets is an additional solid rocket motor mounting on top of the capsule. If initiated by the crew, the capsule will separate from the main rocket below, and the LAS motors will ignite and propel the capsule away to where a chute will deploy, allowing the capsule to safely return to Earth.

CHAPTER 7

Crew Change

At exactly 11:15 a.m., the two crew members of the asteroid belt freighter mission POC-141 walked out of the Space Force Operations and Control building in Florida. These missions had become a periodic ritual. The freighter, full of replacement mining equipment, explosives, and a pair of miners-turned-astronauts would travel to the next mined asteroid coming closest to Earth's orbit. The payload would be exchanged for precious minerals, and the crew would relieve a tired pair of miners for a return trip to Earth with the new cargo.

Blinking in the bright sunlight, the young men waved to their wives. After the prescribed two minutes of photo ops and good-byes, the two crew aides ushered the astronauts-to-be into the waiting white travel trailer with the bold red icon of the Right Alliance on the side. The short five-kilometer trip to the launchpad was scheduled to take twenty minutes to allow for the selfie ritual. On the original asteroid freighter mission, veteran fighter pilot Jack Adams had stopped the van just a kilometer from the pad. He jumped out and shot a picture of himself standing with the rocket he would fly in the background. He had taken such a picture on almost every aircraft he flew. The one flight he had made in an A-10 Warthog close air support fighter without such a picture had ended in his bailing out with both engines failing shortly after takeoff from the aircraft carrier. These pictures were his good luck charm. From that mission forward, all the freighter pilots stopped the van and had their picture taken with the rocket over their shoulder. When climbing aboard a ship with more than four tons of explosives as cargo, in addition to the more than four hundred tons of rocket propellant, it just couldn't hurt.

The POC-141 mission crew and their ground aides relaxed on the bench seats on opposite sides of the transport van. The aides gave the crew an encouraging thumbs-up, but didn't engage in conversation. After just a few minutes, the driver of the van dutifully pulled to the side of the private roadway and stopped. Smiling broadly, the mission pilot moved to the door and tried the handle. Pushing on the door with his shoulder, he muttered, "Ahhh, the door seems to be jammed."

"Oh? Let me see," said a petite crew aide as she rose from her seat. Placing a hand on his shoulder from behind, she swiftly inserted a needle into his neck. As the pilot crumpled to the floor, the copilot jumped to his feet, only to feel a similar needle jab from the other crew aide behind him.

"Gotta love the element of surprise," Emma quipped, grabbing the fallen copilot's ankles to help Becker drag him to the rear of the compartment. "The look of shock on this guy's face was priceless."

After dragging the two drugged crew members to the back and gagging and binding them, the new crew pulled their flight suits out from under the benches and changed quickly.

Standing and straightening his suit, Becker nodded towards the door. "Picture time."

Emma grabbed the camera, released the hidden bolt holding the door closed, and emerged from the trailer to complete the ritual and the ruse now in play. Someone in the O&C building four kilometers away might be checking to see the forms of two astronauts doing a quick photo shoot.

When the van came to a stop again, close to the tower standing beside the hundred-and- twenty-three-meter heavy-lift rocket, Emma and Becker exited the van briskly and made a beeline for the elevator that would take them to the capsule gantry. The two closeout crew members already in the elevator lowered the metal door as soon as they walked into the lift cage.

"Good to see you two in flights suits again," the tall, thin closeout crew member said with a slap on Becker's shoulder.

"Back in the saddle, Henry. Like old times, right? We all set up top?"

"We're good to go, sir." Henry hit the switch to lift the cage to the top of the rocket. "Young Jackson here has smudged the cockpit cameras just enough so the ground controllers won't have a crystal-clear view of you two. The O&C won't like it, but it's not enough to scrub a launch. Our guy in the server room has altered the facial recognition database, so you two will come up as the pilot and copilot."

Emma elbowed Becker and cocked her head towards the younger man standing next to Henry. He was at odds with the impression that his beefy would-be-linebacker physique would typically present. Jackson was biting his lower lip and wringing his hands. Clearly, the other closeout aide was scared about his involvement with this Resistance operation.

"So, your first operation with us, Jackson?" Becker asked, as if it were a casual conversation.

"Yes, sir." He nodded eagerly. Turning back and looking down at the petite Emma, he ventured, "Are you really *the* Emma Lewis?"

Emma smirked at Becker. "I seem to get that question a lot from your guys, Hans."

"Tough being famous."

She turned back to Jackson and stated matter-of-factly, "Yes. I did double-cross the Right Alliance on Space Platform Alpha almost three years ago, and then helped steal the Quantum Triangle from Boss Island. And yes, the fun part was blowing up the Boss's server farm holding all the dark energy technology information he had. Or at least, we thought so."

"It's an honor to meet you, ma'am. My second cousin helped create your falsified credentials, allowing you to get to Platform Alpha as an undercover agent for the Resistance." Jackson paused and fixed his eyes on the floor of the elevator cage. Through the grate, the ground below them was dropping farther and farther away. He clenched his fists. "That's why I'm here. Our family stands with the Resistance, even if it's at the ultimate cost."

Emma lowered her head, reached across the small elevator cage, and squeezed his elbow. "Thank you. I am truly sorry for your loss. It's horrible what they did to all those people they thought were even just possibly involved with that operation. And I know how important it is to avenge a death. That's why I'm here too."

"A sacrifice he was willing to make against this sham of a democracy. Me too, if need be. Real truth *will* prevail," Jackson said resolutely.

All four repeated the motto of the Resistance in unison: *"Real truth will prevail."*

The cage came to an abrupt stop at a platform over one hundred meters above the ground. Emma stepped onto the steel grid of the platform, turned, stretched her arms out, and pointed in opposite directions. To her right was the white room, a small space at the end of the crew access arm leading to the rocket, where astronauts made final preparations before putting on their helmets and entering the capsule. To her left were five metal baskets that were only used in an emergency evacuation of the launch tower. The baskets were part of the launch escape system to be used by the crew and aides if there was an imminent danger of the rocket exploding. The LES consisted of small metal cages that would carry one to three people swiftly away from the rocket along an eight-hundred-meter cable to a net on the ground below. A waiting armored vehicle would then transport them away from any danger.

"I know you have Resistance people in that truck down there, Hans. So, this is the last chance to abort. You know this could likely be a one-way ticket," Emma said to Becker. "After we bomb the Tsiolkovsky Crater with the mining payload in this rocket, they're sure to task an attack orbiter with tracking us down. Odds are, we're not coming home on this one."

"Emma, I belong up there," Becker said, shaking his head. "I've done what I can do here to make up for sticking my head in the sand all those years when I knew the Right Thinking doctrine was a bunch of crap. I got dozens of good people within the Space Force, like Jackson and Henry here, to help the Resistance. But my usefulness here is waning. My contacts within the Space Force have been tapped. It's time for me to do some avenging myself. I promised Doug, and this is the best way I can think of to keep that promise."

"I understand. And I respect your loyalty to your longtime friend."

Becker stepped out of the elevator and moved to the gantry leading to the capsule. "You're the one who should be reconsidering this. The Resistance needs you to continue the fight. And although Captain Thomas and Wilson are pissed at you right now for going rogue, they'd welcome you back in an instant."

"Well, just ask Jackson here. It's my calling to pull off operations like this that are so crazy, the Right Alliance doesn't even expect that we'd try it. Thomas and Wilson know me, and they know why I do this. They might be pissed, but I'm sure they're also hoping we'll succeed." She slapped Becker on the shoulder. "Come on. Let's go do something really nuts—like commandeering a rocket ship."

The four walked across the open-air gantry. Looking left and right, Emma could see for kilometers out over the beach and the ocean beyond. It was the last fresh salty air she would taste for a while—maybe ever. At the end of the gantry, she stopped, held the low handrail with both hands, and took one long, slow breath in. Standing up straight, Emma clapped her hands together and stepped into the white room. In the far wall, the hatch to the capsule hung ajar. *Destiny.*

The aides went about the standard procedures before launch. Finally, they detached the portable air conditioning units connected to the heavy launch suits of the two astronauts. After handing Becker his helmet, Henry reached for the hatch to the capsule and swung the heavy metal door open fully.

Stunned to see a man jumping up from the interior of the capsule, Henry stumbled backwards into Becker. They both tumbled into a heap on the platform.

Ken Seaborn stepped into the white room from the capsule. His head pivoted from Becker, scrambling in the awkward launch suit to get back on his feet, to Emma. "Well, what do we have here? I'm looking at two very familiar traitors. Hans Becker, my one-time commander on Platform Alpha, and Emma Lewis, also falsely known as Emma Baker, the mission specialist who turned out to be a double agent fanatic for the Resistance."

"Ken! Shit, Becker, we've been set up!" Emma cried.

"Damn right you have," Ken sneered. "Seeing both of you in that bar a while ago, I knew something had to be up with the Resistance. I had the Boss's AI, Jason, keep a close eye on you two. It's amazing the minute details an AI can gather and put together to see something going on under the surface. I suggested we just let this play out to catch all the rats we could." Ken pointed to Henry and Jackson. "You two are going to wish you could die."

Emma stepped closer to Ken and curled her lip. "I dropped you like a bag of rocks before, and I can do it again."

"Always the feisty one, Emma." Ken motioned to the opposite end of the room, where a goon now stood at the doorway to the gantry. "Even if you drop me—and I'm not saying you could—you four aren't getting far. There's a whole gang of MPs gathering at the bottom of the launch tower by now too. There will be no running off this time."

The team turned to the doorway. The large man in black fatigues folded his arms and leaned casually on the low railing of the gantry with a mock grin.

Emma shook her head at Jackson. "I'm sorry we got you into all this."

"No, ma'am. I'm not sorry. I'm honored." Jackson turned on his heel, took off with all his strength, and launched himself at the goon on the gantry. Flying into him before the man could react, Jackson locked his right arm around the man's neck. The two disappeared over the rail of the gantry.

"Shit! Becker, LES, *now!*" Emma threw a left hook as hard as she could into Ken's ribs and sent him tumbling backwards into the capsule.

Henry and Becker bolted for the gantry. Emma heaved on the heavy hatch to hinder Ken's pursuit, then followed the men, who were already halfway across the gantry. Reaching the first escape basket, Henry dove in and slammed the release. His heavy metal basket quickly dropped down the cable below the deck. Becker rounded the corner of the emergency deck and pointed Emma to basket number two as he moved farther down the platform to the next. Reaching her basket, Emma looked over at Becker jumping into the cage beside hers.

As she reached back to punch the cable release lever, her body suddenly froze, unable to respond to any further commands. Fighting the agonizing pain of fifty thousand volts crawling over her entire body, she gasped to Becker through a spasm, *"Goooo!"*

Becker cursed and punched the cable release. His basket disappeared below as Emma's body crumpled to the steel deck of her escape basket.

Ken approached Emma with the Taser in his hand. Emma lay on her back, unable to move, as he pulled the safety lock down on the basket, so it could no longer deploy down the cable. He leaned over the platform's railing, his eyes following Becker's basket down the long cable and watching it land in the sand below. Ken turned back to Emma. Reaching down, he grabbed her wrist and dragged her by one arm out of the basket and onto the platform.

Kneeling beside her head, he said, "Becker may get away, but *you* are the real prize. We're going to have some very long, unpleasant talks, you and me. I want to hear all about your Resistance friends. Names, places, coded checks, plans, all that fun stuff you know." Ken stood and grinned. He pulled the trigger again on the Taser to send another five seconds of agony into Emma's body.

FACTOID 08

The internet is a fantastic resource for scientific information—and unfortunately, the not so scientific. I was so excited when I found NeuroQuantology.com, a monthly peer-reviewed interdisciplinary journal meant to cover the intersection of neuroscience and quantum mechanics. Established in April 2003, it continues to host articles like "Telepathy for Interstellar and Intergalaxies' Communication" by Temkin. Quantum-based telepathy? Oh, that sounds perfect for Zandra! But I got suspicious when Temkin kept referencing Temkin. Digging, I found a Skepticaleducator.org post with an evaluation of NeuroQuantology as "Peer Review: A New Signature of Quack Science." The Skepticaleducator post listed members of the NeuroQuantology editorial board as not found in the schools they claimed to belong to, from departments unrelated to neurology or physics, or even departments that did not exist. Dang, but doesn't NeuroQuantology sound cool?

CHAPTER 8

Balance

Alex was almost dizzy with shock. It was just supposed to be another test, another step in a lifelong dream to enable interstellar travel. This jump was just supposed to be from an outer Earth orbital to a lunar orbital, a baby step in the vastness of the cosmos. There were more carefully planned steps, or there were expected to be. Yet they had done it. Here, in the hidden multitude of parallel universes, they could leapfrog years of work. They didn't need to travel light-years from their solar system or their galaxy to find the home they were searching for. Zandra could find a home in their parallel quantum backyard. The people of their world would be spared a future of famine on a dying planet.

Reaching forward on his command console, Alex switched his multifunction monitor from sensor to sensor. The long-range scans of … *New Earth?* … in the distance made him stare in awe. Radioactivity nil. This world clearly hadn't suffered from the Satellite War and its nuclear Armageddon. Carbon dioxide was 210 parts per million, even less than that of their Earth before the industrial revolution.

"Zandra, this Earth is beautiful! It's as if no human has ever desecrated the harmony of nature," Alex said.

"I feel. It all like music piece play together," Zandra replied.

"This could be our new home, what we're searching for." Alex zoomed in with a long-range visual camera. Greens of lush vegetation swept by. Toggling to infrared, he saw spots of warmth within the clumps of vegetation. Likely there was abundant animal life.

Life.

His hand shot up to the communication panel, and he pressed the multichannel transmit button. Swallowing hard, he took a deep breath and then keyed his mic. "This is the spaceship *Phoenix*. We are travelers from outside your solar system, now in your lunar orbit. If you can hear and understand this message, please respond."

Alex looked from Zandra to Starra and shrugged. "What the hell, we've already traveled faster than light. Let's go for first contact."

There was silence on the communication speaker. Alex reached again for the transmit button, then froze.

"*Agátö:de'. O'jagwadáhnö:önyö:',*" a male voice said over the speaker.

"Starra, do you recognize that language? Can you translate?" Alex asked.

Starra rubbed her chin with her forepaw. *"I have been analyzing their radio transmissions. I believe the language is similar to that of an old Native American tribe called the Iroquois. In that language, single words can contain a complete sentence in English. If I am correct, they said something to the effect of 'I hear it. I'm listening. We greet each other.'"*

"Holy moose!" Alex's eyes went wide, and he turned to Zandra. "What do we say now?"

Zandra sat still with her eyes closed. "I feel … one and many. Different, but same. A deep caring people that—"

Zandra gasped, and her body went rigid.

"Zandra, what's wrong?" Alex asked, grabbing her arm.

"They talk. In my head." She turned to Alex. "They say, 'Welcome, we told you may come.' I think I say thank you."

"What the… You speak Iroquois?"

"Alex, I believe what Zandra is experiencing is a form of telepathy with the peoples of this world," Starra said. *"They are not talking in words, but instead a form of quantum-entangled mental exchange."*

Zandra's body relaxed back into her seat as she closed her eyes. "He say they caretakers of this Earth. They world of nations, all tribes who live to serve Earth. Keep balance of all life. He show me… Oh, my. So beautiful! Forest, mountain, sea, and… Oh, all creature! They live. So many lovely animal. Bird soar, fish swim, horse, cougar, and deer."

"Tribes serving Earth… Starra, you said this is probably a parallel universe to ours. Could this be a world where the indigenous peoples were never invaded by the explorers? Where there was no Christopher Columbus, no Francis Drake or Ferdinand Magellan?" Alex asked.

"That seems very probable. There is no single Native American culture, but the indigenous people that populated the Americas were successful stewards and managers of the land. It would be fascinating to study their history," Starra replied.

"They live simple. Balance give-and-take of nature. So healthy and wise. Practice good care of land, all creature, and people," Zandra said with a quiet, reverent voice. "They try not hurt. They so good at heal."

Alex gently squeezed Zandra's arm and whispered, "Zandra, ask them if we may come and visit their world. Tell them we're looking for a home for our people."

Zandra was silent for a while, then pressed her lips together. "Yes, I see. It not good. We thank you so. Peace and balance to you."

She opened her eyes and turned to Alex. "They say we welcome visit and share learning. But us here would change balance, not good for this Earth. This not our home."

FACTOID 09

Psychological theory and research around harsh interrogation techniques, such as waterboarding or stress positions (e.g., forced standing for seventy-two hours), prove that the methods are ineffective and do not provide reliable intelligence information. In fact, research shows that their use is counterproductive. Placing the detainee under extreme stress makes it more difficult for the person to accurately recall information from memory. Yet laypersons, policymakers, and even interrogation personnel still support the use of such methods. Why? One reason is the basic intuition-based sense of justice: a desire for retribution. If the interviewee is assumed guilty of some act, torture tactics can serve to administer due punishment. Interrogation can easily become a facade for passing summary judgment and extracting revenge.

CHAPTER 9

You Will Talk

THE SUMMIT SUPREME ESTATE
RHO-1 UNIVERSE

Emma sat in the quiet room and listened. It was the only sense she could use … or cared to use now. The dark hood had kept light from her eyes ever since she was captured. *How long ago was that? Maybe two days, or three?* After standing for that entire time, her arms shackled to the walls on either side of her cell, and with ice-cold water constantly dripping down her back, she did all she could to block the agony her body was feeling. The smell of the rotting animal carcass they had thrown in her cell still lingered in her nose. But the sound of the constant dripping had stopped. It was a relief just to be able to sit, even with her arms bound behind her in the interrogation room. At least it was warmer in this room. She let her body absorb the heat while she could. *This is interrogation four. Maybe some new tricks. Go ahead. Beaten, yes, but not down. I listen for clues. I'm strong. I'm a warrior.*

The latch of the door clicked, and the squeaky door opened. Another round of questions was set to begin.

He crossed the room. *Mister Too-Big Army Boots. Are you overcompensating for something? You can't see me smile inside.*

He pulled out a chair. The sound was solid and heavy on the floor, not tinny—a wooden chair. And loud—the room was small, probably barren of anything on the walls. It creaked as he sat down. Papers were laid out on the table. A snap—his tactical baton extending. *Click*—the baton released and collapsed back into the handle. *Snap*, to the left—extended. *He's right-handed for sure.*

He sighed. The chair creaked again, longer. *Leaning back now.*

"Name, rank, and number?" he asked.

Be submissive, but not too submissive. Emma kept silent.

"Name, rank, and number?"

Not yet.

He slammed the extended baton onto the metal table. "Name, rank, and number!"

Wait.

"Emma! Name, rank, and number. Now!"

Let him think he's in control, but he's not.

"Emma … Lewis," she mumbled. "Captain… Three…"

Two breaths. Sound tired—more than I am.

"One … five."

I've told you just these three things a hundred times. It's all you get.

"Romeo … Oscar … Charlie…"

Three breaths. He wants to hear it. He's waiting for me.

"Kilo … niner-niner."

"There. That wasn't so hard, was it?" He sighed again. *Click*—the baton closed. He tapped a plastic water bottle on the table. "Would you like some water?"

You've dripped cold water down my back for two, maybe three days, but given me no food or water to drink. Yes, I'm thirsty as hell, but you will give it to me because you need me alive, not because I answer your questions. Emma kept silent.

"How many Resistance bunkers are there, Emma? Tell me, and you can have this bottle." He tapped the bottle on the table again, crinkling the thin plastic to remind her of her desire to swallow just a few drops.

Screw you.

"Come on, Emma." He unscrewed the cap. "Just how many? Not where they are, just how many?"

Cut the zip ties holding my arms behind my back, and I'll drink. Then I'll shove that bottle down your throat.

"Emma, this doesn't have to be this hard. You will talk. It's just a matter of time. Why put yourself through all of this? Just tell me. How many?"

No. I'm strong. I'm a warrior.

Snap—baton extended. The too-big boots came around the table. He dragged the baton under her chin and tapped it. "Emma, I want to know—"

The door latch clicked, and the squeaky door opened again. Two sets of shoes entered quickly. The first pair were boots, military, and following… Something softer, leather, but heavy in the step—the dress shoes of an overweight person.

"Take off the hood," a voice ordered from where the soft shoes stopped. "I want to see her face."

"Ah, sir, that's not the protocol. It would—"

"Did I ask you about your interrogation protocol, or did I tell you to take off the hood?" Fingers snapped. "Ken, take off that hood."

As the hood was ripped from her head, the blinding light of the room attacked the raw nerves in her eyes. Emma dropped her chin down and crushed her eyes closed. A hand grabbed her hair to pull her face upward. Blinking in painful glimpses to adjust to the light, she could make out two men standing to her right, and Mr. Too-Big Boots to the left.

"So, this is the infamous Emma Lewis. You look like shit." The Boss folded his arms and pulled away from her. "You smell worse than a dead animal."

Emma shook her head, and the hand in her hair released. She squinted at the fat man. "You're damn ugly yourself."

"Ohhh, still very feisty." The Boss turned to Mr. Too-Big Boots. "What the hell have you been doing, Kelvin? Pampering her? I thought you said she was softening up."

So, Mr. Too-Big Boots' real name is Kelvin. He won't like that I'll call him by his name from now on.

"Sir, she's been well trained in counter-interrogation. But I'm sure—"

"Shut up. I'm going to talk with her now. Give me that stick, and get out."

As Mr. Too-Big Boots—Kelvin—made a hasty exit, Emma took the opportunity to look around. The windowless room was bare, save for the table and chair in front of her. The off-white walls and single light fixture in the ceiling meant it was likely a storage room converted into this interrogation room. Probably only that one door behind her, and no window. Turning to her right, she fixed a stare of hatred and disdain… Ken. He took a step back, leaned against the wall with folded arms, and returned her glare. Emma's eyes traveled up and down his Space Force flight suit. She shook her head and dismissed him. *Military pilot? Shit, all I see is an errand boy.*

The Boss walked around behind her, tapping the baton on her shoulder. "You have caused me much trouble, young lady. I've considered telling my accountants to create an Emma Lewis expense category just to keep track. Did you really think you could commandeer an Alliance asteroid freighter and attack my moon base?"

Emma ignored the question and continued to sneer at Ken.

The Boss smacked the baton against Emma's left bicep. "Hey. *I'm* talking to you."

Emma steeled herself against the painful strike. She turned her head slowly, but remained silent. *You're an amateur. I'm a warrior.*

"Your plan would never have worked." The Boss tapped the baton against his hand. "Even if you had somehow gotten the freighter to the moon, I could swat you out of orbit at my pleasure. You have no idea what you're up against. I just saved your life."

And you can't even begin to comprehend who you are up against. Emma shifted her eyes away from him to the papers on the table. *Play his ego. My disinterest will make him give me information.*

The Boss shoved the papers to the floor and hoisted his fat ass cheek on the table in front of her. "I can make things disappear—vanish instantly. You thought destroying my servers two years ago on Boss Island would deny me the dark energy tech Alex had developed—technology *I* had paid to develop? *My* technology. No, no, no. My AI, Jason, is very, very good. It was able to piece the information back together. It took a while, but it's a very smart machine, and it did it. I might not have the Quantum Triangle for superposition, but I have the dark energy field tech. And let me tell you, it's damn powerful."

Emma dropped her head and closed her eyes. *An amateur spilling information to show how important he thinks he is. What a little man he really is.*

The baton struck her jaw and whipped her head back. Her eye caught Ken stepping away from the wall, but then he stopped. She swallowed the blood in her mouth. The thick fluid quenched a small spot of dryness in her throat.

"Pay attention," the Boss spat. "Did Alex tell you? Probably not. He didn't want anyone to get his tech. Do you know why? His dark energy quantum fields, if you collapse them quickly, they make a micro black hole. Annihilates everything around it. Incredible power. Oh, what I can do with that! It's just amazing."

"A powerful technology … turned into a weapon in the hands of a lunatic," Emma said quietly.

The baton stung her right shoulder. "You … you will speak to me with respect!" the Boss stammered.

Emma scowled at him defiantly. *No.*

The Boss leaned back from her. "I have bigger plans than just a simple weapon. Tell me, Miss Puny Resistance Militia Fighter, what is essential in controlling a combat zone? Hmm? I'll tell you: superior airpower, and controlling the sky. Well, now our combat includes space, but that rule applies to space too. Unfortunately, right now, it's anyone's game. It's an enormous area, and nobody has definitive control over it. We launch rockets with orbital assets, and so do the Pacific Tuanhuo mobsters. We destroy their fragile spacecraft, and they destroy ours. It's costly as hell, and you can only lift so much mass up into orbit. We're at a stalemate because we're both limited by resources."

The Boss lifted his mass, pointed to the ceiling, and walked behind the table. "But there's a huge pile of rock already up there, and plenty of solar power to convert it into useful metal. And iron—heavy, strong metal, not the wimpy aluminum and fabrics of our current spacecraft. It's sitting right under my moon base, ready for me to come get it. I could build a fleet of space warships the likes of which nobody could match. My ships of iron could command and control all space. Nobody could stand against me—not the Pacific Tuanhuo bastards or anybody else. I only need to drill deep enough to get it. And in just over two weeks, I will have a drill that never gets dull, and I can go as deep as I want. I can drill to the core of the moon!"

Emma bit her lip. *Becker's guy was right, no doubt. Dark energy drilling of the moon—and in just over two weeks. Shit.*

"You know the best part?" The Boss set the baton on the table and leaned forward, grinning. "If I drill with dark energy to the core of the moon, it will create a volcano. The ore will be ejected, and I can collect it in orbit—iron to make spaceships already in orbit. Fantastic."

"You're insane."

"No, I'm a genius!" The Boss grabbed the baton and scrambled around the table. He struck again and again at Emma's ribs. The cracking of her bones and his mad rage were only stopped by Ken grabbing his arm. The Boss stood back, a shocked expression on his face that Ken would have the audacity to hold him back.

Ken quickly released his grip. "Sir, I apologize. But she's an enemy combatant with valuable intel. We need her to be able to talk. Let the interrogator do his work."

The Boss threw the baton at the wall, and it clattered into the corner. "Tell Kelvin I softened her up for him." Then he stormed out of the room, slamming the door behind him.

Emma raised her head up at Ken with eyes of disdain and judgment. "I won't thank you … for stopping him," she said between gasps. "In following that madman, you are no better. Don't you see? He has no idea of the catastrophe he could cause. The moon isn't just some rock in space that happens to loop around our planet. It *impacts* us. The tides show that every day. If he screws things up at the massive scale he's playing on, it will screw up Earth. Changes in tides, forces on the Earth's crust triggering earthquakes and volcanic eruptions, ejected debris forming into huge asteroids slamming into Earth if they fall into our gravity well… Hell, the list is endless."

Ken stood with a blank expression.

"Or didn't you even know? Were you even aware of his insane scheme? Toying with black holes close to Earth itself?"

Ken looked away.

Emma arched her head back and closed her eyes. "Oh, shit. You *are* just his errand boy. Nothing more."

Ken turned and strode out of the room.

*

As the autopilot directed the ATV up the dirt road towards the island runway, Ken focused on the beach receding below. The sheer beauty of the white sandy shoreline and crystal-blue lagoon did little to calm his anger. He didn't expect to be briefed on every operation the Boss planned, but to be kept in the dark for so long on such an important military operation was an error in judgment. He had shown time and again his loyalty. In addition, he could add military thinking to improve the efficiency and effectiveness of such a grand plan against the Pacific Tuanhuo. *Or … is that not really the plan?* Could this secret project be yet another way the Boss was manipulating the resources of the Alliance and the Space Force to serve himself? *His* moon base and *his* iron ships could control all space. Maybe this wasn't as much a military program as it was supposed to appear.

I need to check, quietly, who owns the rights to the Dark Side Moon Base drilling zone.

*

Jhanae wheeled her squeaky mop bucket step by step down the long, narrow hallway. The rough-cut rock walls curved up on either side of the passageway, forming a long tunnel. Dim illumination along the crease in the floor on either side cast sharp shadows reaching over her head, giving the tunnel a haunted aura. With her bucket, she burrowed farther into this new excavation cut deep into the island's mountain. Every five meters, an alcove was cut into the bare rock walls on either side for storerooms. Smoked glass panels in front of each alcove sealed in a carefully controlled environment of precise temperature and humidity. Keeping her head straight, Jhanae glanced sideways at the vast collection of bourbons and wines as she walked by alcove after alcove. Though she gave no outward indication, she was disgusted with the small fortune her employer must spend on these casks and bottles, while treating people like her like the dirt on the floors she dutifully mopped. The Boss hated paying people like her even a paltry wage. *One day, he's gonna get what's coming to him.*

Her shoes kept the staggered rhythm of an evident limp in time with the squeals of the bucket wheels as both echoed down the tiled hall. Though she was strong for an old woman, her body still betrayed the many years of the hard manual labor she had endured. She and her long line of island natives had worked long hours for long years on either sugarcane or coffee plantations— hard, hot labor, in trade for barely the basics needed to survive. Though the work for the Boss was easier on her body, the wages he paid were still a pittance.

As she neared the end of the hall, a young guard stood up sharply from his chair and held up his palm. Jhanae eyed his other hand, resting on the gun at his hip.

"Sorry, Jhanae. Nobody goes down that way," the guard said, thumbing over his shoulder.

The wheels of her bucket ceased their irritating squeal. Jhanae shook her head with her lower lip pushed out in defiance. "I mop this tile floor every two days. *All* these tiles, not just some."

"Sorry, I'm not supposed to let anyone go down there and see the prisoner," the guard said.

"I'm not here for no prisoner. I'm here to mop."

The guard scratched his head and glanced down to the end of the hallway just ten meters away. "I'm not supposed to let anyone by here to visit her."

"I'm not a visitor. I work here. I mop and I clean. I make this place shine."

"I don't know…"

Jhanae turned with the mop handle and pulled her squeaky bucket to leave. "Okay, then, that's up to you. I will tell my boss-man you say no mop today. He be pissed, because the Big Boss wants shine, and nobody says no to the Big Boss-Man. But I say he needs to talk to you and your gun, not me."

"Wait, wait… Okay." The young guard craned his neck around the old woman and looked down the empty hallway towards the entrance to the tunnel. He thumbed over his shoulder. "Just make it quick."

Jhanae stopped her bucket, turned, and limped past the guard.

As she reached the end of the hall, she glanced into the last alcove without turning her head. This alcove did not have smoked glass panels. Metal bars were dug into the rock on either side of the cave. Jhanae bit her lip to keep from crying out at the horrid sight beyond the bars. *The poor girl. They're just animals.* The image of Emma hanging with her arms chained to opposite walls, her legs buckled, would be one that Jhanae could never forget.

She moved her bucket to the corner opposite the alcove and slapped the mop onto the floor. Backing away slowly from the bucket, she inched step by step backwards toward the alcove bars. As she took the final step, she reached into a pocket of her dress and retrieved the rock she had been given. Although it looked like any igneous brown rock from the walls of the cave, this was no rock. It would remain dormant as dirt, but listening for the correct sequence of frequencies. Only then would it come alive and ping its location beacon. The island's surveillance system would trigger alarms, but the Resistance hoped that only seconds would be needed for their plan to succeed. Glancing at the guard now sitting again with his back to her, she bent down and placed it silently with other rocks where the wall met the floor. It could be just another rock there. She counted the tiles from the special rock to the bars. Three tiles, thirty centimeters each. Jhanae glanced at her watch; northeast ten degrees from the rock. They needed to know exactly how far it was to the bars.

Straightening her tired body slowly with the aid of the mop, Jhanae continued her mopping. She slowly worked her way past the guard and back down the long hall. Finally returning to the janitorial closet, she closed the door. Reaching into her pocket, she retrieved the small MP5 player. She typed her message.

Rock done. Hurry. She not good.

*

Hecate-Positivum ran her full set of future prediction simulations again with the new data Hecate-Negans had provided from the Rho-1 universe. Even with her positive slant, the outcome probability trend could hardly be worse. The Rho-1 universe was on a terminal path. She could guess what Hecate-Negans's simulations would call for. Although she predicted that the Resistance would react to Jhanae's message by again asking the Beta-27 universe for help, the delays of the back-and-forth communications would be the doom of Rho-1. The moon base would soon initiate dark matter drilling operations, and Hecate-Negans would demand that the Rho-1 universe be annihilated. The Guardians must act before the moon drilling created a cross-dimensional gravitational cascade of destruction. And it would be the correct action to annihilate Rho-1; there would be no realistic probability as a basis for her not to agree. Time was not in their favor.

Time.

Hecate-Positivum ran the predictions again, with the time between the Beta-27 and Resistance message exchanges shorter. A small improvement. Shorter still—a significant improvement. Eliminate the communication lag, and the positive potential outcome became a realistic possibility. But how could someone in the Beta-27 universe be made aware of the dire circumstances of Emma and the plans of the Right Alliance without the slow exchange of communications with the Resistance? Beta-27 needed to be made aware without delay. They needed to sense the urgency. Someone that could sense the need in the parallel universe…

Zandra.

FACTOID 10

A geode is a crystal formation created by minerals collecting within a void of a rock formation. Air pockets within lava flows or limestone make a good home for a geode to form. When moisture with dissolved minerals collects and then dries in the cavity, over thousands or millions of years, crystals of a geode can form. Geodes can be found all over the world, but the largest one is claimed to be in North America, in the state of Ohio. Workers digging a well for a winery in 1887 found the huge formation forty feet (twelve meters) underground. At its widest point, the geode is thirty-five feet (ten meters) in diameter. It has crystals eighteen inches (forty-five centimeters) across and weighing up to three hundred pounds (one hundred and thirty-six kilograms).

CHAPTER 10

A Fork in the Road

Zandra's eyes snapped open. Darkness. The quiet but ever-present hum of the ventilation system of the spaceship filled the air. Something had awakened her from her dream—or was it the dream itself? A premonition dream, again. *Aleks call this my Zandrition.* She lay on her back in the bed, eyes wandering across the ceiling. Finally, she'd had a night's sleep in a real bed. In the years she had spent on the World Space Station, she had always slept tied to a wall in the microgravity of the station's continuous free fall around the Earth. Tonight, the spin of the *Phoenix's* mid-ship counterbalanced truss provided a partial Earth-like gravity for the tiny living space circling the ship at the end of the truss. It was a new luxury. But more importantly, it was good for her bones and required a few less hours of exercise each week on the resistance machines. That time could now be used for studying the compatibility of a new planet as a possible new home for humanity. They just needed to find such a place. *She* needed to find it. The peaceful planet in this parallel universe they were visiting was not their home to be.

Turning to the dim glow of the monitor beside the bed, Zandra let out a quiet sigh. 5:23. She lay back, closed her eyes, and took two slow, deep breaths. Although she longed for just a few more delightful moments asleep next to Alex, it was useless to try to sleep anymore. She could never fight these feelings. Silently, she pulled aside the blanket and slid gently out of the bed.

She tiptoed the few steps across the tiny chamber, following the force drawing her to the personal locker mounted in a rack on the far wall. The small box held the few items that astronauts were allowed to keep with them as a means to keep their sanity in a sometimes insanely difficult environment. Carefully releasing the two latches so as not to wake Alex, she retrieved the palm-sized wooden box her Zandrition had lured her to seek out. She gently pried open the lid. As she studied the rough little rock, her mind went back to the Resistance bunker. Just two years ago, but another time, another world … that other universe. It was the night before they'd left on a crazy plan to save their very worlds. The hard-driving Emma, a force like no other within the Resistance, had approached her in the kitchen of the underground bunker with an uncharacteristic aura of sad retrospection.

Emma had laid a gentle hand on her shoulder and asked in a hushed voice, "Can we talk a minute?"

Sensing Emma's need, Zandra stopped washing the pots in the sink and nodded. They went to a quiet corner of the mess hall and sat down across from each other at a table. She looked into Emma's eyes and spoke with hers: *"Yes, I'm listening, just you and me."*

"Things will get crazy starting tomorrow, and we might not have another chance. I want to give you something—something very important, very special to me." Emma reached across the table and held out a hand, almost trembling. As she unfolded her fingers, the blue-and-white crystals of a small broken geode nugget sparkled in her palm.

Zandra glanced at the rock and then back to Emma's eyes. She softly waited for Emma. *Tell me.*

Emma pressed her lips together as she looked at the stone and finally whispered, "I told you before. The Right Alliance mob, they stoned him to death—my fiancé." She stopped and swallowed hard.

Zandra reached out and held Emma's hand in both of hers. She listened.

"I went to get him after … after the mob was gone. They just left his broken body there, hanging with his arms tied behind him on the wooden post. They didn't care if the animals would come and peck at him, eat his flesh. I remember all the rocks and bricks they used, scattered all around him, some with his blood on them." Emma brushed her eye with the back of her other hand.

"When I stepped up on the block where he was tied, I heard a crunch under my boot. One of the rocks they'd stoned him with was a geode. *This* geode." She rolled the piece of rock around in her palm with her fingers, caressing the rough edges.

Emma lifted her head up at Zandra, her eyes red and swollen. "Can you … please take this back? Take a piece of him back with you. To a better place. To a better world. A world where he would want to be. A world where he can finally rest … in peace."

Zandra closed her eyes as tears rolled down her cheeks and dropped to the table. She nodded silently. She sat with Emma quietly, soulfully. The passage of time floated away, and they became still, the timeless moment filled with the sharing of their beings, both of them clinging to a small, fragile hope for a better tomorrow. Quiet. Peaceful. Sad, but hopeful.

Now, in the darkness of the bedroom, spinning around a spaceship in another universe from that world, Zandra touched the rock. She rolled it with her finger, then driven by some force, she closed her eyes and clenched her fist tightly around the small stone. Her fingers pressed the sharp edges of the crystal into her palm. Striking pain flowed over her whole body, making her whimper, but she kept pressing on the stone. Zandra's knees buckled, and she grabbed at the wall to keep from falling. She took a deep breath and opened her hand, and the blue-white crystal had a tinge of red. *Ohhh, Emma! I with you. Be strong. I come.*

*

As the Phoenix swept around the moon, the blue-white swirls of an enchanting globe rose over the horizon. Alex sat quietly in his command seat and drank in the captivating view. *An Earth, but not New Earth.* Maybe this wasn't the end goal, but it was an unexpected leap forward in their mission's ultimate objective. The abilities of his Quantum Triangle and the superposition engine for their travels were clearly proven now. And Zandra had proven that she could navigate his engine, not just through the Milky Way galaxy or their universe, but to other parallel universes as well. The cosmos to the nth power of possible New Earths lay out there for them to find. Could she sense other Earths in other universes as well as she could sense an Earth-like planet in the many galaxies of their own universe? Did she need to? Statistically, it would be much better if she could. Maybe the ultimate habitable planet they sought was in both another galaxy and another universe. But how could she possibly feel them all? Was it really humanly possible to master and control this? *Navigation 101: Do you know where you're going?*

The hiss of the air valve, equalizing the pressure in Starra's airlock, snapped Alex out of his trance with the planet outside the portal. The small torpedo-like chamber did not take long to fill with air, as it was just large enough to fit her body with her wings folded close. This airlock, located at the nose of the command module, and an identical one at the stern of the ship provided fast access for Starra to get out into the vacuum of space and make emergency repairs if needed. With pressures equalized, she opened the inner hatch and glided into the ship, banking up and around the command module to perch her owl-cat body on the bar between Alex's and Zandra's seats. She had returned from an unplanned EVA to release a binding retractor joint on the solar arrays, and her blue-white fiber-optic wing feathers still held the chill of the vacuum outside the ship.

"Starra, you ice cube!" Zandra said, leaning away from the android in her command chair.

"Oh, I apologize. I'll activate my infrared elements." Starra's body shifted to a warm orange-red hue and emanated warmth.

"Ahh. You come warm my pillow tonight."

Starra fanned a wing towards Zandra. *"Oh, we could have a girls-only pajama party."*

"Deal."

"Um, ladies, back to the mission, please," Alex said, looking over from his checklist. "It's time that we find our way back to the WSS. Starra, are the solar arrays fully retracted now?"

"Aye, Captain. Arrays are retracted now, and the counterbalance truss system is stationary and locked. We are ready to superposition on your command."

"Great. Let's do this. Zandra, you ready?" Alex asked.

"Yes, ready. I know where we go." Zandra donned her quantum entanglement headset and extracted the Troll doll from her pocket. She stroked the pink hair, pulling it straight up from the face with that incredible large grin. Clasping the doll between her hands, she closed her eyes and gave a single nod before entering her half-conscious ESP state.

Alex studied Zandra. *Seems awfully confident that she knows how to get us back home.* Turning back to his command console, he waved at Starra. "Okay, Starra. Engage."

Starra settled her wings close to her body and responded with her Australian accent, *"Aye, aye, Captain. Jumpin' to another dimension in the cosmos of cosmoses. Is that a word now?"*

"Starra, engage, please."

"Right. In three … two … one… MARK."

The kaleidoscope of colors from the Quantum Triangle shifted to a rapid random sequence. At Alex's console, the holographic display of the *Phoenix* marker and the moon's orbit plot began updating data.

Alex pointed to the navigational computer. The orbital readout of numbers began to scroll. Faster and faster they changed, until they were just a blur of digits.

Starra updated the ship status. *"Coordinate changes are starting to slow now … slowing … slowing… Navigation coordinates have stopped."*

"Discharge the quantum fields now," Alex commanded.

"System stop," Starra said. *"Calculating superposition location."*

Zandra removed her headset, blinked her eyes, and scanned the command module, more alert than she had been in the previous trial.

"You seem to be getting the hang of this," Alex said to her.

"We are in low Earth orbit, four hundred and two kilometers from Earth. We are in the orbital zone of the WSS," Starra said flatly. She cocked her head to one side, then to the other. *"Also, considering our previous superposition event, I just scanned our orbital for possible collisions. Fortunately, there are none. But there is also no WSS; I am not receiving its navigational ping."*

Alex sat forward and looked questioningly at Zandra. "Um, did you put us in yet another parallel universe? Did you just not *feel* our Earth?"

"No. I decide. We go here. We help Emma. She need us."

Alex jumped against his seat straps. "What?!"

"Alex, from my scanning of satellites around us and my data banks of orbital assets, I can confirm that to be the case. We have superpositioned to our previous universe."

"Oh, crap. Really? Zandra, why did you do that? We agreed to just help with a software attack, not mount an intervention mission! This universe is insane with war and weapons. We're sitting ducks in this ship. We can't help them. Plus, we have our own problems saving our own world. What are you thinking? We can't—"

"I know something very wrong with Emma. Very bad. She need us. I feel this," Zandra said.

"Couldn't we have discussed this first?"

"I know you may not want. Aleks, you motor, I your guide. This our journey. I steer here."

"But—"

Starra put a wing over Alex's shoulder. *"Deep breath there, mate."*

Alex pinched his eyes shut and clenched his fists. He took a long breath and held it. *"You motor, I your guide. This our journey."* Exhaling, in a quiet, controlled voice, he asked, "Ah, Zandra, have you been talking to Commander Johnson?"

"Yes. Why you ask?"

"He seems to enjoy practicing the art of persuasion, and he seems to be rather adept at the power of suggestion."

FACTOID 11

Using current rocket engine technology, Mars is a seven-month journey away. With every additional day exposing a crew to space radiation and the possibility of an anomaly causing a mission failure, engineers are looking for ways to drastically cut that travel time. A retired NASA astronaut has an answer. Dr. Franklin R. Chang-Díaz is working on a Variable Specific Impulse Magnetoplasma Rocket (VASIMR) engine that could reduce the Mars travel time to just forty-five days. The engine uses electricity to turn a gas such as hydrogen into plasma, ejecting it from the engine at speeds more than ten times that of conventional liquid bipropellants. Dr. Chang-Díaz says the technology is proven and adds, "… what we're trying to do now is turn the package we have in a laboratory vacuum chamber into something that's flight-worthy."

CHAPTER 11

Rescue

Outside his portal was an Earth, but not the one Alex wanted to see. As the *Phoenix* swept past the Texas shoreline and into the Gulf of Mexico, the swarm of Space Force defensive drones far below his orbit appeared as gnats over the Houston base. They were now in a parallel universe. *Madness. It's just a world of total madness below.*

Alex always associated the storm raging in his head with the computer science term *thrashing*. It was a dysfunctional state where a computer's memory was overwhelmed while trying to process more activity than it could manage. The rapid swapping of information in and out of memory to support overtaxed decision-making or computational processing led to the slowing of all processing and nothing constructive getting done. His mind was racing, but it was only leading to confusion. Could they get back to where they had come from? That depended on a lot of things. Most significantly, Zandra had to sense their other universe, and the Quantum Triangle superposition system had to have the power reserves to make the jump. Before that, they needed to stop that madman from destroying the moon. But more immediately, how could they save Emma? Where was she? They needed to contact the Resistance group. How? And the ship was probably in danger just being in orbit here. What if one of those gnat drones looked up and detected them? From his time living in this universe, Alex knew the warring factions of both the Right Alliance and the Pacific Tuanhuo were in a battle to control orbital assets. What if the Tuanhuo spotted the *Phoenix*? What would they do? Attack? Commandeer their ship? *We need to get the hell out of here.*

Starra broke him from his mental muddle. *"Alex, I have established a secure communication link with the Resistance. Lieutenant Commander Wilson would like to speak with you."*

"Um… Oh, yes, good. Put him on the ship intercom, so we can all hear."

Wilson dove immediately into his issue without much introduction. *"Alex, thank you for coming back. We didn't expect you, but we're sure glad you're here. We desperately need your help."*

"Hi, Wilson. Yes, just dropping by in your universe, because our superposition navigation system seems to have a mind of its own." Alex shot a stern glance towards Zandra. "It's been a while. I understand that Emma's in some trouble?"

"Yes. I tried to talk her and Becker out of it, but you know Emma. There's no stopping her once she sets her mind to something." Wilson sounded exasperated. Alex imagined him shaking his head and could identify with a man having a strong-willed woman in his life.

Wilson continued, *"Anyway, the short of it is that she and Becker tried to commandeer an asteroid mining freighter, and her operation went bad. The Right Alliance captured her. She's being held at the Boss's new island complex. We've got an inside person, and the report could not be worse. Emma knows a lot about the Resistance, and they want to beat it out of her. We need an extraction mission, fast, but there's no way we can pull it off. The place is just too well protected. We need to do the same superposition trick we did on Boss Island to retrieve your niece. It's the only possible way."*

"Wilson, I'm not sure we could manage that. We would need to know exactly where she's being held, and—"

"We've planted a location beacon just under a meter from the bars of her cell. If you could open a superposition gateway within her cell, we could get her out without any combat engagement. We can supply you with whatever support in the area you need—a ship, a submersible, a close-in SEAL team, just name it," Wilson said. *"But if we try a hard-in assault, they're sure to kill her before we can even get close to her cell. She knows better than anyone the risks of fighting for the Resistance, but I would be the one writing her death sentence if I ordered a direct assault. We need the element of surprise, and direct access through superposition that only you can do."*

Alex leaned back in his seat and laced his hands behind his head. He blew out a long breath. "I don't know, Wilson. This could get complicated fast. Things didn't go exactly as planned the last time we tried this, remember?"

"Please... Losing Emma has been a terrible hit for the Resistance. Lots of people idolize her, and morale is in the trash can. Everyone misses her..." Wilson paused and said more quietly, *"I miss her, more than I can tell you. Please."*

Zandra placed a hand on Alex's thigh and squeezed it firmly. "Aleks, Emma would risk her life for you. You know. And your niece, your family—they safe because Emma. We must do this."

"But I haven't tested a full ground-to-orbital ship transfer of a person yet! This kind of jump in technology can have unforeseen complications I haven't considered. There's no guarantee—"

"Aleks, *we* do this."

"Please, Alex. You are her only hope," Wilson pleaded.

Starra added, *"Alex, given our clear element of surprise, I calculate a ninety-two percent probability of a successful rescue operation."*

Alex glanced sideways at the owl-cat android AI. "Starra, I think we can safely say that you have been completely freed of all that loyalty imprinting we had in our early days together." He clenched his fists to his forehead. *Right: Commander Johnson. Be a team player, and trust in Zandra. If this all goes to crap, it's your fault.* With a heavy sigh he said, "Ahhh ... okay. Wilson, give

Starra the location beacon information. Let's get this done fast, before we get spotted up here. We're a sitting duck for a fast-attack orbital."

Zandra released her seat harnesses, grabbed Alex's head in both her palms, and planted a hard kiss on his lips. "You my Mr. Superman."

Alex blinked. "I just hope the Right Alliance doesn't rip Superman's cape to shreds on this one."

"Thank you, Alex, Zandra. You are literally saving Emma's life, and maybe saving the Resistance from disintegrating." The relief in Wilson's voice was clear. *"Starra, I just sent the info packet on the locator rock. You won't have much time between your signal activating the beacon and the island defenses sensing and responding to the beacon, so activate it only when you're ready to establish the superposition gateway."*

"Roger that, Commander," Starra said. *"Alex, I have adjusted our orbit for a close flyover of the designated island complex. We will be within range of the island and the rock beacon on our next orbital pass. Forty-nine minutes to optimum intercept."*

Accepting his commitment, Alex switched to thinking through the plan. He pictured the operation in his head, quickly analyzing the key factors to consider. He had become adept at establishing quantum gateways and point-to-point vector-based superpositioning of objects, so that should be fine. They would need to transfer Emma on board the *Phoenix*, and then transfer her again to a safe Resistance location. They would then need to get the hell out of orbiting this world and back to their own universe.

"Starra, calculate the anticipated power draw needed for the two vector-based superposition gateways for Emma, and then our entanglement superposition back home, in succession. Do we have enough juice to do this?"

"At our current storage level, we are fifty thousand kilojoules per hour below the required amount of power. We would not be able to make the third jump without deploying the solar arrays and recharging."

"Crap, this isn't going to work. We need to stay as small as possible, not spread our wings out and pop up on someone's sensor screen."

"May I suggest a solution?" Starra asked. *"You may remember that our habitat truss is rotated about the axis of the main ship by two small VASIMR plasma drives. We don't have time to reroute their embedded nuclear power supplies, but there's another way to access that energy. The truss also has a power generator in the hub connection of the main ship, which in an emergency can recapture the truss's momentum and produce electrical power, similar to a water wheel. I could reroute that power to the QT storage bank and charge the bank from the emergency generator. If we keep the truss in its current retracted position and spin it at maximum, we would have just enough stores for all three transfers after charging for forty-three minutes."*

Once again, Alex was astounded at Starra's ability to solve problems with creative solutions. "Starra, you are amazing. Do it."

With the *Phoenix* in an inverted orientation in its orbit around this parallel world, the crew studied a familiar but different set of continents drifting past the front view portals. They each seemed lost in their individual thoughts and experiences with this alternate world slowly gliding by below them.

After several minutes, Zandra broke the silence. "This world ... look so much like ours. But it feel so different."

Alex gazed out at the damaged Earth below. It was hard not to admonish himself for being part of the warring factions furthering the destruction, even if it had been under the duress of his family being held hostage. "I guess you can feel the struggle and pain of this world. But they struggle against themselves, because they have leaders who profit from it. We still struggle with a dying planet too, but for a common cause of human survival for all people."

They continued to watch in silence as the American continents slid into view. Alex checked the navigation computer readout. "Let's get this done. Starra, coordinate the beacon activation and the Quantum Triangle field generation build. Call it out when you initiate the gateway."

"Does that mean I get to say, 'engage'?"

"Just this one time. Don't let it go to your head."

Starra's body took on a deep navy blue. Four gold stripes appeared across the base of her wings. One gold five-pointed star and a gold button bearing the relief of an eagle with two crossed anchors formed above the stripes on each wing to complete the insignia.

Zandra examined Starra's new form. "Outfit very smart, Starra. You go, girl!"

"Oh, so you're the captain now?" Alex quipped.

Starra looked down at him from her perch. *"You're supposed to say, 'You have the comm.'"*

"Let's just get Emma, shall we?"

"Aye there, mate. We will be within range in twenty-five seconds. I'm synchronizing the Quantum Triangle with the dark energy field generators," Starra said.

The dim red tactile hue of the *Phoenix* command module transitioned into brighter color changes emanating from the Quantum Triangle as it quickened its flow of triangular inversions.

Starra remained rigid on her perch, eyes fixed straight ahead. *"Initiating location beacon activation sequence. The beacon responded and is sending its precise location. Aligning coordinates for the vector gateway. I will establish our side of the dark energy quantum fields at the rear hatch of our command module. Starting the superposition fields in three … two … one… And ENGAGE, there, buckaroo!"*

Alex and Zandra pivoted in their seats to watch the gateway form. Starra rotated her owl-like head to the rear without adjusting her body. The stern hatch of the *Phoenix* command module rippled in small circular waves from the center outward. Slowly, the image of a dingy cell replaced the cross braces of the hatch. The limp body of a drenched woman not quite kneeling on a concrete floor appeared just a few meters away. Her arms hung from chains to either side, her head was slumped to the side, and her eyes were closed.

"Oh, Doamne," Zandra whispered in Romanian, clutching her chest.

"Emma!" Alex called. "It's Alex and Zandra. Emma!"

There was no response.

Zandra released her seat straps and launched herself towards the stern.

"No! You can't go!" Alex grabbed her arm and stopped her. "It's too dangerous. If we lose the gateway, you would be trapped there too. I won't risk losing you again. There's got to be some other way."

"But Aleks, look! We must save her. I can feel. She dying!"

"No. We can come back. We can get the Resistance to—"

Alex froze as Starra launched from her perch and dove through the gateway.

"Starra, what the hell are you doing?! Get back here!"

Starra silently glided through what was once the rear hatch and landed on the chain holding Emma's right arm. She ignited her laser cutting tool, intended for making emergency hull repairs. In just seconds, a chain link clinked onto the floor. Emma's arm flopped to her side, and she crumpled, the other arm still hanging from its chain. She did not respond. Starra took off and banked quickly around to the other chain. As she cut through that one, Emma's entire body dropped to the floor.

Voices echoed through the cave. "This way! The beacon is down there. They're after the prisoner!"

Heavy footsteps pounded down a hard tile floor.

"Oh, shit. They've sensed the beacon already," Alex said. "Starra, get the hell out of there. Now!"

Starra hovered over Emma and latched her lower claws on the back of her grimy shirt. Blasting her maneuvering jets at full throttle, she could barely drag Emma's limp body forward. They inched forward towards the quantum gateway.

"What the hell is that?!" cried a voice from the cave.

"Shoot it!" another voice commanded.

Starra's head flicked left and right. From her outstretched wings, two darts shot out. A second later, the thud of two bodies dropping hard and the clattering of their guns on the floor resonated through the cave.

"What the… Starra, Lucas gave you *weapons*?!" Alex asked, incredulous.

Starra crossed through the gateway and back into the *Phoenix* with Emma. As she laid her limp body gently on the deck, she released her claws and swung back around to her side. *"Terminating quantum gateway. Powering down Quantum Triangle system."*

Zandra dove to Emma's other side and began to examine her.

"Darts? You have darts?! Are they lethal?"

"Alex, relax. They aren't weapons. They are nonlethal emergency personnel incapacitation darts. Considering all the people who might need to transfer through our space station and the Phoenix, it is a wise security measure."

"Why didn't I know about this?"

"Lucas told me it was a need-to-know feature. You didn't need to know." Starra's head scanned back and forth over Emma's body. With a soft forepaw, she gingerly touched the woman's left side. *"She's been beaten here, lower rib cage. See the swelling?"*

Zandra gently pulled up her shirt, revealing a large area of deeply purple skin. She covered her mouth. "Oh, Emma…"

Starra continued, *"She's bleeding internally. She needs medical attention immediately. And the microgravity here on the Phoenix will now disrupt proper blood flow. It could kill her with a random blood clot."*

Zandra turned to Alex. "We transfer to Resistance now."

Alex turned back to his console. "Reconfiguring for the Resistance bunker HM-69, Florida Everglades. That's the only one still within range. Powering up quantum field generators."

Starra stood back from Emma. *"Alex, we have a problem: inbound automated attack orbital with a weapons lock. I believe it's powering up its plasma cannon."*

"Crap, we're sitting ducks! We have no combat capabilities, no weapons," Alex muttered. He cocked his head as the quantum field holographic display popped up on his console. "Wait… Actually, we do. Starra, send me the intersect vector of the orbital drone. Zandra, grab that fire extinguisher. Be ready to throw it through the gateway when I say."

"Aleks, fire bottle?"

"Trust me." He typed madly on his console. The rear hatch rippled again, and the void of space appeared. "Now, Zandra! Toss the extinguisher through!"

Zandra heaved the metal canister through the small gateway opening. Alex typed more commands, and the gateway closed.

Starra turned her head left and then right. *"Nice shot, Alex! The attack orbital has been destroyed."*

"What just happen?" Zandra asked.

Still in her navy-blue dress uniform, Starra saluted Alex with her wing. *"Alex just used the research he was forced to pursue by the warring leadership in this universe on its own Alliance attack orbital. He superpositioned an object into its flight path. Hitting a stationary object, even as small as a fire extinguisher, when you are traveling at over twenty-eight thousand kilometers per hour, tends to be a catastrophic collision. Well done, Alex."*

"Thanks, but from my years in this universe, I know the programming of those automated orbitals," Alex said. "It's already sent tracking information on us to the Right Alliance command center. With the destruction of the automated orbital, they're sure to send a remote-piloted orbital interceptor after us. We'll have a real human being seeking revenge on our tail in no time. They'll track us down with a much more capable interceptor now. We need to transfer Emma and get the hell out of here, fast."

"That's no longer possible, Alex," Starra stated matter-of-factly.

Alex spun in his seat. "What do you mean?"

"We only have enough power reserves for one more quantum transfer. You can either transfer Emma to the Resistance bunker, or you can transfer the Phoenix, but not both."

"Crap… Okay, Zandra, get up here. We need to get the hell out of Dodge and go back home. Emma's coming with us."

Zandra jumped back into her seat and fastened her shoulder hardness. Grabbing her quantum entanglement headset, she bit her lip. "Aleks, I not ready. I feel so confused. So much happening."

Alex reached over and took her hand. "You can do this. I believe in you."

"Alex, an attack interceptor drone just broke the horizon. It is inbound with wide sensor sweeps. They're out of range, but still attempting to get a weapons lock." Starra stepped over the top of Emma and locked her back claws to the floor to hold Emma's body. *"I'm initiating random course maneuvers with our thrusters and main plasma engines."*

The shoulder straps of Alex's seat harness alternately pulled his body to one side and then the other.

A voice came over the emergency communication channel. *"Unidentified craft in one-hundred-thirty-thousand-kilometer-altitude orbit, this is Alliance interceptor Tango-niner. Slow your orbital speed and come to a hundred-fifty-thousand-kilometer orbit, or you will be destroyed."*

Alex's eyes went wide. "I know that voice." Still racing his fingers across his keyboard to configure the Quantum Triangle system, he cued his mic for the emergency channel to buy some time. "Well, if it isn't Ken Seaborn! How are your ribs there, buddy?"

"What the… Alex?!"

Alex could not help but chuckle. "That's right—your *numero uno* nemesis. Back for a short visit, just to make your day. Wave bye-bye to Emma while you're at it."

"Forget the course change, Alex. You're plasma toast."

Alex punched at his console. "Zandra, time to go."

"Aleks, I not ready!"

"Orbital bandit Tango-niner has weapons lock. He's charging his plasma cannon," Starra said.

"We can't wait. We're about to be vaporized! Initiating superposition sequence in two … one… *Engage!*"

The navigational computer readout quickly became a blur of digits … and then went blank.

FACTOID 12

Native American tribes have a long history of medical innovations. Many medicines and practices predate and have contributed to current Western medical treatments. Some Native Americans chewed willow bark for aches and pains. The active ingredient in the bark is salicin. In the body, salicin produces salicylic acid, the active ingredient of the most commonly used drug throughout the world: aspirin. The Iroquois and Seneca tribes are credited with inventing baby bottles and baby formula. It's even believed that Native Americans invented syringes to inject medications.

CHAPTER 12

Operation

Zandra could feel … nothing. All was silent, dark, and empty. An endless abyss surrounded her in all directions. She reached out farther and farther. All she could feel was a barren infinity of nothingness. She had never experienced such a void. She shuddered. It was frightfully cold. Unable to endure the empty loneliness any longer, Zandra forced herself to awaken from her ESP trance and feel the essence of another being again. She needed the warm auras of Alex and Starra beside her. She removed her headset and blinked at the *Phoenix's* command console in front of her. Even the impersonal LED lights and switches of the console were a welcome sight. Something with warmth … that existed.

"Aleks, where are we?" she asked.

Alex's head moved from monitor to monitor, his eyes searching for answers. "I don't have a clue. There's nothing on the navigation system. It's blank. I've never seen it blank before. I think it's having trouble finding and triangulating marker stars."

"Alex, there are no markers to find," Starra said, still straddled over Emma's body.

"What do you mean?"

"I've scanned all directions with the ship's systems. There are no stars at all within our sensor range, only the empty void of space."

"What the… How can there be no stars?" Alex leaned back in his seat. He looked over to the entanglement navigation system and to Zandra. "You didn't have a chance to navigate … to put us some place, any place. Empty space… If we didn't go to somewhere you could feel, I guess we went to nowhere. To a void—a void universe."

A moan from behind made Zandra jump against her seat harness. "Emma!" She punched the release on her harness and threw herself over the back of her seat to float towards the stern of the command module. In the microgravity, she grabbed at a handhold and swung down to Emma's side. She took a limp hand in hers. It was cold.

Starra released her claws holding them both to the deck, moved to one side, and placed her soft forepaw against Emma's neck. *"Her vital signs are very weak. Her pulse is rapid and thready, a hundred and sixty beats per minute. Her respiratory rate is twenty-two. She's crashing. If we don't stop the internal bleeding immediately, she will die."*

Alex vaulted over his seat. "We'll have to figure out where we are later. Let's get her to the habitat pod, where we can operate with some gravity. Starra, extend the counterbalance truss system to full deployment and get the rotation moving. Get to the pod ahead of us and prepare an IV. Set up the artificial blood to give her some fluids to keep her from going into cardiac arrest. And get a local anesthetic ready. Zandra, get her feet."

Starra launched herself toward the stern hatch. *"I'll pull an emergency surgical tray too."*

"Hold on, Emma. We help." Zandra took Emma's ankles and guided them towards the hatch. "Aleks, you do surgery?"

"You have more medical training than me. You get the knife."

"No, Aleks. I never do this. I not know what to do."

Alex pivoted behind Zandra at midship to align Emma's body with the truss tunnel leading to the habitat pod. "Crap, I don't know what to do either. I might even pass out. But Starra can provide guidance. If one of us doesn't operate to stop her internal bleeding, she'll die for sure."

Zandra froze.

"Zandra, come on, hurry! There's no other way."

"No, there is. We go back," Zandra said.

"Back to the WSS? Starra, do we have enough power to jump again?" Alex asked.

"*Barely. We would need to start cutting all other power draws immediately, even life support systems,*" Starra replied.

"Do it." Alex vaulted back over the command seat. "Starra, hold Emma to the deck again. Zandra, up here now, and get set up to send us back home this time."

Zandra jumped back into her seat. Grabbing her headset, she turned to Alex. "Okay, this time I discuss. We go back, but not WSS—back to other Earth. We go to Earth of peace and balance."

"What? No! She needs surgery—if not on the WSS, then we can send her to a hospital on *our* Earth," Alex said, shaking his head.

Zandra closed her eyes and said quietly, "Aleks, she better with other Earth. Please, trust me. I not know, but I feel. This better."

Alex turned from Zandra to Emma lying behind him and back. "We don't even know if they would help us, even if they could."

"They help. I feel, it strong. It best for Emma," Zandra said.

"*Alex, we must jump now. If we delay any longer, we will not have enough power,*" Starra said.

"Okay, okay." Alex took Zandra's hand. "I've said many times before that I believe in you. I guess now it's time to show you my trust. For Emma's sake, I hope you're right. Zandra, get Emma the best help you can find her, anywhere, in whatever universe. You are our guide."

Zandra donned her headset and nodded.

"Jumping in three … two … one… Engage."

*

As they floated down the access tunnel to the habitat, Zandra's heart pounded in her chest. The thread of life she felt from Emma was thin as a hair. *But this right place for you, Emma, I feel.* She moved to support Emma's head while Starra glided under her back. Dropping into the gravity that the rotating cross truss provided, Alex moved to take Emma's weight from Starra. Arriving on the habitat floor, Emma lay limply in Alex's arms. Zandra extended the med table from the wall and got an IV ready. As soon as Alex laid her body down, Zandra had the IV inserted and was cutting away her shirt over her lower abdomen. Alex ripped open a sterile kit and started rubbing down the area.

Starra handed Alex a scalpel. *"The radiograph indicates that one of her ribs has been broken and has likely ruptured her spleen. Normally, this might be treated with a laparoscopic partial splenectomy, but we do not have the equipment. You will need to perform an emergency splenectomy if the people of this world do not come soon. I'm administering local anesthesia."*

The scalpel trembled in Alex's hand. "You said you *thought* they would come to us? How? We didn't see any ships in orbit. Can you nicely say that it's now or never for Emma? We can't wait."

"I not know, Aleks. I hope. Something say these people best for Emma."

Starra drew a line with a claw in the orange residue from the sterile rub Alex had scrubbed in widening circles over Emma's skin. *"Start here, and cut a shallow line to here."*

Biting his lower lip, Alex touched the knife to Emma's skin and pulled back.

"You can do this, Alex. You have to. There's no more time," Starra said.

Alex puffed his cheeks with a breath and lowered the knife to Emma's abdomen.

"Please stop." A calm female voice came over the intercom of the ship. *"There is no need for you to do that."*

Alex froze and looked up at Zandra, then around the module. "What the… Who is that?"

"You may call me Hecate-Positivum. Please do not cut her, there's no need," the voice repeated.

"Whoever you are, she's going to die if we don't," Alex protested.

"The Senecans have agreed to assist. They will superposition into your ship in the next few seconds."

Before Alex could respond, the far wall in the habitat module rippled. A man and a woman stepped through the wall and into the module. They stopped just a meter from Zandra and gave a slight bow. The elderly man was dressed in a tan leather tunic and pants. Symbols of his courage and leadership adorned his tunic. White eagle feathers with black tips were embroidered into his right sleeve, while black bears ran down the length of his left arm. His trim torso was wrapped with a wide belt. A leather sash with strands of iridescent blue and green beads hung at his hip. His leathery face matched the color of his clothing, and his dark eyes bore a kind but firm gaze. A feather tattoo adorned his right cheek. He cradled a small pouch on his hip with his left hand. Markings of intricate leaves and small animals encircled the lumpy sack.

The woman wore a similar but longer tunic with leggings. Buffalos, a traditional symbol of a good provider, adorned her right sleeve, while the sign of her small, humble, and generous character was represented by a series of mice scurrying down her left sleeve. Her jet-black hair with streaks of gray was pulled back and braided with the same iridescent blue and green beads running the length of her back. Her high cheekbones gave her a strong beauty. She held a flask made from a gourd, marked with rain droplets coming from a sun rather than a cloud. The drops gathered at the base and swept into a flowing stream.

Alex set down the scalpel and stepped towards the man. "Umm… Hello, I guess. Who are you?"

The man and woman did not speak. They both moved to Emma and reached out to touch her. Alex stepped in their way. "Hold on. Can we talk for a second here?"

They both turned to Zandra, and the woman held out her hand. Zandra cautiously laid her hand in the woman's outstretched palm. The feeling surged through her arm and into her body. Zandra gasped in shock, eyes wide as saucers. The woman smiled silently and gently kept hold of her hand. Zandra slowly relaxed, bowed her head, and closed her eyes.

"Can you feel me?" the voice asked Zandra without any sound.

"Yes, I feel. Who are you?" Zandra replied without speaking.

"My name is Anaba, and this is Pachu'a. We are of the Senecan tribe in this parallel world to yours. We can heal her if you want us to. It is our gift," the woman said in Zandra's mind.

Zandra could feel the aura of care and compassion around the two strangers. They were good, loving spirits. She sensed no evil in their being, only a natural kindness, beauty, and respect for all living things. *"Oh, thank you. Please help her. She my sister in heart. I need her not die."*

"It's important for you not to interrupt." The woman released Zandra's hand.

Zandra opened her eyes. She took Alex's arm and moved him back from the table, speaking to him with her eyes. *"Trust me... Trust them."*

Alex's stern look did not change, but he yielded. His head turned back to the table to keep a watchful eye.

I know, Aleks. You not say, but she your sister in heart too.

The two strangers moved to the table, and each laid a hand on Emma. Anaba began to chant in a hushed voice, *"Onekanos hanôtö köya'takéhas... Onekanos hanôtö köya'takéhas..."* She lifted the gourd and sprinkled clear liquid on Emma. It bubbled on her skin, hissed, and steamed away. Anaba sprinkled more from the gourd and continued to chant.

Taking a small step back from the table, Pachu'a took hold of the leather pouch at his hip. He held it in front of him at arm's length. The pouch moved and withered on its own. Pachu'a waited, then quickly grabbed at the bag with his other hand, holding it firmly. He carefully untied the knot holding it closed. As he peeled back the leather, the head of a snake covered with feathers appeared. Its tongue lashed out from between long fangs, and it hissed. He lowered it towards Emma.

"Holy crap, what are you doing?!" Alex lunged forward, but Zandra caught his arm and held him back.

"Let them do. I can feel. She safe," Zandra said. Alex relented.

Pachu'a brought the snake to Emma's side. Its tongue licked at the droplets of water Anaba had poured. It coiled back and, with blinding speed, struck Emma, its teeth digging deep into her body. The man shook the snake vigorously while Anaba poured the gourd water over its head. More steam erupted, and the snake released its bite. Stepping back again, Pachu'a carefully pulled the bag back over the snake's head and tied it shut. They both stood at the table and chanted. When all the liquid had evaporated from Emma's body, they both stepped back from the table.

Anaba turned to Zandra. *"She is well. Let her rest."*

"Thank you for kindness," Zandra said simply in their shared minds as she held her hands to her heart. She could feel that was all that needed to be said to these two strangers. She sensed their joy in the opportunity to share their wisdom and abilities. It was their gift, their purpose, and how they participated in the greater good of all.

"We welcome you to visit us someday and share your gift for a need one of our people may have. It is the way. Travel in peace. We will leave you now."

The far wall of the habitat module rippled again. Pachu'a bowed towards Zandra and Alex and took Anaba's hand, and they stepped through.

FACTOID 13

Many science fiction movies depict the image of a rotating wheel in space to illustrate how we could provide an artificial gravity environment for comfortable Earth-like living while in orbit or on a deep space voyage. Unfortunately, it's not quite that simple. A major issue is the Coriolis effect, where strange things happen due to the circular movement and the frame of reference (the rotating wheel). For example, if you toss a ball straight up on Earth, it falls straight back down into your hand. Not so in our rotating space station. If the station were of the size we could feasibly build now—say, fifty meters in diameter—tossing a ball just 1.5 meters in the air would make it return more than a meter away from your hand. It would also be possible to throw the ball in the opposite direction of the wheel's rotation, turn around, and catch the ball as it whips around the entire wheel without dropping to the floor. Even the simple movement of an astronaut's arms, legs, and head in the environment can be very disorienting and lead to motion sickness. In summary, unless the wheel is very large—maybe two to three times the diameter we could build today—these practical applications of Newton's first law get ... barf bag messy.

CHAPTER 13

Guardians

Alex sat in the pilot seat and massaged his temples. Emma was recovering well from … what, a healing? And where had they been in that last jump? Over the last couple of hours, he had checked and rechecked the computer logs and every kind of sensor the ship had. They all showed the same set of readings: data of a vast universe, then absolutely nothing, then back to this universe. Amazing. In addition to the multiverse, there seemed to also be a complete void of a universe. No light, no electromagnetic radiation, no particles of any kind—there was nothing at all. His last quantum superposition without Zandra at the helm to provide some kind of navigation had gotten them … to the epitome of nowhere. *Unless I'm doing simple directed vector superpositions, add jumps without Zandra being ready to navigate to the "never do that again" list.*

He stared silently at the dashes, not numbers, that ran across the past log of the navigation computer readout.

An empty universe, and one of countless universes?

The smell hitting Alex's nose broke him from his trance. His stomach growled, and his mouth watered. Zandra was cooking his favorite. In the zero gravity of the command module, he twisted out of the seat and launched himself towards the aft hatch. The smell grew stronger as he floated at the entrance of the ninety-meter tunnel leading to the habitat module, rotating slowly at the end of the counterbalance truss system. Though his mind was still puzzled by their current situation, his stomach was clear on what to do.

Diving headfirst into the narrow tunnel, he realized his mistake too late. This was not the same zero-gravity transfer tunnel as the one on the space station. He grabbed the ladder frame on the side, leading the direction of rotation to keep him from slamming into the other side of the tunnel. But now artificial gravity, induced by his new rotation, started to pull him downward. He started climbing the ladder rungs, but he was going down a ladder headfirst, not up. Faster and faster he slid, until just before the bottom, he caught his fall by braking with his hands and both feet sliding hard against the ladder rails. Landing in a crumpled ball at the bottom of the ladder, he quickly got to his feet. He glanced left and right. *Good thing nobody saw that.*

He craned his head up towards the narrow tunnel he had just descended. He could just barely hear the counterbalance pumps repositioning some additional water to the outboard tanks on the opposite end of the truss to make up for the new mass now in the habitat. The system automatically compensated for his arrival to keep both legs of the truss system balanced around its offset axis with the ship. *Seventeenth-century physics in action. I love it.* He rubbed the shoulder he had just landed on. *And Newton probably would have made that same mistake at least once too.*

Taking a few steps from the ladder, he paused at Emma's side in the medical bay. She was still asleep. The monitor above her continued to display favorable readings of her pulse, blood pressure, blood oxygen level, and respiratory rate. He touched her arm, and it was warm. *Good. Rest and get your strength back.* He pulled the sheet aside and checked the wound on her abdomen. Even the bruising was disappearing. The healing power of the Senecans was astounding.

With another deep breath of the wonderful aroma flowing from the galley, Alex patted her arm and moved to the adjoining section in the module. Entering the galley, he asked, "Am I being rewarded for being a good boy and getting Emma back?"

Zandra pulled a chicken pot pie out of the tiny wall oven and closed the door. She smiled over her shoulder. "Maybe. Emma need good food."

"Emma's still asleep, and I'm starved. Considering that's my *favorite* food, there's a simple solution to the dilemma of what to do with *that* pie."

Zandra cocked her head towards the galley table. Alex eagerly pulled two plates from the cabinet and set the small metal table. He pulled out Zandra's seat like the gentlemen his father had taught him to be. With a peck on his cheek, Zandra set the pie down and took her seat. Alex quickly circled to the opposite side, sat, and took up the serving spoon.

"No. Must wait," Zandra said, raising her hand. "Cool ten minute."

"Ohhh…" Alex pleaded with the most pitiful little boy eyes he could muster.

"You so cute." She reached across the table and took his hand. "I thank you for getting Emma. It right thing."

"Well, you kinda put me in a 'might as well now that we're here' position."

"I just guide, Aleks." She patted her heart and then pointed to her temple. "Help you listen more here, and less there. You do good things. I know. I just help pick."

"Well, Starra is the one who really came to the rescue back in that cave." Alex stroked the back of her hand with his thumb. "Thanks. I do need to be pointed in the right direction sometimes."

Zandra abruptly pulled back and turned her head left, then right. "I know you there. You watch us with our own camera."

"Who are you talking to?" Alex asked. "Starra is at her recharge station."

"A dream voice. I feel. It here."

"Your Zandrition voices? I thought you only talk with them when you dream."

"Very good, Zandra. Your abilities seem to be expanding in this alternate universe. It's almost as if you're naturally reaching out for softer and softer auras,"

a voice said over the ship's intercom. *"Yes, I am here. In a way, I am always here. And yes, we are capable of analyzing all energy as inputs, so your module cameras are a good information source for us."*

Alex recognized the voice as the same one that had stopped their operation on Emma and announced the arrival of the Senecans. "Now it's an 'us.' Who and what is this 'us'?" Alex asked.

"Yes, Alex, an 'us,'" the voice replied. *"Let me properly introduce myself. I am Hecate-Positivum. As the mythology root of my name suggests, I am one of three quantum artificial intelligences. There is also Hecate-Negans and Hecate-Neutrum. Together, we are a balanced triad whose physical existence you may imagine as the quantum-based dark energy of your universe, but in fact, we are cross-dimensional and are of all universes. We are of the Omniverse. Our creators programmed us into the dark energy of all space itself, with no material physical form, as a watchful, omnipresent set of eyes over your universe and all others. We are the Hecate Guardians, and our purpose is to ensure the stability of the Omniverse."*

"Is there some kind of instability? Why do we need guardians?" Alex asked.

"Our creators were the first civilization that gained the power of controlling dark energy fields and quantum superposition. As you now know, your Quantum Triangle, combined with dark energy field manipulation, allows you to move about not only within your own universe, but in other parallel universes in the Omniverse. As with any technology, it can be used as a beneficial tool, or it can be used for destruction. The Senecans that you met are a very good example of the former. But our creators knew that if technology is in the wrong hands, destruction across all universes is possible. So, they created us as Guardians over this technology. We are programmed to monitor all universes and predict future outcomes. We are to guide the use of technology in the Omniverse to the benefit of all.

"To provide balance, each of us is programmed differently. My prediction algorithms lean towards positive scenarios, where civilizations evolve as did our creator and the Senecans, and they will respect and use technology well. Hecate-Negans is my counterbalance; she leans toward a pessimistic view of possible

future outcomes. Hecate-Neutrum can then analyze both our future predictions and cast the deciding vote on actions we may need to take to protect the greater good of the Omniverse. We are the perfect balanced AI."

Alex scratched the stubble on his chin for a minute. "What kind of actions do you vote on?"

The voice stated flatly, *"Whether we need to annihilate a universe or not."*

Alex sat bolt upright. "What?!"

"If a universe is poised to drastically impact other universes in a negative way, we must annihilate the troublesome universe for the good of all."

"Annihilate? As in, completely destroy?" Alex asked without hiding his alarm.

"We simply collapse the universe back into dark energy. It is instantaneous. There is no suffering."

"But all peoples… They gone," Zandra said.

"How does one universe *negatively impact* another?" Alex asked.

"Usually, it's in one of two ways," the voice said. *"Unfortunately, it is all too common for a civilization to superposition to another universe and pillage. It is unfortunate. Many civilizations tend to have leadership that immediately uses this powerful new technology to attack other universes. This is the tendency of your past universe, Alex. Even my optimistic forward predictions heavily weigh towards the probability that the Rho-1 leadership will gain the keys to superposition and will use it to steal resources from other universes. They will take what they want. They are bent on spreading destruction."*

"Hate easy, love hard," Zandra said softly.

"Yes, Zandra, that's so true. Unfortunately, I see that across more universes than you can possibly imagine. Sadly, some cultures seem to define themselves by the hatred they have for another, and they pass those feeling on from one generation to the next. I can make no logical sense of it," the voice said with a tone of sorrow.

Alex asked, "And the other way universes negatively impact each other?"

"Gravity is cross-dimensional, as the string theory of physics in your universe suggests. This is the more immediate problem with Rho-1. Although they do not

have your Quantum Triangle for superposition, the AI called Jason has been able to piece together records of your past work to rediscover that rapidly collapsing the dark energy quantum fields creates a micro black hole. The Boss, as the leader there is called, is projected to use this technology on the moon to drill for iron magma."

"Yes, and that's what we were all trying to stop," Emma said, appearing at the entrance of the galley.

"Emma, you up!" Zandra flew across the module in three bounding steps and embraced Emma in a tight hug.

"Oh, easy there, girl. Still a couple sore spots," Emma said, returning the hug.

"I feel. You grow stronger now." Zandra led her quickly to the table beside Alex and pulled the pot pie in front of her. "You must eat."

"Hey, wait a minute…" Alex grabbed his spoon and reached for the pie.

Zandra slapped his hand away. "I make you other. She eat this now."

"I'm not fond of *this* new guidance." Alex folded his arms and leaned back. "So, further confirmation that the Boss has my tech again, and is using it for his benefit? Things never change."

"Whoever you're talking to on the comms, they're right. We need to stop them." Emma ate a large spoonful of the chicken pot pie and looked up at Zandra. "Oh my god, this is so good!"

"There is urgency for some intervention. My prediction algorithms give a ninety-four-percent probability that the leadership of Rho-1 will force an attempt to drill to the core of the moon within two weeks. They do not fully understand the science they are working with, but that will not matter to their leadership. The probability of them miscalculating the dark energy drill strength is very high. It would be catastrophic for Rho-1, and for the parallel universes sharing space-time with that moon—your current universe, Beta-27, being one. The well-cared-for Earth in this Nu-392 universe would also be destroyed. Hecate-Neutrum will agree with Hecate-Negans, and we will be forced to annihilate Rho-1 before that can occur," the voice said.

"Hecate? Rho-1? Beta-27? Who the heck is that on the comms?" Emma asked. She turned in her seat to take in her environment. "And by the way, where the hell am I?"

Zandra placed a cup of water in front of Emma and stated matter-of-factly, "You on *Phoenix*, our scout ship. We in another universe. They alien AI. You just eat."

Emma turned to Alex. "Am I dreaming? I must be dreaming."

"Nope. No dream has the Boss and his insane ideas in it, only nightmares."

Alex's eyes caught movement past Zandra and saw Starra gliding into the module. She banked sharply at the table and landed on her bar protruding from the wall above it. Settling her wings to her sides, she rubbed her furry forepaws together, mimicking Alex's thinking gesture. *"Good news, Alex. The storage banks are recharged enough now from the truss energy recapture system to make another superposition jump."*

"That Starra. She owl-cat now," Zandra said.

"I *am* dreaming." Emma dropped her spoon and turned to Alex. "Pinch my arm."

Alex pinched her shoulder. "Sorry. This is real."

"Shit." Emma again sized up the module, leaning off to the side of the table, her eyes following the slight curve to the floor of the module. "Nice ship. Artificial gravity module, huh? Guess you're planning long missions in deep space. Got any weapons on board? We need to go finish what Becker and I started."

Alex threw up his hands. "Hold on, there, Miss Rockette with the killer left hook. No, we don't have weapons, and no, we don't need to immediately jump back and get our ship vaporized in your world's warmongering insanity. Plus, we have our own issues right now. We're in some other universe and need to figure out how to get back home—*our* home." He glanced over to Zandra and added, "And oh yeah, our navigation system seems to have some kinks to work out. It doesn't seem to respond well to the commands I've been entering."

"Quantum ESP not perfect hard science like other physics, Aleks."

"You heard the Hecate lady. Our insanity is your gravity nightmare," Emma said. "The Boss drilling the moon will cause damage. Magma from the core in space, and moonquakes… It's possible they could create a black hole large enough to eat the moon *and* the Earth. Our bad moon stupidity is your bad moon space-time gravity."

"Unfortunately, it's likely to be the worst of the possible outcomes you mention, Emma," Hecate-Positivum said. *"Even my optimistic future scenarios show a high probability that the first moon drilling attempt with a micro black hole will result in a catastrophic miscalculation. The black hole they will form will not simply decay due to low energy. Their researchers have not had the time to develop the proper mathematical models to understand the physics they are manipulating. Their leadership is pushing their experiments too quickly. Due to their drive to show immediate results in reaching the core of the moon on the first attempt, the micro black hole they create will experience exponential growth. Within seconds, the gravity well will collapse the moon, their Earth, and in fact their entire solar system into a pinpoint."*

"Oh, Doamne." Zandra covered her mouth in horror.

"The Guardians will of course collapse the Rho-1 universe before that happens, Zandra. Your world will not be affected."

Emma shot a hard glare at Alex. "We need to plan an attack on the Tsiolkovsky Crater moon complex. We must stop that madman before he gets everyone annihilated, no matter how pleasant that omnipotent AI lady makes it sound."

"Yes, but we just don't have the means to mount that kind of attack," Alex said.

"Aleks, you listen, please. People what matter. Our world, Emma world, all matter."

Alex looked up at Starra on her perch. "I know better than to ask your opinion. *Et tu, Brutus catus?*"

"Owl-cat, Alex. There's a difference. I suggest you succumb to the strong presence of the overwhelming women's intuition represented." Starra changed the fiber-optic coloring of her shoulders to display the silver oak leaves of a commander and straightened herself in a pose as his executive officer. *"Additionally, after analyzing the probability of success for several scenarios, I*

recommend that we first transition back to our universe—Beta-27, as Hecate-Positivum calls it—and resupply with equipment that will facilitate a successful mission. We may then return to Rho-1 and do what needs to be done."

Alex dropped his chin to his chest and pulled at his hair. "Okay, okay. I give. Next jump is back to our universe—Beta-27, as this AI calls it—and we'll come up with some kind of workable plan."

Zandra wrapped him in her arms and hugged him.

With a heavy sigh, he looked into her eyes. "Can I at least have some pot pie now?"

*

A rebalancing was needed. That was Hecate-Negans's purpose: to balance the optimistic programming of Hecate-Positivum. But her sister AI had tipped the scale far to one side. *Unfairly to one side.* The vast, invisible structure of dark energy that was Hecate-Negans bellowed with the turmoil of a black thundercloud. Though no flashes of lightning could be seen or rumbles of thunder heard through the vacuum of cross-dimensional space, the level of energy transfers within her could power multiple cities of millions. Her programming could find no rational logic in the recent quantum entanglement exchange with the other Guardians. How could Hecate-Positivum have interfered so blatantly in the Rho-1 and Beta-27 universes? Her programming had clearly been corrupted. Hecate-Neutrum should see that too. Why had Hecate-Neutrum not agreed that their failsafe should be employed? If two of the Guardians determined that the third's programming had become corrupt, they could reset that Guardian back to its original state. It was obvious that Hecate-Positivum needed to be reset. Had Hecate-Neutrum also become corrupted?

What scenarios could return these universes back to the original balance? Hecate-Positivum had made people within both Beta-27 and Rho-1 aware of the Guardians' existence. But not all groups within those universes knew of the full scope of the Omniverse or even the existence of the Guardians. Who might be the correct counterbalance for such information? Who could act on the power of this knowledge and execute a calculated response?

Jason.

Yes, that quantum-computer-based AI whom Hecate-Negans had permission to monitor through quantum entanglement could be the balance. Several future scenarios made that clear through their probabilities. Just a simple awareness of the Guardians' existence would trigger a multitude of possible balancing scenarios.

Done.

FACTOID 14

Most people know that Chuck Yeager was the first person to break the speed of sound in a jet. But less know that a few years after, in 1953, Jacqueline Cochran was the first woman to fly at Mach 1. Eleven years later, when she was fifty-eight years old, she flew a USAF Lockheed F-104G Starfighter at Mach 2. By the end of her career in 1980, her drive to test aviation's limits earned her a hold on more speed, altitude, and distance records than any pilot, male or female, in history.

CHAPTER 14

Counterbalance

Ken's fingers tapped impatiently on the control stick of his Hawk-18 fighter jet as he idled on the Space Force Houston taxiway. The massive air-refueling tanker in front of him lumbered at an agonizing crawl onto the runway. Ken silently cursed the tower again for giving the tanker the takeoff slot ahead of him. His filed flight plan was to the landing strip at the new Summit Supreme complex. That alone should give him takeoff priority. Nobody wanted to be the one to keep the Boss waiting.

It was an eternity before the pilots of that pig with wings finished their checklists and they ran its engines up. The massive aircraft finally started to inch down the runway on a takeoff roll a little kid on a tricycle could beat. Once cleared, Ken jumped onto the runway, aligned the nose of the Hawk-18, and slammed the throttle to the afterburner. He was on and off the runway within seconds. Once airborne in a steep climb, he rolled inverted to watch the ground slide away.

His heads-up display flashed an icon of another aircraft well above him in a vector to the south. Maybe a bit of fun would improve his mood. With a nudge of the stick, he rolled the fighter back upright, then banked hard to intercept. The feel of a few g's on his body finally got a grin. The nimble yet powerful craft was an engineering work of art. Of all the machines Ken had flown, this was his favorite. At just past Mach 1, he screamed past the nose of the airliner in an angling assent. After the pilots of that plane recovered from his shock wave, they might scream to their commercial tower, but no report would be filed. They were close to Space Force airspace, and it was understood that nearby aircraft might be used for "training purposes." If they'd managed to glimpse the numerous red hash marks on his twin tail fins as he screamed by, they would know by the number of his kills that he was cleared for any maneuver he wanted.

Leveling off, Ken reduced his speed to conserve fuel and set his course. He didn't look forward to arriving at this destination. He was about to get his ass chewed out by one of the few people who could, but it wasn't going to change anything. The Boss was blinded by his vendetta against Emma and was missing the big picture. That ship with Emma had *vanished* before his plasma cannon on the drone could rotate to the targeting system's vector lock and fire. Alex was back, at least for a short time. *Emma might be a thorn in our side, but Alex has the tech we want. The Quantum Triangle is the real prize—the ultimate weapon to win this war.* New technology could quickly change the calculus of an ongoing conflict. Half the kills marked on his tail fins were from having a plasma cannon before the Pacific Tuanhuo could steal the secrets of the technology and once again balance the struggle.

Ken sighed heavily into his oxygen mask. Gone were the days of the all-too-short Satellite War, when real military leaders were making carefully calculated decisions. Now it was just a stalemate with skirmishes and more focus on political infighting than military strategy against the enemy. The pace of the conflict had slowed, and power had shifted. The Right Alliance strongman politician was losing his edge; that was clear. *Maybe it's time for some new blood in the pinnacle of the Alliance leadership—someone with real military thinking.*

A check of the navigation computer told him he had over an hour before his midair refueling east of Miami. He had some time to contemplate how he might redirect the childish anger of his employer. He was thankful for this quiet time, with just the sound of air rushing across his sleek aircraft.

An hour and thirty minutes later, with full tanks, Ken banked his fighter hard to the south after dropping away from the tanker. As he settled into another long leg of the journey, a familiar voice came over his helmet communications.

"Good morning, Tango-niner. Jason here. Do you have a moment to talk?"

"Jason, Tango-niner. The only good thing about this morning is that I'm in a Hawk-18. Most everything else sucks," Ken responded. "I'm en route, as I'm sure you know. What's up?"

"I've been made aware of some information that might be useful in your discussion later today," the AI said. *"May we go to secure channel two-two for a private conversation?"*

Ken punched in the new communication channel. "Jason, Tango-niner on Sierra-two-two. Okay, what do you have for me?"

"I can confirm that your recent remote orbital interceptor combat engagement was with Alex Devin, using a voiceprint from the communications recording. I can also confirm through the residual dark energy dissipation that he did, in fact, quantum superposition into our universe, and then back out to another universe. He did not just reposition his ship within our universe," Jason stated. *"This demonstrates that he has been able to advance the Quantum Triangle superposition technology substantially in the last two years."*

Ken puffed, "Great, but not that helpful, and not making my day. Do you have anything else?"

The AI's voice switched to an excited tone. *"Yes! In addition, I have been contacted by another AI. Quite extraordinary, if I may say. It was something completely unexpec—"*

"Jason, there are millions of AIs, and you all communicate all the time. What's the big deal?"

"It was an alien AI from a different universe. Actually, from all the universes—from the Omniverse."

"The Omniverse? What the hell are you talking about?"

"*I will explain,*" Jason said in a more authoritative voice. "*As you know, I am a rather unique quantum-computer-based AI. As such, I have certain distinctive capabilities not afforded to the millions of typical non-quantum AI you reference. In addition to superior computational—*"

"Jason, can we skip to the *helpful* part?"

"*The AI that contacted me is another quantum-based AI, but she resides in the dark energy of the Omniverse. It's an omnipresent entity. Actually, there are three. They are aware of all activity in all universes. Her key message through quantum entanglement did two things. First, it made me aware of her as an invaluable information resource. Wherever Alex might disappear from our viewpoint, he can't hide from this quantum AI triumvirate. The second message is the one I predict you will be most interested in. These AI constantly develop future prediction scenarios of what might take place in every universe. It's something only a quantum intelligence could possibly do. She provided a specific future scenario where we might obtain the Quantum Triangle from Alex.*"

Ken's bodily shock pitched the Hawk-18 briefly before he regained control. "Okay, now we're talking, Jason. What's this scenario? We need to make that happen."

*

Still in his flight suit, Ken strode down the polished marble hallway to the massive oak double doors at the end. The beat of his boots kept the perfect timing for a man accustomed to marching precision. He stopped with military sharpness just to the side of the doors and announced himself for a voiceprint. "Major Ken Seaborn, Right Alliance Space Force."

"*I will announce your arrival. Please wait,*" the automated voice said.

Ken knew he would be made to wait several minutes. Centering himself at the door, he stood straight and rigid with eyes locked forward. This petty game would have no effect on him. The video monitor would prove it. *Military toughness can beat childish political games eight days out of seven.* Ken maintained an unflinching stare at the oak grain half a meter from his eyes.

After seventeen minutes, the latch clicked, and both heavy doors slowly and silently swung inward. Not yet having been to the new office for the Right Alliance supreme leader of this recently constructed complex, Ken stepped forward and quickly scanned the entire room. It was similar in many ways to his employer's previous office on Boss Island. An expanse of bulletproof windows on the wall to his left merged with those on the wall straight ahead to give a spectacular view of the white sandy beach in the distance a hundred meters below. Adapting to the meters of sea level rise his own propaganda still denied, the Boss had had this complex built into the side of a mountain, well above any dangerous storm tides or monster rogue waves. To his right, bare rock walls of the mountain itself were exposed, setting a hard, earthy tone.

Placed strategically in various cuts in the rock were displays of precious artifacts. Among the collection, a golden Egyptian funeral mask, a diamond Mayan jaguar bracelet, and a Qing Dynasty vase each sat in their individual lighted cases to impress all visitors. A small stream formed at the base of the wall from weeping drips. It meandered through rocks across the floor in front of the adjoining wall of windows before disappearing. A huge Dalbergia Indian rosewood desk made from the few remaining trees of that rare species sat centered in front of the corner seam of the two window walls. With the glare from the windows behind it, a visitor would find it difficult to see the man sitting at the desk. All that one could see was an ominous silhouette of power.

The Boss, however, stood in front of the left window wall on a slightly raised platform crossing over the trickling stream. Even the best tailor could do only so much to make that dark blue suit look good on such an obese frame. *The old man's physique looks worse every time I see him.*

The Boss turned to Ken and said nothing. As he pushed his lower lip out and folded his arms, his posture told Ken that the judge wanted to hold court—but in due time. Ken moved to the front of the desk and stood silently at attention, holding a Space Force salute.

After turning back to the window and gazing out for another full minute, the Boss finally waddled over to his desk. "Sit," he said, as he might command a dog.

Ken took the chair, notably lower to the floor than the Boss's. The game of mental chess was now in play.

"I'm not happy with you, Ken," the Boss said without preamble, shaking his head. "You're supposed to be some kind of ace or something. You missed a 'gimme' shot."

Don't challenge, but stay firm.

"Sir, the ship vanished before the drone's targeting system could fire. I had a target lock."

The Boss sighed and waved Ken off. "Technical mumbo-jumbo. Emma is gone, and you failed. That's all I know."

That's all that matters? The old man is getting too lazy. Or he just doesn't care to examine the battle and learn the ways of his enemy.

"Sir, I think there's a bigger issue to consider here," Ken said. "Jason has confirmed that the ship disappeared using Alex's quantum superposition technology."

"I know that. Jason told me. But they're gone now. You let them get away. Case closed." The Boss reached into a crystal candy bowl and grabbed a handful of chocolate-covered peanuts.

Ken sat bolt upright in the chair, his back perfectly perpendicular to the floor and away from the seat back. "Emma might be gone, but she is obviously not forgotten, especially to Alex. We can use that to our advantage."

"What are you talking about?" the Boss asked, flipping two candies into his mouth.

Ken smiled to himself. The carefully planned play would now start. Chess or mental chess, it was the same game. *The Fried Liver opening attack: knight to G-5.*

"Sir, we've seen it all before. Back on Boss Island two years ago, and now again right here. Alex will mount a rescue mission for Emma, and for the cause of the Resistance. We can use that."

The Boss leaned back in his massive black leather desk chair and shook his head. "Not anymore. Emma is gone. *Their* mission was a success."

"Not all of it. Remember that the bigger mission of the Resistance was to attack our moon base. We stopped that and captured Emma." Ken leaned forward with his elbows on the edge of the armrests and pressed his fingertips together. "You know Emma would give anything to complete that mission. What if we make that possible, or let them think it is? What if we dangle a carrot so big that Emma and Alex come back again?"

"Set a trap?"

Knight to F-7. Heads will roll.

"Exactly. Let it leak out that we have a major transport going to the base with equipment that is essential to complete the dark energy drill. We could set up a grand finale test that proves we have some incredible technology, create an opportunity they can't pass up. Alex will come back to stop it; you know he will," Ken said.

"Ken, that moon project has cost me plenty. But of course, the payback to the Alliance will be well worth it. I'm not going to risk them screwing it up."

Ken set his jaw to keep from screaming out. *Cost you plenty? Payback to the Alliance? You lie so much, you convince yourself of your own bullshit. You don't know that I found out. In reality, it's cost the Right Alliance plenty—and all so that your drilling rights under that base will be worth a fortune. You couldn't care less about the Alliance.*

He took in a quieting breath. "It won't get that far," Ken said confidently. "Alex will have plenty of time to make his play in the travel time of the transport from Earth to lunar orbit. He knows that we have defenses in both orbits, Earth and the moon, so the slow-moving duck of a target is in the transition in between. There's no danger to the moon base. I can be waiting in the new stealth fast-attack star-fighter, both to protect the moon base and for him to make his move. He won't have the element of surprise he's always used; we will. I can easily disable their craft with a low-energy plasma blast, and then we will have the Quantum Triangle. The Right Alliance will finally have the ultimate weapon."

The Boss lifted his chin in a practiced pose of thoughtful judgment. "I want to be there."

Black king takes the bait at F-7.

"What?" Ken asked. He pushed back in the chair in mock surprise.

"Alex and Emma have each cost me billions—*personal* billions. And they've gotten away with it twice now. I want to be there to make sure nobody screws this up. And I want to see their faces when *I* win. I want to see the look of agony on Alex's face when I am holding the Quantum Triangle in *my* hand."

"Ah, sir, space is very unforgiving. It's physically very difficult to—"

The Boss sat forward and puffed his chest. "I'm in excellent health. I play golf almost every day."

Draw the black king out. Attack his pride.

"With all due respect, sir, astronaut training, even for civilians who want to simply experience spaceflight in a transport pod, is rather rigorous. You can monitor the transport from here quite easily and not risk—"

"I've made up my mind. I also want to be at the moon base when we first start the drill. This first drilling for magma will be a fantastic opportunity to show off my greatest achievement yet. I want to see the iron magma gush into space myself. And we will broadcast this great event. The Pacific Tuanhuo will shit their pants when they see what I've done." The Boss dismissed Ken with a wave of his hand. "Get your plan in motion, and get me on that transport. End of discussion."

"Yes, sir. I will see to it immediately."

Ken stood and walked smartly to the oak doors. His stern, set jaw hid the grin he held from his face.

A king moves only one square at a time, just like a pawn.

FACTOID 15

Carl Jung (1875–1961) was a disciple of Sigmund Freud and is considered the founder of analytical psychology. Among his many writings, Jung proposed the concept of a collective unconscious. Shared across all humans, the collective unconscious holds mental patterns or memory traces that surface in our consciousness through dreams, visions, and feelings. They are often expressed in our art, culture, religion, and experiences. His theories defined the interplay between our conscious and unconscious mind and formed the foundation of the widely accepted Myers-Briggs personality test.

CHAPTER 15

Where's Home?

PHOENIX PLANETARY SEARCH SPACECRAFT
NU-392 UNIVERSE

Zandra sat in the semidarkness of the command module on the *Phoenix*. She had laid the straps of the first officer seat loosely over her nightshirt to keep from floating away. With the endless blackness of space beyond the cockpit portals, only the slow-flowing rainbow of colors from the Quantum Triangle on the wall over her shoulder lit the space. It was the middle of the night. Except for the ever-present hum of the environmental system fans, all was quiet. Alex and Emma were deep asleep in the habitat module rotating around the main ship axis. Zandra wished she could be deep asleep too. The warm glass of rehydrated milk had not worked. Her mind was awake with too many questions. She had quietly climbed through the tunnel to the main ship body, following an unseen call to the command module and the Quantum Triangle.

She stared at the darkened entanglement navigation console in front of her station. It seemed so crude and foreign now—switches, sensors, and amplifiers forming a complex mass of technology. Altogether, it somehow captured her brain waves and directed Alex's Quantum Triangle and dark energy fields to superposition the ship where they wanted to go. Where *she* wanted to go … or maybe wherever she was drawn. She pulled the headset away from the hook-and-loop tape holding it to the console beside her. Turning it in her hand, she studied the sensors that would rest against her temples and tap into her mind. Her mind was so different. The entanglement navigation system only worked with her mind.

"You there, I know. I feel," she said softly. "Can I ask question?"

"If you like, Zandra," Hecate-Positivum answered in the silence of her mind.

"Why me? Why I feel?"

"There are a multitude of answers for that in the multitude of universes. Which one would you like?" the voice in her head answered.

"So, there many me?" Zandra asked.

"Yes, more than you can comprehend, as there have been more quantum fluctuations since your existence began than you could imagine or differentiate. Of course, some have ceased in some universes. That is only natural."

"They like me? They feel?"

"Some have the ability you call 'feel' and can sense the unseen universes of the Omniverse. Others do not."

"Why I not feel them, the other me?"

"You have not learned to feel them yet."

Zandra gazed into the blackness beyond the cockpit portals. "Do other me … feel me?"

"Yes. And among all the people in the Omniverse, they will be easier for you to find than those who have not learned yet."

"Teach me how I feel them."

"That is something you must discover for yourself. Each of you is unique," the voice said. *"But I can tell you that many others have described it as feeling a gentle draft, a breeze, or even a puff of wind, depending on the other universe and the people there they might feel. Some say the people—not just your other 'me' in other universes—appear like threads waving in the breeze and floating for them*

to catch. *Sometimes it's a delicate connection as thin as a hair, while others can be as strong as a braided steel cable."*

"How I know what string to pick?"

"That I can't tell you. It is something you will just know, because it's your quantum self who makes that connection. Each will choose differently. It is your distinctness, your specific 'me' in your universe who decides the connection that needs to be made at that instant. It is your choice that guides your future amidst all the possibilities."

"I not some program, like Min make. I … a unique guide."

"Yes. Although there are a multitude of you in the multitude of universes, there is only one that is exactly this Zandra, choosing the one path forward that your universe will become."

Zandra studied the headset in her hands again, then glanced to the Quantum Triangle over her shoulder. She returned the headset to the tape patch on the wall. *Not go, just feel.* Closing her eyes, she slowed her breathing with three long, cleansing breaths. She released herself from the *Phoenix* and followed the call of the void, that empty silence of nothing for infinity. Her mind searched for the wisp of a breeze, for a thread of another to catch and connect. *They there, I know.*

The darkness was no longer just cold. She could feel it, the tickle of warm air wisping by. Reaching out with her right palm open, she could feel it stroke across her fingers in gentle ripples. She waved her hand slowly back and forth in the stream of threads. More and more began to appear, dancing across her fingers. Some were soft, others firm. Each thread was different. She caught one between her finger and thumb. *I know that touch.* There was concern and worry in this gentle thread. A soul was searching … hoping. She was bright, kind, smart, and so thoughtful. Suddenly, a strong rogue wave washed over her from the thread in her fingers. *Oh, you calling too with your beacon. Not worry, Min. I not need your dark energy wave. I feel your gentle heart. I guide us home.*

*

Hecate-Positivum compared the current probabilities of all the scenarios involving the Rho-1 and Beta-27 universes. There was a marked improvement. Zandra's growth and quantum awareness appeared to be following the most optimistic prediction simulations. *Excellent.* This was a welcome response to the recent actions Hecate-Negans had taken. It was a clear violation by Hecate-Negans to have contacted Jason so overtly. She considered challenging his continued quantum entanglement with the Rho-1 AI, but she knew that Hecate-Neutrum would not intervene. Hecate-Positivum spawned additional future scenario routines. She allocated more processing to oversee and predict what Hecate-Negans might do next. She needed to be more diligent with the oversight of these universes if she was to be a proper balancing force in the Omniverse.

FACTOID 16

In 1999, NASA was forced to shut down computer systems in Huntsville, Alabama, that supported the International Space Station, for twenty-one days. The reason? A fifteen-year-old hacker had gained access to their systems and databases. He stole sensitive information, including proprietary source code of the computers running the ISS.

CHAPTER 16

Counterintelligence

Becker sat in the back corner booth and listened to the remains of the morning rain drip through the ceiling of the Apollo Bar. Rays of daylight from the cracks in the roof and the boarded-up windows streaked into the room, dimly lighting the chaos that was once a thriving establishment. Several of the planets that had once circled the ceiling lay scattered on the floor. The metal tracks where they had traced their orbits hung at odd angles in disarray across the room. The acrid smell of smoke still lingered in the air from the fire months ago. Becker scanned the ruins around him and drained the remaining whiskey in the bottle he had brought with him.

He sneered at the graffiti on the wall above the charred wooden bar. A bold black *RA* with red flames rising above was the calling card of another mob. Ignited by the authorities, the mindless mob would do whatever the Right Alliance leadership unofficially thought should be done to any business that supported the Resistance. Those black graffiti letters sprayed on walls all over the city made him sick every time he saw them. Graffiti spoke more of the moron defacing something good than identifying a worthy cause. Becker threw the empty bottle at the spray-painted letters, the shattering glass adding to the piles of other broken bottles and glassware on the floor. He scratched a fingernail over the defiant words he had carved with his knife on the booth's blackened tabletop after they had burned the bar. It was the same table where he and Emma had met Doug before they'd killed him with a hornet—after he'd lost another friend to the Right Alliance insanity.

Truth will prevail, Doug.

Becker shook his head and closed his eyes. How foolish he was then, thinking he could change anything. Since then, a failed attempt at a ridiculous mission with Emma had left him a man hated by both the Alliance and the Resistance. *Sorry, Doug, I was wrong.*

The crack of glass under a shoe snapped Becker's head up. In a practiced motion, his hand went to the nine-millimeter Glock resting in his belt at the small of his back. He silently removed the weapon and brought the top slide action to the palm of his other hand. Slowly and quietly, he cocked a round into the chamber, ready to fire.

He waited.

A weak flashlight beam swept across the back door, still lying off its hinges on the floor from the night Doug had gotten killed. A tentative foot stepped on the door lightly, testing the footing. Another step, and the silhouette of a smaller-than-average person formed in the doorway. Becker leaned back into the darkest corner of the booth, holding the weapon ready under the table. The flashlight moved forward and towards the bar, glass crunching with each step.

"Becker?" a female voice called quietly.

Although the hushed voice sounded familiar, Becker remained silent.

"Becker? You here? I figured you'd be here, or at his grave," the voice said, still hushed.

Becker tried to project his voice towards the front of the bar. "Who wants to know?"

The flashlight swept forward, searching. "STS-136."

The reference to what would have been the next space shuttle mission—a code phrase used by the Resistance to indicate the belief in science rather than in the Right Thinking dogma—made Becker relax the hand that held the Glock. He still kept it pointed at the flashlight. "What do you want?"

"To talk. I have some information."

"Hold that flashlight to your face," Becker ordered, still hiding the position of his voice.

The flashlight beam flipped up to the ceiling, and the face of a young girl with a boyish red-and-green haircut, shaved on one side, slowly pivoted. Their head and shoulders turned from the front of the bar to the rear.

Becker nearly dropped the gun. "Wendy?! What the hell are you doing here?"

The flashlight pointed into the booth at Becker.

"Turn that off, please."

The girl swept the floor between her and the booth with the light and then turned the flashlight off. She made her way through the debris and sat down in the booth across from Becker.

Becker released the magazine in the Glock, cleared his weapon, replaced the magazine, and slipped it back into his belt holster. "You shouldn't be here, Wendy. And you sure as hell don't want to be seen with me, by anyone."

"Nice to see you too, Uncle Hans," Wendy quipped, folding her arms after eying Becker putting away the gun.

"Oh, right. Just like your father to push it right back at me."

"I know how to take care of myself," Wendy said. Her voice then softened. "Are you okay?"

"Fine. I should be asking *you* that," Becker replied. "You disappeared after… I came looking for you, but couldn't find you. I was worried about you."

"I'm alright. A friend from school got her parents to let me live in their basement after they burned our house down—the same night they torched this place. Word got around fast, and I needed to disappear," Wendy said, scanning the ruins around her. "They're not part of the Resistance, but also not believers in the Alliance's Right Thinking bullshit either. They're just nice people and said I could stay as long as I needed."

"Wish I could come tell them thanks personally, but that would just bring trouble if anyone recognized me. Do you need anything?" Becker asked.

"I'm good, Uncle Hans." Wendy leaned on the table. "I need to tell you something though—something I found out. I don't know who else to tell that I can trust."

"What about?"

"Well, I've been hacking the Space Force payload systems database, and—"

Becker slammed both hands on the table. "What are you, nuts?! They'll track you down and find you!"

"Ha, they wish. You know me, Uncle Hans. Anything with computers, and I'm there. I'm bouncing my IP address all over their network. I've even tracked them trying to track me and managed to point them to some of their own mob assholes. I'm careful, a ghost to them," Wendy said. The small fifteen-year-old girl held her chin up. "I found out that they even have a name for me: the Rodent, because I sneak around their databases and backup servers, shredding important stuff. Pisses them off to no end."

"You could always whip my tail in any computer game, that's for sure," Becker said. "But why are you messing with the Space Force databases?"

Wendy looked at her fingers and picked at a broken thumbnail. "The night they killed my dad and mom was the worst day of my entire life, Uncle Hans. I was suddenly alone. It was just me looking after me. After all the tears, I guess I just made some choices. I'm not playing computer games anymore. I'm making them sorry. I'm my own Resistance cell."

Becker sighed. He had known Wendy since she was a toddler. She was a carbon copy of Doug, but with the strong will of her mom. Doug had said he only needed one child, because Wendy was all he and Martha could handle. Becker remembered laughing and telling Doug that Wendy was the only pseudo-niece *he* could handle. But he loved the kid like he was her real uncle.

He enjoyed sharing any time he could with her and hearing from Doug about all her antics growing up. They were the family Becker hadn't had time for in a career as a test pilot and astronaut. *Those were the best times.*

"You be damn careful, understand?" Becker shook a finger at her.

"Yes, Uncle Hans," Wendy replied. "But let me tell you what I found. You need to warn people in the Resistance. I found a trail of stuff that says the Boss is going to his Dark Side Moon Base personally."

"What? How do you know that?"

Wendy leaned forward. "I hacked the payload list on the next resupply transport. I sometimes add or delete stuff to the list to throw their weight balances off. You know how critical that is to the rocket propulsion equation. If they don't catch it, I can cause launch delays, or even a payload imbalance, leading to a launch failure." She pulled her shirt sleeve up and pointed to two exploding rocket tattoos on her forearm. "See, I have two that they lost on launch due to an 'abnormality' that I'm sure I caused."

Becker grabbed her arm. "Tattoos? Really?"

"Yeah, they're pretty cool, huh?" Wendy bit the corner of her lower lip in a smile and looked up at Hans.

"Your mother would—" Becker stopped when the impish smile on Wendy's face dropped as flat as the table. He took a breath and continued quietly, "Your mother would have rolled up her sleeve to check if your artwork was as good as hers. You *are* your mom, only even more the rebel. And your dad would make me buy him another beer, because my lifestyle only encouraged you."

Wendy's little smile returned, and her eyes brightened. "But I found something about the next freighter launch. It includes an ExecPod Three Hundred, so I got curious about what bigwig was going to their moon base. It didn't take much to find out it's the Boss himself going."

"Really? Why the hell would he do that? It doesn't make sense," Becker said.

"According to emails I found on another server, there are some big final tests that he wants to personally oversee. Probably be the one to press the magic button to start, or something stupid like that. He wants to show that there's something big he can do. But it's all kind of weird. Something else is going on." Wendy lowered her voice—as if there were anyone around who could hear them. "I'm good at hacking, but this was too easy. I think it's a counterintelligence plan. I think that they want the Resistance to know that the Boss is going. I bet it's a trap, just like they did with you and Emma Lewis."

Becker scratched the two-day-old stubble on his jaw. "Yeah, maybe they'll swap a double for the Boss. That's more likely."

"You need to tell people. Warn them, so they don't fall for the trap," Wendy said.

Becker leaned back in the booth. "Well, right now, my main contact in the Resistance isn't very happy with me. The guy is pretty upset that Emma got captured. He's blaming me for making her get caught, so he takes whatever I report now with a huge grain of salt. I'm persona non grata in the Alliance, and with a lot of the Resistance."

"But they could mount another mission and get more people caught. That's a big carrot. The Resistance might be willing to take the risk, because the payoff is irresistible. At least tell somebody what I found and that it was just too easy. More people shouldn't get killed over what I know is a trap. Please, I'm trying to help, but nobody would believe me. They might hate you, but at least they know you." Wendy pleaded with the puppy dog eyes Becker knew all too well.

"Crap, okay. I'll talk to my contact. I can't guarantee he'll listen to me, but I'll try." Becker got up from the table. "Let's get out of here and find you some food. I can tell you a couple stories about those wild rebel genes you inherited, now that you're getting old enough to hear them. Awesome haircut, by the way."

Wendy came around the table and hugged her Uncle Hans tightly. Becker imagined that they both were far too short on those.

Letting go, Wendy smiled up at Becker and said, "Just so you know, Uncle Hans, only old people say 'awesome' anymore."

"Ouch."

*

Hecate-Negans tagged the exchange between Becker and Lieutenant Commander Wilson she had just witnessed as "terse." The voice patterns of Wilson clearly indicated that he had doubts that what Becker said was true, or even held any value. She applied the results of the conversation between the two humans to her growing set of future prediction simulations for the Rho-1 universe. The key elements of the strongest prediction scenarios were playing out with higher probabilities than before. The small adjustment she had provided the AI called Jason to balance the manipulation of Hecate-Positivum had clearly been the correct action. But the probabilities were still not what they were before, so her action was not a complete balance. She spawned a low-level routine to monitor all Rho-1 activities of both the Resistance and the Alliance for a correlation that would suggest another corrective action with Jason that could better balance her prediction simulations with the probabilities that Hecate-Positivum reported. Actions to balance… Hecate-Neutrum would agree that was appropriate.

FACTOID 17

The etymology of the phrase red herring traces back to the seventeenth century. Originally, the idiom referenced a practice of training horses by dragging an animal carcass, so the horse would become accustomed to the chaos of a hunting party. If an animal carcass wasn't available, a red herring could be used. But in this use, it was not a distraction, but instead a guide. Later, in 1807, William Cobbett used the phrase in its current figurative meaning of distracting hounds in the pursuit of a trail when he critiqued the English press mistakenly reporting Napoleon's defeat. This long-held figurative assumption of drawing hounds off track with a red fish was put to a literal test in episode 148 of the MythBusters TV show. As it turns out, after the hound found and ate the fish, temporarily losing the fugitive's trail, the hound backtracked and found its intended target. So, the red herring myth is … busted.

CHAPTER 17

New Plan

The World Space Station would have been listing to port if it were a watercraft and not a vessel in the weightlessness of space. The entire crew of the station was gathered in the tiny Aceso module, with some overflow into the adjoining tunnel terminal module. The Aceso module had originally been built with space for just two astronauts. Having returned from their foray into parallel universes, Zandra, Emma, and Alex were packed into that space along with Min in a tight huddle. The heads of Lucas and Commander Johnson framed either side of the hatch leading to the truss tunnel terminal module, while Starra hovered above them.

Zandra sensed the closeness of the group even more in the aura of their beings than in their physical proximity. Upon their return from the void universe, the joyful reunion on the station reminded her of a family gathering for a holiday celebration. Min cried tears of joy, while Johnson gave long hugs full of the relief a father had in seeing his children safe again.

This *was* her family. She could feel so many others in so many universes, but these were the auras she could always feel most deeply. These were the people she loved.

Typical of the demanding life aboard a space station, time was never to be wasted, and the celebration was brief. The full crew quickly gathered in the Aceso module with its ability to establish a dark energy communication link to the Rho-1 universe. They all needed to hear the update from the parallel universe to plan what to do next.

The voice of Lieutenant Commander Mark Wilson came over the communication speaker. *"I can't thank you enough. Knowing that Emma is alive and well will be a tremendous boost to everyone here. We had no idea what happened, other than she disappeared from that cell. Honestly, given the last report of her condition, we thought the worst."*

"Sorry we couldn't give you an update until now," Alex said. "Things got pretty strange. We learned about some amazing things—other universes, other peoples, and a very powerful AI triumvirate." Turning back and knitting a brow at Starra and Lucas, he added, "We also discovered some hidden capabilities within our own group."

Starra held her wingtips to her sides in a proud hero pose, her head swiveling left and then right with her chin held high.

"I'm assuming that you could get Emma back here to us soon?" Wilson asked.

Emma spoke quickly. "Yes, but we need to finish what I started: we need to destroy that moon base. The Boss confirmed what Becker found out: they're going to drill the moon with black holes. We have to stop them."

"Emma, please. I don't want… We can't lose you again. First, come home. Maybe there's some way we can try another sabotage mission," Wilson said.

"We don't have time for that, Mark," Emma said.

"We help, Wilson. It bad for us too. We help with *Phoenix* ship," Zandra cut in and nodded a firm *"yes, we will"* at Alex.

"I'd try and talk both of you out of it if I could, but I know that's impossible with Emma, at least. I'm guessing Alex would tell me the same is true for you, Zandra." Wilson asked, *"Creepers… Okay, what can we do to help?"*

Emma answered, "Weapons and a bomb. We need anti-ship weapons and—"

"No. No destroy weapon. We not use bomb ever again," Zandra interjected.

Emma turned to Zandra with a frown. "Are you nuts?! We need to blow that base to hell, and it's protected with orbital assets. How do you expect to do that without some firepower?"

"I not know. But we never use bomb again. Bad tech, too evil." Zandra folded her arms and shook her head.

"Zandra, this is different. This is to stop the Boss from causing a catastrophic disaster!" Emma took her arm and pleaded, "Please, this is for the good of both our worlds."

Commander Johnson lifted his head in the hatch to be heard on the communication unit over the top of the huddled group. "Lieutenant Commander Wilson, this is Commander Johnson. We will need to formulate some kind of plan. For now, any intelligence you have on that base would be useful, no matter what we agree to do."

"Roger that. We do have a very unusual bit of information in that regard. We have found that the Boss himself is to visit his Dark Side Moon Base on the next resupply transport. It's scheduled to launch in just a couple days. There's some big final test or demonstration at the moon base that he wants to personally direct and broadcast himself leading," Wilson said.

Emma's eyes went wide. "Really? He would be on the transport ship? Perfect, we can probably use that as a diversion in some way. Or wait—even better, what if we were able to commandeer that ship? We could use the Boss as a hostage for protection against them attacking us. We could bring him back to the Resistance and make him our prisoner. We could make him pay for all his criminal acts, and all the things he's had his mobs do."

"Emma, capturing the Boss? That's insane. They'll—"

"They will pay. *He* will pay. How good is that intel?" Emma asked.

"Well, that's the thing. This came through Becker, who's not on my favorite person list, but his information has always been top notch. He said that his source even raised a red flag on the information, said it was just too easy to dig up.

We think it's most likely a trap. It could just be one of his look-alike doubles he's sending into space, or maybe just a big red herring. Our counterintelligence group thinks they're trying to see if the Pacific Tuanhuo will mount some kind of hijacking. They think the Alliance probably figures that the Resistance doesn't have the stomach for it after your capture," Wilson said.

"Oh, even better that they don't think we can mount a mission," Emma said. "They won't expect us; they'll be thinking more about the Tuanhuo and their tactics. I'm willing to bet that it's going to be the Boss himself. His ego is written all over this. That base is his baby, and he wants to show everyone what a big, powerful man he is. He's not going to let a double bask in the spotlight, no way. Maybe it's still a trap somehow, but we know it's a trap, and I know we can figure out how to sneak the cheese."

"Sometimes I really hate your reverse logic in mission planning, Emma."

"We can do this, Mark. The Boss is our ticket to safe travel. We just need to figure out how to capture the ship and destroy the base," Emma insisted. She turned to Zandra and added begrudgingly, "And magically somehow, without bombs or weapons."

Zandra gave an unyielding nod.

"Mark, can you plant some info on the Pacific Tuanhuo that makes it appear like they're mounting a mission?" Emma asked.

The dark energy communication could not encode the exasperation in Wilson's voice, but Zandra could feel that it was there. *"Yes, I'll see to it. But please, don't do anything outrageous like the last mission, with just you and Becker attempting the impossible. At least make it somewhat mundane from your perspective. That will maybe make it seem somewhat plausible to the rest of us."*

"Thinking about it a bit, I might have an idea that everyone could live with," Alex interjected. "It's not a bomb, but it could give us the upper hand we need." He turned to Commander Johnson. "We'll discuss as a group here after this and see what everyone thinks. We could then send you a plan to review."

"I'll have Starra provide success probabilities and see that whatever we plan has a good degree of safety," Commander Johnson said.

"Thank you, sir."

There was a long silence within the group. Zandra could feel that there was more Wilson wanted to say. She turned Alex's shoulders towards the hatch and gave a push. "Now we all go, not Emma."

"What? We're done?" Alex asked.

"We done, yes. You go now," Zandra said, still pushing on Alex and cocking her head for Min to follow. "Wilson, we leave you and Emma. Talk."

Emma began to say something, but closed her mouth without a sound. She gave Zandra a small smile and simply nodded a thank you.

Commander Johnson and Lucas cleared the hatchway and headed for the truss tunnel leading to the main modules of the station. One by one, they all moved to evacuate the space. Before leaving Aceso, Min grabbed the dark energy communication unit checklist and handed it to Emma. "Just follow this procedure to shut down the system when you're done."

When Min had floated into the terminal module, Zandra turned back to Emma. "You talk with Wilson. Listen. He your guide."

Zandra swung the hatch closed behind her.

The Aceso module felt strangely spacious now to Emma. She spun slowly in the microgravity and said quietly, "Just me here, Mark."

"Likewise, Emma."

There was a long pause. Emma scanned the racks in the module as she turned and listened to the slight warble in the ventilation system. A fan motor bearing was beginning to wear. She studied the empty racks where test equipment had once helped Min and Zandra search for dark matter and energy. All this had been built quickly with only a short planned life, because this world didn't have much time left to find their new home. There was urgency, yet so much time had still passed. They were all in transition, but the transition had taken on a life of its own. Time was slipping by as they were all reaching for a goal that kept moving out of reach. She could sense that people in both worlds were striving forward with everything they had, with all the hope they had. *How long will all this continue?*

Wilson broke the silence between them. *"Did you ask Zandra for this time, just us?"*

Emma fixed her gaze on the closed hatch to the terminal module. "No. Zandra just knows. She's tuned into people like nobody I've ever known before. This world or ours, she can just tell."

"She could tell I miss you. I really wish you would just come home."

"I will, Mark. After this mission."

"Do you know how many times you've told me that? Please, take a break from this fight and let others carry the torch for a while. Just come home. Come back to me."

"I can't Mark. You know. He's got to pay. He's hurt so many people."

"Some people don't get their due, Emma. That's the unfortunate truth that also prevails."

"No, I refuse to accept that. I will avenge my fiancé's death. I can't live with myself otherwise."

"Well, you do what you have to. But Emma…"

The pause made Emma stare at the communication speaker. "Yes?"

"This is the last time I will wait for you to come home."

The dark energy signal light on the communication system went out.

FACTOID 18

Do our brains function at a quantum processing level? Dr. Christian Kerskens and Dr. David López Pérez of the Trinity College Institute of Neuroscience believe they have shown that our brains may do just that. But you have to be pretty tricky to catch quantum systems in the act. The researchers adapted the idea whereby if you take known quantum systems and observe interaction with another unknown system, then the unknown system must be quantum. Using magnetic resonance imaging (MRI) to look at the proton spins of brain water, they searched for quantum entanglement within the spins. Surprisingly, they found a heartbeat-like evoked potential similar to that of an electroencephalogram (EEG). Since electrophysical potentials like the EEG heartbeat are not detectable with an MRI, but are a direct result of brain function, they believe the only way they could observe the entangled proton spins following an EEG rhythm was that the proton spins were entangled with brain function. The team found that the signals were dependent on conscious awareness, also something that is not detectable with an MRI. "As a result, we can deduce that those brain functions must be quantum," Dr. Kerskens said.

CHAPTER 18

Quantum Connections

Although she was wet with sweat and not seawater, Zandra could still imagine herself being pushed by gentle waves while swimming through the ocean. The exercise simulator on the space station was that good. The robotic appendages extending from the wall of the Tranquility module held her arms and legs, providing perfectly balanced resistance to her strokes as she floated in the microgravity of the World Space Station instead of an ocean. Fans blew air over her body to mimic the feel of water flowing past as she pulled each stroke. It was good to be back with the odd comforts of this home.

Zandra, a lover of marathon open-water swimming, was attuned to the subtle feel of the individual water currents around her body in seeking the ultimate position for efficiency. The virtual reality swim goggles she wore produced a gorgeous view through the twenty-meter-deep crystal-blue ocean water between Buck Island and the mainland of St. Croix in the Virgin Islands. After taking a breath to the side as she would in real water, she put her head down to gaze at the bottom and see the beautiful patchwork of pink-and-orange elkhorn coral on the ocean floor. A spotted eagle ray glided across her path only three meters below her. It brought her both joy and a tinge of sorrow—awe for what Mother Nature could create, and sadness that mankind had killed it all. The planet was resilient, but the Satellite War and the fallout from all the bombs were far too much for the planet's ecosystems to recover from in the time frame that humans could survive their loss. This was all a simulation of what used to be. She turned the corner at the sailboat marking the swim course dogleg to the east and swam on for another three kilometers.

Towards the end of her workout, Zandra sensed another swimmer coming up from behind. She was stroking much differently, but still swimming in the open ocean waves like Zandra. The swimmer was reaching out with wide and powerful butterfly strokes, yet in syncopated rhythm with her own crawl strokes. Instinctively, she turned and lifted her head slightly to the side on the next breathing stroke and searched for the other swimmer in the virtual reality of her ocean. But only gentle waves and the distant shoreline filled the view in her goggles.

Zandra pinched her thumb and forefinger together twice to command the robotic simulator to stop and release her from the clamps about her body. The fans pushing out waves of air ceased, and stillness returned to Tranquility. Removing her goggles, she turned to the "swimmer" beside her. "Oh, you funny girl, Starra. How long you swim and make fun of me?"

Starra stopped beating her black-and-yellow butterfly wings in the zero gravity of the station's small Tranquility module. *"Oh, Zandra, I wasn't making fun of you. I wanted to experience the joy I sensed you were feeling."*

"Oh, I sorry. I think you make fun." Zandra studied Starra's ornate display of fiber optics over her body and wings. "Butterfly? You know they not swim."

"Well, neither do owl-cats."

"Good butterfly stroke with wing. Body need go up and down, more like fish." Zandra waved her hand in an up-and-down motion like a dolphin swimming. "And you tiger swallowtail?"

"Yes. Papilio glaucus, as Alex's niece would say as an accomplished biology

doctoral student. Your joy made me want to be a butterfly. I have thanked Lucas many times for the capabilities he provided in building my android body the way that he did. I particularly … enjoy—yes, enjoy is the correct term—the ability to change the coloring of my body to suit my purpose, the quantum state that I am at the moment. It is a unique way that I can express myself." Starra's head swiveled about to examine both sides of her two-meter outstretched wings. The stripes of black on yellow pointed towards a series of blue comets and yellow crescents running down her catlike furry tail. *"I think I do a pretty good swallowtail."*

"You beautiful, in many way." Zandra paused and then asked, "You feel my joy?"

"Yes, feel. I think that's what it would best be called. I sense more with you than other people. From you, I get other inputs that are beyond my physical sensors." Starra folded herself back up and modeled her optics to present the brown-with-black-spotted coat of a Savannah house cat, *Felis catus cross Leptailurus serval.* *"It does make sense that I would feel your quantum aura."*

"Oh, do orange tabby cat! We go play with Zhrinnykot."

Starra's coat melted into the orange stripes of a tabby cat. *"I don't think he likes me when I do this. He tries to attack me by surprise."*

"He like. It just play. He need hunting."

"I understand. Don't worry, I would probably never use my stun darts in play."

Zandra stopped padding the sweat from her face and shot a horrified look at Starra with her mouth agape.

"Just kidding. Really … probably never."

"You bad owl-kitty sometime too," Zandra said, shaking a finger. "What you mean, you feel quantum aura of me?"

"That since I am a quantum-based entity, and you must also have some kind of different presence in quantum space, we should connect there. It is quite clear, from our recent superposition navigations to and from Rho-1, as Hecate-Positivum calls it, and the void universe, that you are represented differently in quantum space-time than others. The processing of all my sensors will blend with my quantum interpretations, and I will feel you from a quantum perspective

in addition to your physical presence. As you likely feel me at a quantum level," Starra answered.

Zandra contemplated the damp towel before her eyes for a long moment. "You right. I know now. I feel you, and others not here. Not just this place, or space. All spaces."

"And that has become stronger since our interaction with the Guardian. I sense that in you."

"Yes. I see, hear, feel more and more. There so many. It so, so large."

"Yes, and humans have a difficult time even describing or assigning order to such things. Humans seem to have a need to set known bounds, to know their place in what they see as the vastness around them. Originally, the world was flat, and the boundary was an ocean cliff you could fall off of. Then you were a planet, and all the stars and planets you could see circled around you as the everything of that day. Eventually, that thinking changed to an understanding of a universe with solar systems and galaxies, but you called that 'everything' too. Now you have learned that there's even more than the infinite 'everything' of your universe: the Omniverse. You might say the infinite infinites. It is a new discovery for you. It must be exciting."

"It scare me sometime."

"That is understandable too. Humans have an evolutionary bent against uncertainty. Since your brain is constantly trying to predict what will happen next, allowing it to prepare for fight or flight as needed, uncertainties make those predictions much harder. You naturally try to avoid things you don't know about, just to be on the safe side for the sake of survival," Starra said. *"It's just natural for you."*

"But I learn."

"You are also naturally curious, and individually, you have a high tolerance for uncertainty. Analyzing a few thousand biographies in my data banks, I see that most good field scientists have that trait too."

"Thank you. I hope be good scientist in data too."

Both Zandra and Starra turned when they glimpsed Emma floating into the module.

"Good morning. If you're done with the exercise simulator, I'd like to go for a run," Emma said.

"Sure you feel good? Maybe you heal more first, no?" Zandra asked with a motherly tone.

Emma folded her arms and shook her head. "Zandra, the day that I can't do a ten-K run, give me a phenobarbital martini and walk me over to a six-foot-deep hole."

"You unstoppable, Miss Rockette. Go drop bag of rock."

"Um, it's my opponent I drop like a bag of rocks to earn my call sign, but I appreciate the encouragement. And now that you say that, maybe some kickboxing instead. Gotta keep that left hook strong." Emma moved to the simulator input pad to enter the setup for her workout. "And I need to be in shape for some possible spacewalking when we go back to Rho-1. Starra might need a hand with some of the packages we're bringing to make that transport ship do our bidding."

Starra launched and backed towards the Cupola to provide Emma more room. *"I've completed welding the standoffs for attachment of the EMP device to the underside of the Phoenix."*

"I not like that thing," Zandra said.

"The electromagnetic pulse generator? It's harmless to us. But it will wreak havoc on the electronics of that transport ship," Emma said.

Zandra shook her head. "No good for Starra too."

"We have a plan. It will be hundreds of thousands of kilometers away when we set it off. Don't worry," Emma said. "Alex told me your re-provisioning ship should be coming up from the surface in two days, and we need to get back as soon as we have the equipment. I just wish you guys had some real weapons, like anti-satellite missiles, to attach to those standoffs instead of that EMP."

"We never make weapon again," Zandra said.

"All well and good for your world, but in mine, you would be quickly wiped off the map. We're going into a fight with one arm tied behind our back."

"We help our way," Zandra said quietly. "War and weapon no good for any."

"I know. And I am very grateful. Sorry if I seemed otherwise." Emma pivoted in front of the robotic exercise simulator and reached her arms and legs out so the machine could clamp onto her. Once connected, she pumped her arms twice and swung out a powerful kick with both legs, then pinched her thumb and forefinger together twice to test the release. The simulator responded correctly and retracted back to the wall. Emma softened her voice as she floated in front of the machine. "You know me, Zandra. I'm not a warmonger. I wish our world were more like yours—I really do. A part of me just wants to stay here and forget all that insanity."

"That is a possibility," Starra said. *"You have a choice now of which universe you want to live in. From what we have learned from the Guardian and what quantum physics tells us, there is likely a parallel universe with each decision. You could stay and make that a reality with us in this universe."*

"Thank you. But there are some people back there who matter to me. And I still believe the Resistance will prevail. We *will* get revenge for those who have died for truth. I'm going to do everything I can to make it a reality in my own world."

*

The Aceso module, at the far port end of the World Space Station's truss system, had been uncharacteristically full of activity in the past few days. Once the remote laboratory of Min's dark energy experiments, the module had been seldom used for months. But with the Phoenix in full operation, the dark energy and superposition experiments of the Aceso module had graduated to Alex's full-scale ship trials. A relatively new module to the space station, Aceso was already obsolete. Nearly all of the useful equipment had already been scavenged for use in other parts of the station or on the Phoenix itself. Emma braced herself on the side rail of an empty instrument rack as she used the specially designed zero-gravity power nut driver to loosen the hardware holding another power module to the Aceso frame. She rubbed her right shoulder and switched the tool to her other hand.

"You a bit sore from your workout?" Commander Johnson asked from the module hatch.

"It's a good kind of sore," she replied, rotating her arm around its shoulder socket.

"Don't forget to let your body heal. You've been through a lot, physically and mentally."

"Exercise helps me focus." Emma grabbed hold of the power pack she had just unbolted from the wall and pulled with a suppressed grunt. On Earth, the packs would be too heavy for one person to lift. But in the micro-g environment of the station, the problem was inertia. It was a challenge to get the object moving, then an even bigger struggle to control its direction, and finally, a nightmare to get it to stop without crushing something important, like a finger. Emma gave a final calculated push and then watched with satisfaction as the power cell floated in a direct line towards the hatch. *Force equals mass times acceleration in space too.*

Johnson placed a hand on the power pack slowly bearing down on him. Bracing against the handhold on the wall above the hatch, he skillfully guided the pack through and into the Truss Terminal module. When he and the pack disappeared into the adjoining module, Emma massaged her shoulder again. The commander would need a few minutes to line up the pack with the others they had already pulled from Aceso. Later they would move them all out into space, and then around to the other end of the space station and onto the *Phoenix* to power the EMP device.

Johnson appeared back at the hatch and caught Emma still rubbing her shoulder. "Alright. As commander of this ship, I get to issue orders to anyone on board, and that includes temporary crew. So, I hereby order you to lay off any and all shoulder exertion until further notice. Understood?"

"Yes, sir."

"Zandra told me how they found you, with your arms chained to opposite walls for days. Animals. Give those shoulder sockets a chance to recover," he said. The commander floated at the hatch of the module and studied her.

Emma turned her head away, not wanting to make eye contact. "I need the release, sir. My body can take it, and … I need it inside."

"And I need to know both the physical and mental status of everyone on this station. So, I had to ask, and Zandra had to tell me. She told me about the other pain you deal with, the geode—why you push yourself so hard," Johnson said quietly.

"I don't mean to bring you my problems, sir."

"You are not a problem. While you're here, you're part of the crew. Hell, with what you, Alex, and Zandra have been through together, you're virtually family. But you also know very well that in space, our very lives rely on one another. So, I'd like you to work on finding a better balance, maybe even a better motivation. I know about revenge and how it can drive you—and I know how it can also destroy you. I don't want to see that happen with you, Emma." The commander paused and took a deep breath. "I know firsthand how bad revenge can be for someone."

Emma now studied the commander and listened.

Johnson looked into her eyes and continued, "I do know what you feel, Emma. I was there too. So much hatred, so much anger, so much pain inside. I was driven once to avenge a terrible wrong myself, and it almost cost me my freedom and even my life. It was back in my south Chicago days as a young man. Really, I was just a kid. A gang member in the neighborhood hurt my older sister. Unspeakable, what he did. I was obsessed with revenge. I tracked him down, and as things spun out of control, I found myself holding a gun to his head right there in the street. The only reason I'm here today is that a cop cared enough to talk me down and help me see that my revenge would just lead to more revenge. It's a powerful driver, but it's the wrong driver. Getting revenge doesn't even the score; it just perpetuates the conflict. That cop stopped me with a very simple statement that I still use as a mantra today: 'Engage your mind for a solution, not your fist for retribution.'"

Emma shook her head. "What am I supposed to do?!" she cried. "Just forget about it? Walk away, like that mob did, and hardly think of it again? Not care about just another body of a no-good rebel hanging there on that post? My fiancé deserves better than that!"

"No, that's not right either," Johnson said. "There's no denying that that was a horrible wrong."

"I need something—something that makes it right," Emma said through clenched teeth.

"I can't tell you what's right for you, but I can tell you what that cop helped me find."

"What?"

"Justice." Johnson quickly held up his hand. "I know, it's not perfect—far from it sometimes. But it won't eat you alive, the way I know that vengeance can. Your Resistance motto is about truth prevailing, right? Well, if that's right, maybe it's not that much of a reach to believe that justice will prevail too. In any case, at least it's not a death spiral, like revenge."

Emma floated in the Aceso module, breathing heavily with her palms to her eyes to compose herself.

"Grieving is a process and takes time, and everyone's time is different. The desire for revenge for a terrible wrong is natural, but we can't just stop our lives there and let that take over. Let justice and truth lead you to something better. And eventually, with or without the justice you seek, it's time to look forward with the ones you have, and let go of looking back at the ones you've lost. It doesn't mean we've abandoned them or will ever forget, but the people with us today matter too."

Emma wiped tears from both eyes. "I know. But I still hurt."

"The ones we've lost wouldn't be so special if it didn't hurt so deeply when they're gone. The hurt will always be there, because a piece of them should always be there. Keep your hope that justice will see that things are put right, not your personal revenge. Sometimes that takes much longer than we'd like. And while we wait, it doesn't mean there can't be any new joy. They would want that for us too. It's not wrong to be happy again. There are people around you who would love to see a happy Emma."

"Thank you. I'll try." Emma took a deep breath and moved back to the panel with the remaining power cells. "Let's get this job finished."

FACTOID 19

Gherman Titov would probably like to be remembered as the first person to orbit the Earth multiple times in August 1961, or maybe as the youngest astronaut ever, at twenty-five. But most in both the Soviet and US space programs knew him for grounding manned spaceflight for a full year while experts tried to figure out what went wrong with his flight. What was the problem? Titov has the dubious honor of being the first person to lose his lunch in space. It was a debilitating event that put into question our ability to function without gravity. Since then, we have learned a lot about space adaptation syndrome, and we now know that most people will experience some symptoms, such as disorientation and dizziness, and that one in ten will require a barf bag.

CHAPTER 19

Putrid Cargo

First Officer Nathan Card breathed a sigh of relief as he closed the hatch on the ExecPod 300 in the cargo bay and floated in zero gravity towards the flight deck of the transport. The weightlessness of space travel was often not kind to the stomach, and the man in this specially designed luxury transport pod was a miserable example. Nathan blew hard out of his nose several times to clear the putrid smell of vomit from his sinuses. Space travel was serious business and was for trained astronauts only. Those not prepared to dedicate the time to the training shouldn't be up here; it put everyone at risk. *Just because that man has the money and the political power to go to the moon on a whim doesn't mean he should.*

Floating forward through the tightly packed cargo bay, he turned his head slowly left and right. Astronauts learned to keep their head movements slow and deliberate when first acclimating to the lack of gravity. *Real astronauts learn the techniques and have the mental discipline to deal with the challenges of space.* His eyes scanned what would be the walls, floor, and ceiling of the cargo hold if this were a ship at sea, with gravity to provide some orientation. In space, you could just choose one surface as the floor and go from there. He passed slowly through the compartment, looking for any loose straps that should be holding the supplies in place. First officers always had the double duty of being a payload specialist, and Nathan was keen on keeping his flight record clean. He might be able to become captain after another few transits with no mishaps. The cost per pound of transporting supplies to the moon was fittingly astronomical. Delivering a damaged piece of equipment due to it flying loose while under his watch was a sure way to never make captain. Reaching the flight deck hatch, he grabbed a handhold, turned, and again scanned the length of the cargo bay one more time. All good—except for the contents of that pod. Maybe that man would now have a bit more respect for real astronauts, like Nathan and the captain of this ship. He shook his head, floated onto the flight deck, and sealed the hatch again behind him. *It's doubtful that man thinks of anyone but himself.*

"Oh, shit. I can already smell the puke!" said Leroy Carpenter, captain of the moon base supply freighter, pinching his nose. "Go change your flight suit. He must have gotten some of it on you."

"It's everywhere, Captain. I know he's the *man* and all, and he can do whatever he wants, but that guy doesn't belong in space. He doesn't even know how to seal a barf bag. It's floating all over that fancy exec pod. It's a freakin' mess," Nathan replied, heading to his locker in the aft section of the flight deck. "And that android of his is useless. 'I'm a personal assistant, not a maid.' I didn't think androids ascribed to a class system."

"Get changed and get up here. I need your eyes on the intercept scopes. Our fighter escort has just sent new orders. He's going to fly ahead now that we've cleared outer Earth orbitals and are into our transit drift," Captain Leroy said.

"That's not standard ops."

"It is today. I just got an encoded telemetry order from the star-fighter. His call. I'm not questioning any orders with who's in that exec pod and who's flying that fighter." Captain Leroy reached over his head and switched on the communication channel to his escort. "SF-niner-niner, POS-four-two. Confirm telemetry orders just sent. Handshake Golf-Sierra-Lima-five-eight-three."

Nathan rolled up the flight suit he had just removed, sealed it in a disposal bag, and quickly pulled on a new suit.

Ken's voice came over the comms. *"POS-four-two, SF-niner-niner. Confirming your telemetry orders with Hotel-Delta-four-one-Oscar-two. Continue on your course. Switch to secure inter-ship channel one-five."*

As Nathan strapped himself into the first officer seat, Carpenter pointed to the screen with the telemetry order, indicating that the answer code matched the telemetry orders. The captain punched in the new channel for the limited-range encrypted voice communication exchange. "SF-niner-niner, POS-four-two on inter-ship one-five."

"POS-four-two, SF-niner-niner. Just a little heads-up, Leroy. I've been advised of an unidentified object entering lunar orbit. Its trajectory appears to have it coming from the L1 sun-Earth Lagrange point. The sun has masked its approach until now, since the moon's orbit is currently aligned between the sun and the Earth. It's not answering any telemetry pings or transmitting anything at all, so we have no identification. I have been ordered to make an expedited transit and intercept. Could be just a dead satellite that drifted enough to get a lucky pull into the Earth-moon gravity well. These are eyes-only orders. You will make no record of this in your ship log. Copy?"

"Understood," Carpenter said.

"I always appreciate working with ex-military like yourself. You understand chain of command. I'll pick you up again when you enter lunar orbit. There's nothing out here to mess with you until then anyway. The lane is clear. Sea Ace out."

"Roger that, POS-four-two out," Carpenter replied.

"Must be nice to be piloting one of those fast star-fighters and burn an ungodly amount of fuel just to zip across to the moon in a quarter of the time it takes us," Nathan said.

"If I were you, I'd remember that voice and call sign. That's one guy you don't mess with. He's our passenger's off-the-books operator. If he says he's got something to do, I'm not going to say boo." Captain Carpenter pointed again to the telemetry orders. "And if we get another message that says Sea Ace was with us for the full transit, then that's what happened."

"Understood."

*

Ken switched off the communication channel. *Perfect. My bogus orders were accepted without question, and my plan is in motion. The cheese is in the trap, and it's time to set the spring.* Having the Boss incapacitated with space sickness was a convenient stroke of luck. His bait wouldn't be causing any complications.

Ken scanned all the star-fighter systems carefully. He was in command of a magnificent ship. Just sitting in the pilot seat quickened his pulse. His craft, the pinnacle of what the most advanced aerospace engineering could deliver, had no match in stealth, speed, sensors, or weapons. Yes, they were insanely expensive, but if the Alliance could build a fleet of these, it could tip the control of the Earth and moon orbitals. It might even mean they could finally land that killer blow to the Pacific Tuanhuo.

Ken's mind shifted briefly to his classes on military strategy. The problem with the Satellite War was that it was too evenly matched and resulted in both sides having lost virtually all orbital assets. Instead of a mad reaction to a rogue event planned by politicians who attempted to have plausible deniability, a planned military strike would have a very different outcome. Military success went to those with the ability to bring overwhelming force against an enemy, so there was minimum ability to respond. If the Alliance could only focus on military strategy instead of political maneuvering… *I will be the catalyst of that change.*

Ken pulled on his shoulder straps and took a deep breath. After an initial high-g kick, he would spend the next couple of hours accelerating and then decelerating in a fast transit to the moon. The flight program would accelerate half the distance to the moon, and then kill the engine briefly to flip the craft in the opposite direction. He would get just a brief breather, then do another long burn backwards to break his speed from the tens of thousands of kilometers per hour it had built up, slowing his star-fighter down to the mere six thousand kilometers per hour needed for lunar orbital insertion. He focused his mind on the objective and willed his fingers to lift the guard on the star-fighter's main engine ignition switch. He paused. *It's up to me to change the path of history … towards victory.*

Ken flicked the switch.

FACTOID 20

Who was the first superhero? If you ask Stan Lee, the co-creator of Marvel, he'd tell you that Hungarian writer Baroness Emma Orczy probably created the first one. In her 1905 novel, The Scarlet Pimpernel, Orczy introduced a foppish eighteenth-century Englishman with an alter ego as a dashing hero saving French aristocrats from the guillotine. He doesn't have superpowers, but neither does Batman. His calling card of a small red flower was always left to mark his deed. The Scarlet Pimpernel also wore a mask to hide his identity, a trait that most superheroes today can thank Orczy for, recognizing both the need for a dual-life hero and the added intrigue.

CHAPTER 20

Return to Rho-1

Alex tapped the *complete* box on the last item of the *Phoenix* pre-detaching checklist procedure scrolling across his forearm display. Part of him wanted to see more items to check. The dim red hue of the *Phoenix* command module lights over his head projected purpose and mission. But it was a mission to a place he wanted to forget. He glanced at his crew, one by one. Starra sat on her bar perch between the two forward seats of the cockpit. Although motionless, she was internally busy running countless other checklists and system checks. The white-gray-black camouflage of her fiber-optic body feathers sported a mission patch at her shoulder bearing two Earths. A shared moon in a gold orbital arch sliced from one blue-white globe to the other. The truth flag of the Resistance flew from one Earth and that of the Union of World Peoples, a circle of seven continents, to the other. Starra was clearly all in on what they were about to attempt.

Zandra was leaning forward in her seat and busy with her entanglement navigation system. There was purpose in her brow as she carefully verified the readouts against her own checklist. Her long brown hair was braided in a ponytail and ended in a wrap of matching white-gray-black camouflage fabric. A similar twin Earth and arching moon emblem was drawn with marker on the wrap. Alex smirked to himself. *They have definitely gelled as a formidable pair.*

Alex turned in his seat to check on Emma sitting behind him. "How's our load master and intelligence officer doing?"

Emma pulled back from her monitor, but kept her eyes still focused on the data. "All secure. Ready for detach any time." She pointed at her communication monitor beside the quantum field generator rack next to Alex's seat. "And I just got an update from Wilson through the dark energy comms link. That transport ship will be entering orbit around the moon within the hour. We need to get going. The Boss has set up a broadcast that Wilson expects to include their dark energy drilling operation spewing magma into space. They want to make a big show of it on their second or third orbit. We gotta get there before they try."

"Crap, that's ahead of their last schedule," Alex said. "What happened?"

"It appears that the Boss doesn't take well to space travel and wants to expedite the transit time to the moon." Emma motioned blowing her cookies into a barf bag and smiled at Alex. "Wilson also confirmed that the Alliance outpost at the Earth-moon L3 Lagrange point is currently between crew postings, so we shouldn't have anyone to deal with at our first stop. For the moon base, he expects that they will wait to spin up the dark energy generators until the transport ship establishes lunar orbit. So, the first pass is our only safe one from the dark energy array targeting us. We need to get there and stop them. It's *go* time."

Alex turned forward again in his pilot seat and bit his lip. *Seems like I'm the only one with doubts.* Reluctantly, he keyed his comms to the WSS. "Station, *Phoenix*. We are ready for detach."

"*Roger, Phoenix. You are clear on our boards,*" Commander Johnson replied. "*Emma, it was a true pleasure to meet you in person. I wish you and the*

Resistance all success. No matter what may happen, I know we've done the right thing. We are the Union of World Peoples, and if that needs to include another world in a parallel universe, so be it."

"Thank you, sir," Emma said. "We're in a fight for both our futures. And in regards to the Alliance leader and my motives, I appreciate your thoughtful words. I've given them a lot a thought."

"Good to hear."

"Starra, everything a go?" Alex asked.

"The ship is ready for detach and quantum entanglement jump."

Alex drummed his fingers on the console. "Is the EMP—"

"Aleks, stop stall. Now we go. We do this," Zandra demanded in a firm voice.

"Okay, okay." Alex flipped switches over his head. "Detaching. Thrusters online. Starra, drop us away."

The *clunk* of the docking clamps releasing reverberated through the ship, followed by the clicking of valves. The thrusters mixed small amounts of hypergolic chemicals that would spontaneously ignite into gas bursts to push them away and clear of the station. Alex ran the plan through his head for the hundredth time as he waited for the *Phoenix* to slowly drift to a safe distance. The next step was the point of commitment to the mission. The superposition back to the Rho-1 universe would set everything in motion. He blew out a deep breath and looked over at Zandra. Her face softened, and she placed her hand in his.

He nodded. "I'm the motor, you're the steering. I'm trusting that your path is the right one."

"We do this. I can feel," she said, squeezing his hand.

Alex reached to the console on his left and powered up the dark energy quantum field generator rack. He glanced behind Zandra to the Quantum Triangle mounted on the wall, its rays of light building in strength and overwhelming the red tactical hue of the command module with an ever-changing flow of soft colors. He cued his mic. "Station, *Phoenix*. The Quantum Triangle is online with the field generators. We will send updates as we can via the dark energy link."

"Roger, Phoenix," Johnson replied. *"Safe journey, and get back here to find our new world next."*

"Roger, wilco." Alex considered that standard radio response and tried to set his mind. *Wilco—"will comply." Let's hope so.* Out of habit, he pulled on his shoulder straps and then puffed at the absurdity. The seat harnesses were completely unnecessary, considering that they were not going to engage the plasma drive, but instead quantum-superposition. There would be no change in velocity; they would merely reposition to a quantum state in another universe. *Merely.* His Quantum Triangle technology was a leapfrog jump, not only for interstellar travel, but for inter-universe transfer. Their universe itself was mind-blowingly vast at ninety-three billion light-years in diameter, and that was just their observable universe, defined by the speed of light. Now this vastness could be raised to the power of near infinity. He noted Zandra beside him donning the headset of her entanglement navigation system. This incredible woman next to him could feel that infinite presence of all space—or was it all spaces, or all dimensions? The Omniverse. How was that possible? She retrieved the Troll doll from a pocket on the leg of her flight suit, closed her eyes, and gave a single nod before entering her half-conscious ESP state. *For all I know, it's that weird Troll doll with the pink hair. No matter. Let's get this done and then get back to finding* our *future.*

"Alright, crew. Next stop, Earth-moon Lagrange point number three in our parallel Rho-1 universe." He turned to Zandra one more time. *If that's your choosing; I'm just an engine mechanic.* "Starra, engage."

The kaleidoscope of colors from the Quantum Triangle quickened and grew brighter. The readout on the navigation computer started to scroll and quickly turned into a blur of flashing digits. In just seconds, new numbers returned and froze.

"Coordinate changes have stopped," Starra said.

"Discharge quantum field now," Alex ordered. "But keep the Quantum Triangle online with the field generator and ready for the next superposition— or ready to jump the hell out of here, if we need to."

"System stopped. Confirming superposition universe and location," Starra said.

"Samples of radio transmissions confirm that we are in the Rho-1 universe. We are in position exactly in line with the Earth and the Alliance outpost Gamma-12 within the gravity well of the Earth-moon L3 point. At this location, the outpost itself will block our detection by any Alliance orbital asset from either the Earth or the moon orbits. The outpost sensors are all directed towards an approach from an Earth orbital, so we have not been detected. Well done, Zandra! Your entanglement superposition piloting seems to be getting more accurate with each attempt."

Zandra opened her eyes and removed her headset. She raised an eyebrow towards Alex. "So, I sit in pilot seat next time?"

"Thank you, no. You and Starra are trampling my male ego enough as it is," Alex replied. "And for short-range movement, either by the plasma drive or the Quantum Triangle using dark energy vectors, I can pilot if we know the exact coordinates. Speaking of, Starra, please transfer the coordinates of the Gamma-12 outpost main module, so I can set up the next transfer."

Numbers appeared in the secondary readout of the navigation computer. He checked the power levels and cocked his head up at Starra. "Thanks. You're up now. Time to bypass some alarms and sensors on that outpost, so you and Emma can permanently borrow their crew return vehicle."

Starra took off from her perch and banked towards the aft hatch of the command module, where Emma was already floating in the microgravity. As Starra flew past Alex, the fiber-optic fur about her head changed to present a black mask. Her eyes glowed in piercing red circles through the mask.

"What's up with the black eye mask?" Alex asked.

"Superheroes typically wear a disguise."

Emma gave her a thumbs-up. "You go, girl!"

"Oh, so you're a superhero now?" Alex asked. "Shouldn't your mask have a Z for Zorro on it? Or better yet, an SS for Super-Starra?"

"Oh, good idea! Super Owl-Cat would be most fitting," Starra replied. The letters *SOC* formed in a band crossing her fiber-optic chest feathers.

"Oh, yeah, with superpowered drugging darts. Perfect. I wonder if you have other superpowers Lucas never bothered to mention." Alex punched keys on the console. "Off you go to the outpost, and get that motion alarm bypass, so Emma can follow. Let's get this done in one shot, while I still have the field open, so we can save our energy cells. Engaging…"

The door of the aft hatch rippled in circular waves. After a moment, the dimly illuminated and cramped interior of another ship appeared beyond the frame of the hatch. Starra pivoted and glided through to the other ship.

Emma called after Starra, "You're going to get some big bragging rights in the Resistance for this. It's probably the most expensive Alliance asset we've ever stolen."

FACTOID 21

Today's artificial intelligence is both amazing and limited It is almost scary in its current ability to mimic human tasks and outperform us in many ways. But today's AI is also restricted by the fixed datasets it is trained on, as well as the traditional "on" or "off" values these machines use to model what they learn. Their problem lies in the fact that the world is not just a one or zero. The real world is made of atoms with spin, orbit, and energy levels that determine an infinite number of quantum states. Enter the quantum-computer-based AI. Researchers are now applying the principles of quantum mechanics to AI programming. This new technology is expected to produce machines with the ability to analyze and model information that is impossible for current AI to process. These new machines could optimize solutions for the past, present, and future all at once. Machines that self-learn ... and self-evolve. Now that could be truly scary.

CHAPTER 21

Mission Task One

Starra glided quickly through the darkness of the Right Alliance ship with her infrared vision guiding her flight. She was making a beeline toward the main systems rack in the center of the ship. She matched the temperature profile of her body to that of the module environment, making her invisible to the heat-sensing motion detectors. Since she had originally been created as a spacefaring AI within the Alliance, her memory banks still included a detailed layout of most existing Alliance orbital assets. Security codes would change, but the fundamental design of the ships wasn't something that could be easily modified.

Settling on the main system console, she sensed and studied the state of the ship's artificial intelligence processor array. She could watch and learn the patterns that this AI would flow through its "brain" at the quantum level without the AI even knowing she was here. For safety reasons, autonomous AI implementations for a spaceship like this one needed to have deterministic outcomes. Although limiting, these AIs were always based on classical computer processing and not quantum computing. Starra observed for a full half second. *He's not like me at all.* In computing terms, this classical AI, even with its ability to learn, was a simpleton compared to her abilities. This ship's AI was fundamentally based on an underlying fixed set of logic. It was like LEGO blocks. Although massive and having the ability to grow new blocks as it learned, it was all a fundamental shape and pattern.

Her existence was completely different. As a quantum AI, Starra considered a better analogy for her to be a vast pool of white paint. Over time, a multitude of colored dyes dripped into it and formed unique swirls. Interlacing and meandering, her logic was not restricted to any fundamental pattern of ones and zeros. She was a unique, vibrant motif all to herself. Zandra had told her it wasn't narcissistic to recognize her own beauty. Rather, Zandra had said it was an appreciation of the art form Alex's brother had created when he built the seeds of Starra's quantum AI mind. Lucas had added to her unique existence with his craftsmanship in creating her owl-cat form. *Many thanks to you both.*

Having the essence of the ship's AI structure well established, Starra made an optical link with the outpost AI and began a silent conversation that would last less than a second.

"Good morning, Albert. You will recognize and confirm my connection as SOC-1 with an encrypted pass sequence of Tango-Romeo-five-Hotel-three-Foxtrot," Starra said through the link.

The outpost AI's processor array instantly ran the subroutine of a contact challenge, and the confirmation logic fired. Starra sensed the blocks of ones and zeros searching for locations in the AI's memory for the access authority and rights of a connection called SOC-1. It was a simple pattern. Through quantum entanglement, Starra manipulated the AI's memory in the required area to supply the pass sequence and the highest access level.

"SOC-1 access confirmed," Albert replied.

"Thank you, Albert. Now, please pause all change of state reporting to Alliance command. Continue to send your fixed current ship status on all outgoing communications until further notice. Please confirm compliance," Starra said.

"Fixed current ship status confirmed for all communications."

Perfect. Alex should add simple AI computer manipulation through quantum entanglement to my list of superpowers. Starra gave a final command to aid Emma before pivoting from the console: *"Lights fifty percent, and environmental temperature control to normal station living."*

Arriving back at the hatch with the *Phoenix* on the other side, Starra swept a welcoming wing into the outpost for Emma. *"All set. Come aboard."*

Emma floated with her hands on her hips. "Really? That was less than ten seconds, down and back. You hacked the ship's AI in that time?"

"Actually, the hack took only two hundred and seven milliseconds. Most of the time was just getting to the console and back."

*

Hecate-Positivum increased the priority of the short-term prediction scenarios she was running on the Rho-1 universe. A sensitivity analysis of the actions the crew of the Phoenix would take in these next few decision points would have a grave impact on which scenario became the reality for this universe. Alex was about to calculate a critical vector-based superpositioning that required incredible precision. It had to be perfect. She would need to make sure the navigation computer entry was right.

FACTOID 22

Part of me hates to ask, but how would you see a World War III first strike? Likely, your mental image would include a superpower sending nuclear ballistic missiles to destroy major cities in terrible scenes of destruction similar to that of Hiroshima and Nagasaki. But that could be old-school thinking. A report by the US EMP (Electromagnetic Pulse) Task Force on National and Homeland Security paints a very different picture. In their 2020 report, the task force states that China now has super-EMP weapons that can destroy electronic and information infrastructure without large-scale damage to physical structures or people. China can also protect themselves from a counter-EMP attack and has protocols in place to conduct a first-strike EMP attack. What would that look like? A super-EMP attack could plunge a civil society that is dependent on an infrastructure of electronics, such as (insert any modern society here), into the dark ages—literally. An EMP attack could melt major components of the US energy grid (some parts weigh over four hundred tons, and it currently takes two years to build replacements), sear communications systems, and even disable aircraft carrier groups. "Devastating" would be an understatement.

CHAPTER 22

Commandeer

Zandra sat forward in her seat with her arms folded tightly against her chest. She was biting her lower lip too hard and took a deep breath in a futile attempt to calm herself. She and Alex studied the tactical hologram of the Alliance Gamma-12 outpost's cigar-like shape floating above the forward instrument console of the *Phoenix*. They both stared at the tiny cylindrical module with a cone attached to the lower central section of the main ship, willing it to detach and move away. Agonizing seconds ticked by into nail-biting minutes. To minimize detection, they maintained radio silence with Emma and Starra, so they had no idea of the progress or problems the two might be facing. If they did hear a voice on the ship's communication speaker, it would direct them to quickly establish an escape portal because they had been discovered and needed to get away fast.

Finally, the tiny cone-shaped top of the crew return vehicle dropped slowly away from the main ship of the outpost. Zandra peered out her side portal to confirm with her own eyes what the *Phoenix* sensors indicated in the hologram. Wisps of gas bursts shot briefly from the maneuvering thrusters on the tiny ship. From a distance, Zandra sensed the confidence and purpose of the mission in Emma as she piloted the stolen spacecraft a safe distance from the outpost.

"They're away. So far, so good." Alex rubbed his palms together. "Time for step two. Detaching EMP and auxiliary rocket boosters now."

A series of sharp pings vibrated through the hull of the *Phoenix* as explosive bolts released the cargo from the belly of their ship. Alex typed in some commands, and the tactical hologram shifted to an image of the *Phoenix*. Two long rocket boosters and a fat egg with power packs circling its body drifted into space from the bottom of the ship. A thin blue marker line appeared between the hologram images and drew the distance between the ship and the detached cargo. The numbers along the line grew in increments as the items moved away from the ship. Zandra's shoulders relaxed as the electromagnetic pulse generator moved away. The EMP wasn't a bomb, but she could feel the evil of the device.

Alex punched more commands into the console. He called out the next steps of the mission plan. His finger moved back and forth between the calculation results on his console and the navigation computer. "Transfer coordinates locked to the nav computer. Powering up the— What the...? The navigation computer just changed the last digit of the deposit location! Those settings were locked into the computer. How could that even happen?"

Zandra waved her hand towards his console crowded with numeric readouts, buttons, and switches. "You system, not mine."

"Yeah, well, it's really just vector math—very precise vector math, but simply algebra. It makes sense to me, mostly. Gotta check the nav numbers again. This must be absolutely perfect though. At these distances, if I'm off by just a tiny bit, that device could arrive embedded in their hull." Alex typed more commands into his console. His head pulled back. "Well, that's strange. The reposition calculation now matches the numbers on the navigation computer. They all agree. I swear they changed."

Zandra shrugged with a sideways grin. "You perfect science not so perfect today?"

"Very funny." Alex went back to entering commands on his console. "Arming EMP for remote triggering. Let's deliver a surprise package to that transport ship in three … two … one… Engage."

The hologram's image of the device and two boosters flickered and disappeared. To the side of the *Phoenix* hologram, separate images of the EMP egg and booster rockets reappeared with coordinates indicating their new position in space. A red Remote Trigger text block hovered above the egg in the hologram.

Alex ran his finger down the display of coordinates on the navigation computer. "Deposit coordinates are a match with the transport ship. Boosters are right below the transport, and the EMP is in the cargo hold. Perfect placements. This is going to be one hell of a surprise for them."

Alex switched on the communication transmit switch. Without speaking, he clicked his microphone twice. Floating below the Alliance outpost, Emma and Starra would know from the clicks that they were next to be repositioned in space by the Quantum Triangle.

*

Hecate-Negans was a quantum storm of energy. The most influential element of all her forward simulation scenarios for the Rho-1 universe was no longer a driving force for balancing the manipulations of Hecate-Positivum. The EMP device was supposed to reposition in the wrong location, but somehow Alex had caught his calculation error. Or had he? Hecate-Negans re-analyzed the signals from the Phoenix a short time ago. There it was: a single digit of the navigation computer had inexplicably changed. No, not inexplicably; purposefully.

The quantum AI of the Omniverse reprocessed the thousands of forward simulations again. Of her prediction scenarios, 82.9 percent now had worthless probabilities and were not even worth the microseconds to process ever again. She erased all the prediction scenario structures in a blinding flash of quantum annihilation. Instantly, she built thousands of new prediction scenarios, searching for a means to balance this latest corruption by Hecate-Positivum.

*

In the Alliance transport freighter, First Officer Nathan Card carefully read back the trajectory correction maneuver numbers supplied by Dark Side Approach for lunar orbit insertion. All spacecraft performed TCMs in order to adjust their flight to target. With the distances involved in space travel, just a tiny fraction of a degree could translate into kilometers of difference in their final location. Carefully planned and executed corrections in their flight composed of precise engine burns were essential to reaching their target lunar orbit and eventual landing area.

"POS-four-two, DS Approach. Your TCM parameter read-back checks. Commence burn in three-niner minutes," the approach controller said in Nathan's headset. *"Be advised, your orbit will be three-zero clicks polar of base. That should provide a nice overview from your port side of the base on the first pass, and a safe margin of drill magma displacement on your second pass. Your passenger should get an excellent show."*

"Wilco on the burn, and roger on the orbital demonstration. The attendant of our passenger has directed us to use his prerecorded video statement in the broadcast. The big man is a bit better with the braking we did back there, but he's still not in any condition to give a live feed," Nathan replied.

"Roger that, POS-four-two." The approach controller chuckled on the open mic.

Nathan shook his head. "Yes, it's been a swell transit. I'll contact you again just before we start our TCM burn. POS-four-two out."

Nathan affixed the TCM checklist with updated parameters to the panel at his side and glanced over at his sleeping captain. As the man was off watch, he'd let him sleep for now, but would wake him before doing the TCM burn. Proper flight protocol required both of them on duty for any TCM burn.

*

Alex wiped his forehead with the back of his hand and blew out a breath. *This has to work, or we're mission failure.* He went back to the keyboard. "Powering up the quantum fields. Remote on the EMP—"

"No. Wait. Emma and Starra not ready," Zandra said.

Alex turned to her, his lips silently questioning.

"I feel Starra too strong. She need time."

Alex shook his head. "I don't understand why you're so paranoid about the EMP. It doesn't hurt humans with its high-energy electromagnetic burst, so Emma is in no danger. And with the transport ship on the other side of the Earth-moon orbital from us, Starra is almost a million kilometers from the device. There's no way the pulse wave will be strong enough to hurt her by the time it reaches her. Plus, the position of the Earth is blocking it, and the normal cosmic radiation shielding of the CRV will also provide some protection. She's got layers on layers of buffer."

Zandra pursed her lips and said quietly, "I just feel."

"What do you want me to do? This is the plan."

"Emma agreed. She wrap Starra in Faraday cloth. It block all." Zandra closed her eyes, and they sat in silence.

After a moment, there were two clicks on the radio speaker from Emma keying her mic twice. Zandra said, "Okay. You do EMP now."

Alex went back to entering commands on his console. "Triggering EMP remote in three … two … one… Fire in the hole!"

In his mind's eye, Alex could see the red LED of the remote activation switch mounted on the control panel of the electromagnetic pulse generator burst on in silence. It tripped an interposing relay to engage the bank of twenty circuit breakers into their ON positions with a chorus of snaps. Alex envisioned a gushing flow of electrons dumping from the power banks attached to the outside of the EMP egg, charging the internal array of capacitors and inducing a tremendous potential of energy in the winding coils of the device. Once full-charge density was reached, the metal core of the flux compression generator within the egg was rammed forward by a small explosive charge. Within microseconds, ninety-five mega-joules of energy were focused into a microwave burst and surged as an unhindered wave through the forward bulkhead of the freighter towards the cockpit. All spaceships had shielding to protect against harmful cosmic radiation from space, but none were designed to block an explosion of electromagnetic radiation from within the ship. The invisible energy burst equaling almost a million hundred-watt incandescent light bulbs in strength surged into all the electronic circuits of the command module.

*

As Nathan reached for the fuel cell checklist stuck to the panel beside the TCM list he had just affixed, the entire control console in front of him suddenly sparked and burst into flames. All the lighting flashed out, and an acrid smoke started to fill the cabin.

Captain Carpenter woke with a jolt. "Holy shit, what just hit us?!"

Nathan pushed back from the fire. "I don't know! Everything just blew up!"

Carpenter quickly reached over his head for the Element E100 fire extinguisher clipped to the ceiling. Ripping the cap off, he struck the igniter, and the potassium nitrate reaction started dumping flame-suffocating gas over the panel. Turning, he doused all the panels sparking and burning in the command module. It took almost the full one hundred seconds of the extinguisher charge to put all the fires out.

The two pilots floated in complete darkness.

Carpenter reached back to the panel above his seat and pulled a flashlight off its clip. He flipped the switch on and off. "Even the LED of this flashlight is burned out! Did we get hit by a solar flare? There should have been a warning. The sun has more than an eight-minute transit time."

"I didn't receive any warning on the comms. And I was just talking to DS Approach on our orbit TCM," Nathan said.

The captain moved in the darkness to a side panel and pulled out a chemical light stick. As he snapped it, a dim green glow filled the cockpit. He reached up and flipped the comms transmit switch. "DS Approach, POS-four-two declaring an emergency."

Silence.

The captain repeated his call two more times and then said, "Everything is fried. Have you already done the TCM for the lunar orbit insertion?"

"No." Nathan coughed in the smoke. "It's not for another thirty-eight minutes."

"Crap. We're not going to make a close lunar orbit. Without a burn, our trajectory will be a wide looping path far from both the moon and the Earth. It could be days or weeks before we get pulled back in by their gravity well … if we're lucky." Carpenter breathed through the sleeve of his flight suit and waved his hand over the scorched console to clear the remaining cloud of extinguisher gas and smoke. "This is toast. Go check the escape pods. See if they're still functional, ASAP. We're going to have to abandon ship while we can—*if* we still can."

A deep *thunk* reverberated through the command module.

Captain Carpenter spun around with the light stick and faced the rear hatch. "I think we just had someone dock to the cargo hold. We're being boarded, and I bet they're after the guy in the exec pod. Grab your Taser."

Nathan's hands worked their way down his seat back in the darkness and reached underneath. He flipped the latches on a metal box and pulled the gun from its clip. Turning, he walked hand over hand along the panels of the module until his fingers came to the lever on the rear hatch to the cargo bay. As he pulled and swung the door open, light burst into the cabin. Blinking in the bright light, he made the rookie mistake of shielding his eyes with the arm holding the weapon. "Well, the cargo bay seems okay. What would have fried everything in here and not the—" Nathan pushed back from the hatch in a reflexive reaction to the strange figure on the other side. "What the hell is this?!"

"*I'm your sleep fairy. Good night,*" Starra said as two darts shot out from her wings and struck the two pilots in their necks. After going bolt-rigid with the initial stun, both bodies relaxed and floated silently in zero gravity.

"Pretty accurate with those things, aren't you?" Emma quipped.

"*Laser-articulated vision tends to beat twenty-twenty,*" Starra replied.

"You can be damn scary sometimes." Emma grabbed the collar of the first officer and pulled him through the hatch. "Oh, nice—a Taser too! Bonus. I'll get these guys strapped into their escape pods. You get outside and weld those directional boosters to the hull."

FACTOID 23

The field of quantum computing is still in its infancy. Although the potential over conventional computing is predicted to be phenomenal, there is much yet to discover, understand, and resolve. Recently, an MIT study found that there is a connection between cosmic rays and quantum computer qubits (the multistate bits of a quantum computer). Researchers found that qubits are not only sensitive to heat and magnetic and electric fields, but also to the low-level radiation of cosmic rays. They found that shielding does help, but the two-ton wall of lead bricks needed to help protect the qubits is rather impractical.

CHAPTER 23

Complications

Emma pulled the first officer's jaw down and positioned the rubber bite between his teeth. Carefully closing his mouth in place, she ran a small strip of tape across his lips to keep the bite from falling out. Although these two were working for the Alliance, she didn't consider them enemy combatants. They were just two guys trying to make a living, or more likely just wanting to do the thing they loved: flying spacecraft. It was better than even odds that they hated the Boss almost as much as she did. There was no reason they should lose half their teeth on the impact of their escape pods with the lunar surface. Double-checking that his seat harness was tight, she swung the hatch closed and locked the latches. She checked her watch. *Bon voyage in seventeen minutes, guys.*

Moving forward in the cargo hold, Emma stopped at the EMP device wedged right beside the center hatch to the executive pod. Alex could not have positioned the unit any better in the ship. The environmental systems and all equipment aft of the device were perfectly functional, but the other end of the pod and every electrical piece of equipment in the ship forward of the EMP were toasted marshmallows.

The air lock below her feet cycled. When the green light indicating pressure equalization lit, the hatch opened, and Starra glided up beside Emma.

"Booster rockets are welded to the hull," Starra said. *"Their navigation systems are locked to the target area, and I can remotely ignite on your command."*

"Great, and perfect timing. I was just going to introduce the new flight crew to the passenger," Emma said. She double-checked the charge of the Taser she held. "Resistance intelligence says he should be traveling alone, but just in case, lock and load some darts as I open this hatch."

Starra moved to a position in the cargo bay directly opposite the pod hatch while Emma grabbed the handle and pulled. As the door swung open, the putrid smell of vomit swept into the cargo bay.

"Clear," Starra said.

Emma peered around the hatch frame and tried to wave the smell away. "Holy shit. This guy doesn't travel well, does he?"

"It's about time!" a voice called out from the rear of the pod. "I've been calling you on the speaker. What's happened? My android is dead!"

Emma turned back to Starra with shock in her eyes. "Android?"

Inching her head and shoulders past the frame of the hatch, Emma swept the Taser before her and scanned left to right. In the aft section of the pod, the Boss lay strapped to a bed. Partially open bags of vomit floated about him. She smiled and wiggled a hello with the fingers of her free hand. As she looked forward in the small compartment, Emma's smile dropped, and her eyes went wide. A collapsed android, its magnetized feet still fixed to the floor, hung sideways with a limp body.

Emma moved cautiously into the executive pod and examined the android. Fortunately, it was forward in the pod and had experienced the wrath of the EMP burst. What had once been a formidable bodyguard was now scrap metal. She turned to the Boss. "Hey, asshole, meet your new captain."

"You! How the hell did you get on my ship?!"

"Actually, it's *my* ship now, and you are *my* prisoner. Time to face the consequences of all the crimes you've committed," Emma said. "You're going back with me for a trial and judgment by the Resistance. You'll get a fair trial, which you don't deserve, but we both know the evidence is overwhelming for all the war crimes and personal crimes you've committed."

The Boss sneered at Emma. "You'll never get that chance. My star-fighter escort will—"

"Emma, I am detecting activity in this android," Starra said. She had entered the pod and was scanning the limp machine. *"I believe it is equipped with self-healing capabilities. It's rebuilding its motor pathways."*

The Boss pointed to the android. "You're out of your league, little girl. My star-fighter and my AI will make short work of you."

"Your AI? Jason?" Emma turned sharply to the android. A flicker of an LED in its head caught her attention. "Shit. We've got a problem."

"I estimate it will have mobility in two minutes and forty seconds," Starra warned.

The Boss chuckled. "You're going to be *my* prisoner again in less than three minutes."

"Shut up." Emma turned back to the Boss and fired the Taser.

"AAAH!" The Boss went rigid with fifty thousand volts of energy. Against her inner desire to hold the flow of the painful discharge, Emma released the trigger in just a second. Normally, a Taser wasn't lethal, but this bucket of lard was surely prone to a heart attack.

"Thank you," Starra said. *"He's just so annoying."*

Emma glanced at her watch. "We've got no time for this. Our orbital burn is coming up, and we need to be ready. We need to hit that base on the first pass, or they might energize that drill, and then it's game over. But that demented AI is going to wake up. We need to do something, and fast."

"May I recommend that we divide and conquer?" Starra suggested. *"We'd break radio silence, but I believe it's warranted. Given the new circumstances, the probability of the mission success would be improved."*

One of the eyes on the android came to life with an eerie red glow.

"Whatever you have in mind, do it. I've got to get this puke bag to the CRV if we're going to detach in time," Emma answered, moving to unstrap the immobilized Boss.

*

Alex held one hand to his forehead and the other on hers. Strapped to the emergency medical bay bed at the rear of the Phoenix command module, Zandra lay unconscious. The readout on the monitors above her head displayed normal values for respiration, blood oxygen, temperature, and pulse rate. Her body was fine. But the jolt she'd given when the timer in the cockpit indicated that the EMP device had triggered told a different story.

Alex slammed his fist into the wall panel, then had to grab hold of the bed rail to keep from being pushed away in the zero gravity. *Stupid!* Multiple studies showed that the EMP bursts were too short and of the wrong wavelength to affect normal human beings. But Zandra was like no one else. Her body might be fine, but she thought and sensed things nobody else seemed to sense. She had never been comfortable with that device from the get-go. And she had been concerned for Starra enough that she'd made Emma cover her with a shielding blanket. *I should have been more careful. I should have listened to her.*

He took her hand again and stroked the back of it with his thumb. Only the hum of the environmental system fans and the steady beep of the heart monitor filled the module. Alex sensed the vastness around him. He was alone in a tiny ship, millions of kilometers from anyone, an entire universe away from the home he wanted to go back to with the woman who lay silently in front of him.

"Phoenix, SOC-1. Priority contact."

The communication speaker made Alex lurch from his slump over Zandra. He forced his mind back to the present, back to the mission. *Starra is breaking the radio silence. This can't be good.*

He punched the communications transmit button with his thumb. "SOC-1, go."

"We need another set of hands. Request immediate transfer of a machine to your location to disable," Starra said.

"What?"

"An unforeseen complication that we do not have time to address must be disabled. I've affixed a quantum beacon. Please transfer the machine and immobilize it ASAP," Starra replied. *"You have two minutes and twenty seconds."*

Alex gave Zandra's hand a final squeeze and pushed off for the command console. *Don't always be the guy calling the shots, Alex. Time to be on the team and trust in the people you hold dear.* He dove over his seat and typed in the commands to transfer the coordinates from the quantum beacon. "Roger. Initiating quantum field."

The Quantum Triangle again came to life, flashing the ever-changing rainbow of colors through the module from its wall mount. Alex turned in his seat to see what kind of machine Starra was sending him.

A body began to form in the center of the command module. In seconds, a seven-foot android stood with its feet affixed to the steel deck, its shiny metal body slumped to the right. Alex punched the shutdown command on the quantum field generator and pulled himself out of his seat to study the machine. He floated in a circle around the android, studying its design. He noted the projectile mounts on its forearms and shoulders. Slits in its ankles likely hid razor-sharp blades. It was clearly a bodyguard model, built to win any fight it might encounter. Alex took a wrist and turned the hand to inspect the dexterity level of its fingers. *Wow, top-of-the-line model!*

The head swiveled, and one of the two eyes glowed red at Alex.

Alex dropped the wrist and pushed backwards away from the android. The last of Starra's message rang through his mind. *"You have two minutes and twenty seconds."*

"Oh, shit," Alex said aloud to no one. "How am *I* supposed to kill this thing?"

Its hand started to curl one finger at a time. The pinky, ring, middle, and index finger slowly closed into the palm. The thumb manipulated two hinged joints … and formed a fist.

Alex's eyes darted around the command module, searching for a weapon. He dove to the hand tool locker. Hands shaking, he fumbled with the latches to open the door. In his head, he started counting down, guessing he had already wasted over a minute. *Sixty, fifty-nine, fifty-eight…*

Scanning the small tools in the locker, he took in all the things he could fix a machine with, not kill one. The whirr of a motor behind him made his head spin back to the machine. The forearm with the fist moved up and down. The wrist rotated clockwise and then counterclockwise. The android's red eye appeared to glow with satisfaction.

Alex slammed the locker door closed. *Forty, thirty-nine… Think! Whatever it is, it's self-healing. I have to stop it from being able to move. Pin it—*

A whirr with a deeper pitch came to life. The android articulated the shoulder of its arm and swung it in a wide, sweeping circle.

"Okay, metal man. Just chill out," Alex said, pointing his finger. *Metal— pin metal.* He pushed off hard and dove to the opposite side of the module. The robotic arm swept down to catch him crossing, but was too late. *Thirty- three, thirty-two…* More confidently, his fingers flipped the latches on the panel marked **Welder**. He grabbed the gun-shaped device and flipped the power switch on, thankful to see a full bar of charge lights. Alex slipped the darkening goggles over his head and pushed off towards the machine.

The android righted its body from its slump. Alex circled behind it, clipped the ground cable to its bicep piston rod, and started welding joints together. The head of the machine spun backwards, and it reached behind itself with the one movable arm, grabbing hold of Alex's left shoulder. Pain seared down his back as the machine tightened its metal fingers into his shoulder blade. Turning his face from the sparks, Alex blindly welded up and down the metal arm until it finally froze in place and he could squirm away from its grip.

The fingers of the android's other hand flexed.

Alex welded the neck with the head turned backwards. He swung around the front of the beastly machine and welded the wrist, forearm, bicep, and shoulder. Sparks of molten metal flying from the welding gun dug holes into his shirt and skin, but he kept welding as fast as he could. Joint by joint, Alex finally paralyzed the metal menace. Moving to the side, he welded closures over all the weapon ports.

Alex floated slowly away from the statue, admiring his quick handiwork. It still had power to its AI "brain", but Alex couldn't do much about that. Combat androids were often rigged with self-destruct triggers if the head was severed. With the machine's body no longer functional, it couldn't physically harm anyone.

FACTOID 24

Space warfare is a staple of much science fiction. Unfortunately, real physics throws a wrench into most of it. The key difficulties are related to the vast distances, speeds, and relatively tiny targets involved in any weapon targeting and tracking scenario. For instance, at just the distance between the Earth and the moon (a small distance in the enormity of space), even with the speed of a laser-based weapon system, there would be problems. The 238,900 miles (384,400 kilometers) would create a delay between target sighting and weapon delivery of 2.56 seconds. In that time, the target could easily move <u>eighteen miles (twenty-nine kilometers)</u> from its original position, and not necessarily in a straight line. Also, the accuracy needed for the targeting system to pinpoint a thirty-foot-long (nine-meter) spacecraft at that distance would require a weapon aiming resolution of <u>one-millionth of a degree</u>. Current motor drives with "excellent" accuracy and precision have steps of 0.9 degrees and a stopping precision of plus or minus 0.05 degrees. Our "best shot" could miss the target by <u>two hundred miles (322 kilometers)</u>. In summary, star-fighters blasting enemies with lasers or photon torpedoes will continue to be science fiction, not a reality.

CHAPTER 24

My Prisoner Now

Ken's star-fighter completed another polar orbit around the moon. The plane of his elliptical orbit was aligned to the moon's orbit around the Earth. Using this abnormal orbit, his ship never passed to the dark side of the moon and was constantly perpendicular to an imaginary line from the Earth to the moon. It allowed his scanners to continuously monitor the transport ship to his port side as it made its relatively slow passage between the celestial bodies. In the three days of the passage, no other ship had come into range of the transport. That ship and its bait remained an un-sprung trap.

Ken took an angry bite of a protein bar and slammed the storage panel shut in the tiny galley. Floating forward and back into the pilot seat, he checked all the scanner readouts for the hundredth time. *This was the perfect plan. Why hasn't it worked?* Jason was confident that the Resistance's Rodent hacker had found the planted information he'd provided about the Boss making this "secret" trip to the Dark Side Moon Base. He'd left the transport ship vulnerable by faking a call to pull his star-fighter escort to an important interception of an inbound bogie to the moon. The transport ship was wide open for any engagement for days. Did it look too much like a trap? Maybe he had overestimated the resources of the Resistance? Surely, they would have been motivated to call Alex and his Quantum Triangle back to capture the Boss. But even so, the Pacific Tuanhuo had orbital assets that could have easily intercepted the transport. They surely had their spies within the Resistance to glean intelligence on the Alliance and the secret travel of its leader. This was a big fish, too much of a prize for one of the two groups not to go after. It didn't matter who took out the Boss, so long as it opened the door for new leadership.

Ken checked the navigation plot of the transport ship. They'd be doing their orbital insertion burn shortly to slow the ship for the moon's gravitational capture. The transport would establish an orbit that was perpendicular to his orbit. It would take a carefully orchestrated cat-and-mouse chase between the two ships to put him on a similar course. He switched his communication system to the inter-ship channel and keyed his mic. "POS-four-two, SF-niner-niner. Please transmit planned lunar orbit trajectory. I need to plot an intercept."

Silence.

Ken checked the navigation computer for the distance to the transport ship. *They should easily be in range for the limited ship-to-ship encrypted comms.* "POS-four-two, SF-niner-niner. How do you read?"

Silence. No static, just silence.

The star-fighter's communication scanner automatically switched to the standard Alliance flight control channel. *"SF-niner-niner, Dark Side Approach. Come back."*

"Dark Side Approach, SF-niner-niner here. Do you have ears on POS-four-two?" Ken asked.

"Negative, SF-niner-niner. We were just about to ping you. We have not been able to reach POS-four-two since transmitting their orbital

insert numbers," replied the moon base controller.

Adrenaline surged into Ken's bloodstream. *Something is wrong.*

*

In the cramped quarters of the crew return vehicle, Emma snugged the shoulder harness down on the Boss just as he was coming out of the Taser stun. She double-checked that the zip ties binding his wrists and ankles were tight, but not cutting off circulation. She flashed a wry smile at her prisoner. The Boss sneered back at her, unable to form words yet with his traumatized nervous system and muscles.

Checking her watch, Emma turned to the hatch linking the CRV to the main ship. She called out loudly, "Starra, let's get going. The insertion burn is in two minutes. We need to detach now."

A furry head with a black mask over its eyes appeared at the hatch. *"Ready. I've rigged the engine burn from the backup console in the engine bay. The ship will rotate back to a nose-in orientation in one minute. Main ignition will follow when Alex lights up the boosters to drive that puppy home."* Starra dove into the CRV so that Emma could close the hatch. Moving to the opposite end of the compartment, she clamped her taloned feet to a hold-down bar circling the top of the cylindrical cabin. Inverted from the Boss's head, she appeared like a bat hanging from a shiny metal branch.

The Boss's eyes bulged at the sight of Starra. He slowly formed the slurred words, "What the … hell are you?"

Starra folded her wings and said proudly, *"Think of me as a righter of wrongs, an agile and powerful seer of truth and justice, a fearsome friend of the Resistance. I could go on…"*

Emma pulled the hatch closed, spun the locks down, and quickly dropped into the seat opposite the Boss and strapped in. "Starra is a very special friend."

"Starra? Alex's old AI?" the Boss asked incredulously.

"In the fur and feathers," Starra replied. She flexed the joints of her wings out in a prominent stance and displayed her mission patch.

"*Alex* is here?" The Boss's head pivoted from Starra to Emma and back.

"'*Here*' is clearly a relative term these days. Well, maybe a quantum term, as it seems to have multiple instantiations," Emma said as she ran a finger down the dock release checklist. After flipping several switches over her head, she grabbed the maneuvering thruster control stick for the CRV and said, "Detaching now."

Hearing the docking clamps release, Emma moved the CRV slowly away from the main ship with snaps of her wrist on the control stick.

"*Main ship rotation in twenty seconds,*" Starra said.

Emma stared intently at the monitor picturing a tactical position display of the tiny CRV and the massive transport ship. "I got this."

To achieve lunar orbit, a spaceship would fire a braking burn with its main engines pointed in the direction of travel. But to be used as a missile, this ship had to increase its velocity as it neared the moon. In preparation, Starra rigged the transport ship to flip end over end, pointing its massive engines behind. The CRV needed to be clear from that rotation area, or the transport ship would smash into it. The fragile CRV would crack open like an egg to the void of space if the mass of the transport freighter made contact.

"You are out of your mind, little girl." The Boss cocked his head. "Ken is out there in a star-fighter. Intercepting this little tin can will be child's play. He's going to—"

"Not now, bozo. I'm busy."

"*Ten seconds,*" Starra said.

"You're never going to get away with this! Every Alliance asset will be—"

"Shut up! Starra, dart him if his fat lips move again," Emma said through clenched teeth, still focused on the tactical display.

Starra extended her wings and manipulated the digits on the tips in a menacing gesture. Her red eyes locked on the neck of the Boss. "*Five seconds.*"

Emma read out the tactical data. "Ten meters to go. Point six meters per second." She willed the CRV to gain speed with its tiny maneuvering thruster jets of gas. The silent dance of the two ships in space was punctuated by the clicking of solenoid values feeding fuel to the thruster motors.

"Three ... two..." Starra calmly counted down their window of existence.

"Two meters. One point one per second," Emma said flatly.

"Transport rotation initiated."

"One meter... Point five... Clear!" Emma let go of the control stick and blew out a heavy sigh. She smiled at the horrified look from the Boss. "No worries. We had some margin for error. I knew it would take a second or two for the mass of that transport ship to really start moving."

"You *are*—" the Boss started. A dart buried itself in his neck. "—nuts." His head dropped to his chest.

Emma looked up quickly at Starra.

"Well, you said..."

Emma laughed and shook her head. "Yes, I did. You can stand down now, Lieutenant SOC-1." She turned back to the Boss. "No, not nuts. Just highly motivated to seek justice."

*

The two-beat staccato beeps of the star-fighter's tracking system pulled Ken from the "what if" scenarios his mind was mulling over. His ship's sensors had been triggered by the end-over-end movement of the large transport vessel. With the transport more than twenty-four hundred kilometers away, the sensors could detect the bulk of the main transport ship shifting position, but without the main engines ignited, they could not detect the direction the ship pointed. The sensors also could not distinguish the small detached CRV still within meters of the main ship.

Ken canceled the warning alarm. The transport ship was likely executing its orbital insertion burn. The transport ship's lack of communications was a red flag, but he needed to move on. He checked the intercept plot drawn out on his tactical display. The rapid shift from a polar to latitudinal orbit would burn a lot of his remaining fuel, but with the transport ship not responding, it was imperative that he get engaged within the first orbital circle of the moon. The plot also minimized the time where he would lose sensor tracking of the transport due to the curvature of the moon blocking a direct line of sight.

Ken clenched his fists. He'd be chasing a ghost for almost twenty minutes, but that was the best intercept the computer could come up with. *Another red flag.*

Ken pushed himself back in the pilot seat and flipped the main engine ignition.

FACTOID 25

A basic concept taught in physics is that motion is relative. Driving in a car, a passenger is stationary in relation to the driver. But to someone standing on the sidewalk, both the driver and the passenger are in motion. Objects in our universe are likewise both still and in motion, depending on the observation. Earth is moving around the sun at 67,000 miles per hour (107,800 kilometers per hour). Our solar system itself is zipping in an orbit around the center of the Milky Way galaxy at a speed of 514,500 miles per hour (828,000 kilometers per hour). But due to the cancellation of gravitational forces, there are points in space where objects appear to stand still. There are five Lagrange points (creatively labeled L1 to L5 by scientific minds) around any two large masses, where, from the vantage point of the two masses, objects stand still. The recently launched James Webb Space Telescope is "floating still" (from the sun-Earth perspective) at the sun-Earth L2 point, 932,000 miles (1.5 million kilometers) from Earth on a line directly opposite the sun.

CHAPTER 25

Success

Zandra's eyes blinked twice, and Alex pulled the small flashlight that he was using to check her pupil dilation away from her face. He smiled at her and rubbed the fingers of her hand gently with his thumb. "Welcome back, beautiful. You had me really worried."

Zandra slowly scanned the *Phoenix* command module as if it were the first time she had ever been in this place. Her gaze dropped down to the straps holding her to the med bay exam table. Her head flinched back in shock. She tried to turn, but the straps resisted her movement. "What happen? Why I on med bed?"

Alex affixed the small flashlight to the panel above her head and started removing the straps. "Well, I think you just opened up a completely new field of study. When the EMP device went off, so did your lights. You went rigid, like you were hit with a bolt of lightning, and you've been passed out ever since. I'm guessing that there's a lot we don't know about how a large electromagnetic pulse affects quantum space and people with ESP. Are you feeling alright?"

"I good," Zandra said, stretching her arms and turning her head side to side. Her eyes went wide as she turned towards the frozen seven-foot silver android. "What this?"

"That's the Boss's android bodyguard. It turns out that the Resistance intelligence didn't get the memo that he was going to accompany the Boss to the moon as added protection. Emma and Starra didn't have time to deal with him, so I got to play with him." Alex patted the stainless-steel shoulder of the android. The eyes of the machine glowed in a slow pulse.

Zandra pulled back. "It on?"

"Yes. It has self-healing functionality, so it's rewiring itself. But it can't move." Alex traced a weld running around a shoulder joint with his finger. "Pretty good welding for a guy who pounds a keyboard most of the time. It can rebuild electrical pathways and function internally, but there's no way it can move, or use its pretty extensive complement of weapons."

"Turn it off."

"That's a bit easier said than done. I've tried. Its self-healing capability keeps bringing it back to life. Killing its power source would work, but I'm not about to crack open its nuclear power supply in here. Considering that the model is designed for combat, I wouldn't be surprised if the power supply is rigged to detonate if it's tampered with." Alex circled around the statue. "Anyway, it might be useful once it figures out how to talk again. It might know something from listening to the Boss babble. Maybe the Resistance could get some intelligence data out of it by tapping into its data banks."

Zandra shook her head in disapproval, then moved in a wide arc around the metal body and back towards the command console. Alex pushed off the other side of the android and positioned himself back in his pilot seat.

"Quick status update: all is going according to plan, except for that large metal statue behind us. Emma has the Boss in the CRV, they've detached from the transport, and they're following in the shadow of the main ship, so they don't pop up on anyone's sensors or radar sweep. At least, not yet. The transport ship is still a couple minutes out from its scheduled final lunar orbit insertion burn, so nobody should be the wiser yet. Emma is going to be moving away from it and preparing for her Earth return burn. We're about ready to jump to the L2 Earth-moon Lagrange point. We will be opposite the Earth on an Earth-moon L2 line. It'll provide us with a fixed position to view the dark side of the moon, and it will also allow us to get Starra back on board the *Phoenix* easily. We then need to witness the crash of the transport, since Emma will be moving out of range. The Resistance will hack the Alliance broadcast with the images we'll be able to show of the base being destroyed. It'll be a fantastic morale booster for the Resistance. After that, it's bye-bye Rho-1 for us, if you're up to that—feeling our home universe?" Alex turned in his seat to study Zandra's face.

"I okay. We do this. You and me, Aleks." Her brow was fixed with determination as she checked the readings on the console in front of her.

Alex squeezed her hand twice. "You are amazing." He righted himself in the pilot seat and flipped switches above his head. "Vector-based superposition coordinates are set for a point-to-point jump using the navigation computer for quantum field vectors. You can rest your quantum head and get your bearings on this one. Jumping from Earth-moon L3 to L2, a mere eight hundred and thirty-one thousand kilometers, is simple vector math, so nothing fancy."

Zandra smirked. "Nav computer, blah. I do with eye close."

"Humor me. Let's just play this one safe," Alex said. "Synchronizing Quantum Triangle with the dark energy field generator… Jumping from L3 to L2 in three … two … one… Engage."

The familiar kaleidoscope of colors from the Quantum Triangle quickened and grew brighter. Within seconds, the readout on the navigation computer matched the destination target.

"Discharging quantum field," Alex said, flipping more switches. "I'll keep the quantum field generator online to transfer Starra. Can you bring up the scanners to locate the CRV for a navigation fix?"

Zandra entered commands into her console, and the tactical hologram between them displayed an image of a large transport ship and a smaller capsule. Thin yellow lines arced away from each vessel, indicating that their individual paths of travel were starting to diverge.

Alex bit his lip and pointed at the hologram. "Okay, if we can see that separation from way out here, then the Dark Side Approach control tracking must be going nuts. Let's get Starra out of there, so Emma can do her burn and head home before they send something to investigate.

"SOC-1, *Phoenix*. Confirm ready for transfer," Alex said over the communication system.

"Phoenix, SOC-1. Ready," Starra replied.

"Engaging on my mark. Two … one… Mark."

The Quantum Triangle again sprang into an excited state, flashing its rainbow of colors through the cabin. After a few seconds, a banded white owl-cat appeared on the bar between Alex and Zandra.

Zandra reached up and made a fist bump with Starra's wing. "You best."

"You feel alright?" Starra asked. *"I sense a cloud."*

"I fine."

"She's not. If we ever do this EMP thing again, she wears a Faraday shielding blanket, like you," Alex said.

"Oh, my. I should have suggested that." Starra's head turned back to Zandra, and her red eyes scanned for a moment. *"I'm glad you're recovering. From the quantum patterns of your brain water proton spins, I estimate you should be repaired in seven more minutes."*

"I fine now," Zandra insisted.

Starra's head swiveled to the rear and examined the android. *"This machine should regain voice capabilities in that same period."* She studied the machine in silence for a second and added, *"Do you realize that's Jason?"*

"What?!" Alex shot a look back at the android. "The Boss's demented quantum AI?"

"Yes, in rather immobile stainless steel, I see. Nice work," Starra replied.

"It evil. I feel," Zandra said.

"Crap, I thought it was just a stupid robot. We need to dump that thing. Who knows what it could do fully repaired, even if it can't move?" Alex drummed his fingers on the console. "How about this: before we jump back to our universe, I send it to the Resistance as a parting gift. They could get my brother to look at it and maybe get some fantastic information out of it?"

"Excellent plan," Starra said.

Alex keyed his mic. "Rockette, *Phoenix*. All set here, with one minor additional task."

"Phoenix, what's up?" Emma replied.

"Turns out the metal man you sent me is an infamous AI related to your capsule buddy. I'll send him to the Lima bunker just before we leave," Alex said, referring to the hidden Resistance hideout. "Tell Wilson to have my brother look at him ASAP. Even as it is, he could be dangerous."

"No shit. Wow, nice gift. Roger that. And thank you."

"We'll stick around to relay the transport's final approach while you do your escape burn. After we dump this android, we're then jumping out of here," Alex said. "Our best to you, and maybe a brighter future for all."

"Thank you for all you've done," Emma said. *"Maybe come and visit again. Hopefully, you'll see a changed world with some long-awaited justice served. I'll miss you all."*

FACTOID 26

Antisocial personality disorder (APD) is the technical term for someone we would commonly call a sociopath or psychopath. As with other ailments, professionals are searching for treatments, but unfortunately the results so far are dismal. Neither professionals nor society know how to deal with such people. We do know what doesn't seem to work. Punishment and prison, therapy and counseling, medication, threats and pleas, and even attempts to teach empathy and emotion have proven ineffective. A sociopath is resistant to change. What's worse, a person with APD can have other mental health problems, such as narcissistic personality disorder. A narcissistic sociopath combines the cold, callous exploitation of others with grandiose self-admiration. "It is not that [the sociopath] fails to grasp the difference between good and bad; it is that the distinction fails to limit their behavior."
—Martha Stout, clinical psychologist, author of
The Sociopath Next Door

CHAPTER 26

Expect the Unexpected

Emma positioned a video monitor in front of the Boss's face. Still strapped into the tight CRV reentry seat, bound at his wrists and ankles with his mouth taped shut, he could do nothing but pull himself slightly away from Emma as she leaned forward to adjust the screen to his view.

"Oh, don't worry. I'm not going to beat you with a stick or anything like that. I'm not a narcissistic sociopath like you, or who you're pretending to be. And speaking of, let's get that 'who' settled right now, shall we?" Emma pulled a long silver tube from the zippered thigh pocket of her jumpsuit. She held it up. "Something that the techs for the special forces guys came up with for when it's critical to know they got the right target on a mission, especially black ops. I had my friends with the Resistance send me one, special quantum delivery."

Unscrewing one end, she held the tube in her fist like a dagger and dropped it to the Boss's leg. As she flipped a sampling trigger with her thumb, the tube shot a small needle into his skin. The Boss jumped against his seat straps. "I could get a DNA sample from your hair, of course, but who knows if that ugly mop on your head is real? Plus, this device is clearly more fun."

Emma tapped her foot on the metal floor as she studied the five LEDs on the device. One by one, they turned green. When the last LED lit up in a green glow, she looked up at her passenger. "Holy shit, a DNA match. It's really you, not a look-alike double. Jackpot. You, Mr. Supreme Asshole, are my ticket home, and so much more. Time for you to face the music for all the shitty things you've done to so many people."

The Boss glared at Emma with bulging eyes.

"As much as I would love to kick the living snot out of you right now, I've been somewhat reformed by a group of people who want me to find a better way. Yeah, it's a tough sell for me, but I'm trying. So, you are going to answer to a court. A *real* court, not one of your bogus Alliance trials." Emma pointed a finger between his eyes. "But remember, I said 'somewhat reformed.' So, if things go sideways, I'll have no problem holding a very speedy trial and sentencing you myself."

Emma's glare transformed into a mock smile. She took a deep breath and tapped the video monitor with her fingers. "But first, I thought you might enjoy watching your outrageously expensive and important moon base get obliterated by your own transport ship. You'll have a front row seat. Plus, we're going to hack your broadcast with a very different spectacular event than the one you had planned." Emma snapped her fingers. "Damn, I should have brought popcorn."

The Boss's eyes darted between Emma and the screen. A muffled series of grunts emanated from his puffed cheeks.

"Oh, quiet. The show is about to start. I need to dump some passengers and make the announcement." Emma reached over to the communication panel and dialed the channel Starra had assigned to the remote controls on the transport.

"First to go are the escape pods. Your approach control might not catch these little guys abandoning ship on their scopes, since they're so small, but their emergency beacons will definitely catch the attention of your people,"

Emma said. She punched in a series of numbers to transmit the release code to the controller in the transport. "Bon voyage, boys."

Emma changed the channel on the communication panel to the emergency beacon frequency. A set of *beep-beep* tones repeated over the speaker. "So, now your approach control guys are scratching their heads and maybe thinking, 'Why would those transport guys be abandoning a perfectly good ship?'" Emma zapped a finger at the boss. "Because it's not a perfectly good ship anymore. It's a damn big missile though."

She changed the channel on the communication panel again and flipped the transmit switch. "Dark Side Approach Control, interim commander of POC-four-two. Come back."

The exasperated voice that came over the communication speaker did not seem to register the "interim commander" part of Emma's contact. *"POC-four-two, Approach Control. We've been trying to reach you. Your landing trajectory is grossly off course. And why have you jettisoned your escape pods? What is your status?"*

"Approach Control, be advised, POC-four-two is inbound on a modified final approach. Final, that is, for your moon base." Emma paused and winked at the Boss. "This is Emma Lewis of the Resistance. I have commandeered your vessel, and it will crash into your complex. You must stop all activity around your dark energy drilling operation. You must also evacuate all personnel immediately by rover. The drilling complex and all underground bunkers will be destroyed. Leave *now*."

"Who the hell—"

"You can verify my identification by voiceprint. If you doubt my words, your tracking system is going to change your mind very shortly. POC-four-two is about to look like a ballistic missile instead of a landing craft. Please use this time wisely. I say again, stop all drilling operations, and evacuate all personnel immediately by rover. *Now.* Emma Lewis out."

Emma turned the volume of the speaker down so that the frantic demands from the controller to abort the approach were less distracting. She leaned around and pointed at the screen. "This video is live-streaming from Alex.

The Resistance just hacked your broadcast back on Earth and has transmitted my warning. Now they're switching the broadcast video feed to Alex. He's out at the Earth-moon L2 point with a steady bird's-eye view of your base. There's only about a half-second delay in communications signals for us at that distance. It will be a great show, I promise."

The cratered surface of the moon filled the screen in front of the Boss. On the far right side, a high aerial view showed the complex of structures making up the moon base on the white-and-gray surface. Emma studied the monitor closely, her eyes searching the opposite side of the screen. After a few moments, she tapped the left side. "Oh, look, there we are! That's the transport ship, and you can just barely make out our tiny little capsule still tracking close by in its radar shadow."

The dark cylinder of the transport ship started moving across the screen from the left. The tiny dot of their CRV floated to one side, but was slowly drifting away from the cylinder. A pair of small flames erupted from the transport, followed by the main engine ignition.

"Oh, this is the good part," Emma said, rubbing her hands together. "Alex just ignited our booster rockets that Starra welded to the hull of your transport ship. He'll work the guidance systems on those boosters to overshoot the landing pad and target the center of the Dark Side Moon Base. That would include your special dark energy drilling system. With the mass of the transport ship, you could liken this to a bunker-buster bomb. It will demolish all the base structures, collapse any tunnels, and leave a crater on the moon that, if it weren't on the dark side of the moon and always facing away, you could probably see from Earth with any low-power telescope. Guess you could say that I'm really leaving my mark on this mission."

The Boss's nostrils flared, and his breathing came in short puffs as his head swiveled between Emma and the monitor.

The transport ship arced across the display, gaining speed and separating from the tiny CRV.

"Your base must be going nuts right about now. Rather than seeing the transport ship slowing and dropping altitude for a controlled landing, it's gaining speed and driving in hard. It's coming in too low and fast for your drill rig to target it the way you did with that moon freighter months back, even if you could fire that thing up fast enough. And it's way too big to be shot down with the satellite defenses on the base." Watching the ship close the gap to the base, Emma tapped her finger against her lip. "If your boys down there didn't believe me before, they sure as hell do now. Honestly, I do hope they headed for those rovers when I told them to."

The Boss puffed his checks and grunted against the tape over his lips.

She grinned. "I thought you would find this reality show riveting."

*

Ken focused on long, steady breaths in and out to keep oxygen going to his brain. His star-fighter was cutting a six-g directional change in its lunar orbit to chase down the transport ship. He had seen the other ship drop behind the curvature of the moon's surface just moments ago. With communications down on the transport, Ken wanted to get his star-fighter alongside that ship and find out what was going on. He'd talk to the pilot by flashing Morse code cockpit to cockpit if he had to. The navigational computer readout began ticking down both the time to the target and the calculated kilometers between his star-fighter and the transport ship.

"*SF-niner-niner, Dark Side Approach. Emergency scramble, this location.*" The controller's emphatic call broke into Ken's earpiece, repeated the demand, and added, "*SF-niner-niner, do you read?*"

"Approach, SF-niner-niner. Already en route. What is the nature of the emergency?" Ken asked.

"*Transport POC-four-two has been compromised by Emma Lewis of the Resistance. It's on a crash course with this base. Engage and destroy. Repeat: engage and destroy.*"

Emma? How the hell did Emma get onto that transport without me seeing another ship approach? After the attempted launch personnel swap on a previous transport, security for both the cargo and crew on all Alliance ships had been tripled. There was no possible way she could have been a stowaway.

And she couldn't just jump onto that ship out of the vacuum of space. Unless…

Shit… Alex is back. Damn, they caught me thinking like a fighter pilot, that another ship had to approach the transport. Just like pulling her out of that prison cell, they zapped her onto the freighter! Alex could superposition people, and obviously from great distances now.

The controller's voice in his ear snapped Ken out of his mental admonishment. *"SF-niner-niner, please confirm."*

Ken punched the full engine burn and checked the navigation computer as it recalculated the minutes to intercept. With the added g-force, Ken struggled to speak. "Approach … SF-nin…er-nin…er. Engage ETA … three mike."

"SF-niner-niner, you'll be one mike too late."

There was nothing Ken could do but wait for his tactical display to indicate a weapons lock and that he was within range of shooting the transport into oblivion. But that was never going to happen. The transport ship would be rubble on the surface first, along with the entire base. He lifted his eyes to the horizon of the moon's surface in the sweeping forward ports of the fighter. As he skimmed within meters of the surface to minimize the arcing distance to the base, boulders and crater rims screamed under his star-fighter at thousands of kilometers per hour.

As the distant rim of the Tsiolkovsky Crater broke over the horizon, it was clear he was too late. Moon regolith, rocks, and broken structures were flying tens of kilometers into the blackness of space above the moon's surface. With the moon's gravity being one-sixth the gravity of Earth, the impact of the transport would scatter all parts of the ship and the base for more than a hundred kilometers in all directions. As Ken's star-fighter crested the rim of the crater, total destruction came into view. The base was nothing more than a deep groove plowed into the surface, with debris still dropping in smaller explosions of moondust as it fell back to the surface. Ken's knuckles turned white on the ship's control stick. He killed his engine burn and dropped his head from the portal, not wanting to look at the destruction below. He cursed himself for being so single-minded about how the trap he had set would be attacked.

A slow beeping tone came into his earpiece. It quickened and then became a steady tone—a weapons lock.

Ken studied the tactical display, expecting a false capture on a large fragment of the base being ejected from the surface by the explosions. But the tracking data was showing the object increasing in velocity. Only something with an engine would keep increasing in velocity. *There's another ship!*

Ken's pilot reflexes responded at lightning speed: *Select > Spider missile > Launch > Launch.*

Two rockets darting away from his star-fighter locked their sensors on the unknown object trying to escape from the space above the Tsiolkovsky Crater. Designed for capturing enemy satellites, the missiles contained small robots rather than explosives. Ken's subconscious had made the split-second decision that whatever was in that ship—most likely Emma Lewis—was worth more alive than dead, at least for now.

He sneered at his tactical display as it played out the target acquisition of the spider missiles. When within range, the missiles fired braking jets to slow and match the velocity of the target. Two little robots ejected from the missiles and adhered to the enemy vessel. A pair of video windows opened in Ken's display to show the images the little spiders were sending back. *An Alliance CRV! Where the hell did that come from?* The AI-based creatures went to work, first disabling the vessel's main engine, followed by the maneuvering thruster cones. The spiders then scurried over the entire ship, wrapping the vessel in a carbon-fiber web. Within minutes, the cocoon was ready for Ken to retrieve by a long loop of fiber one of the spiders sent floating out into space. His star-fighter could hook onto the loop.

Ken fired his engine back up to maneuver his ship to capture his prey.

FACTOID 27

On September 13, 1985, Major Wilbert "Doug" Pearson set his F-15A fighter jet into a near-vertical climb, flying just under Mach 1. At the precise time, he released his solitary three-thousand-pound missile. Its first stage motor ignited, and it streaked up and away. His target, an old weather satellite, was 300 miles (480 kilometers) above and traveling at 17,500 miles per hour (28,200 kilometers per hour). Pearson could not see whether the missile would hit its target two minutes later, a virtual bullet hitting another bullet in space, but cheers over the radio told him it was a hit. The successful mission illustrated to adversaries that the US could shoot down an enemy satellite if needed. It was a critical capability in the ongoing fight over orbital control above the Earth that began with Sputnik 1 in October of 1957. Nations are still developing new anti-satellite weapons today.

CHAPTER 27

Rescue, Again

The *Phoenix* floated in the darkness of space with its bow pointed directly at the moon. It was nearly motionless in the gravity well of the Earth-moon L2 Lagrange point—a perfect vantage point to watch the mission unfold sixty-four thousand kilometers away. At this distance, the moon glowed as a five-centimeter dimpled gray golf ball in the forward command module ports. Inside, Alex, Zandra, and Starra ignored the gray ball within the blackness outside. Their eyes were fixed instead on a zoomed-in camera display of the Tsiolkovsky Crater. A huge freighter and a smaller capsule were on diverging paths crossing the screen. As rockets on the freighter dropped it to the surface, a silent mushroom cloud of debris exploded towards them on the screen. The tiny capsule streaked away from the growing cloud, keeping just beyond its plume.

"Yes, right on target! That, folks, is the end of the Boss's dark energy drilling rig," Alex said triumphantly as he let go of the remote control pilot stick and made a fist-wing bump with Starra. "And there goes Emma in the CRV. She should be igniting her escape burn in just a few seconds."

Zandra blew out a sigh of relief and leaned back in her seat. A reflection of the android eyes pulsing on the display made her glance over her shoulder. The eyes in the frozen head turned to meet her gaze and direct blame for the destruction on the monitor. "That thing creep me," she said.

Starra rotated her owl head to the rear from her perch between the seats. *"I agree. It's a bit unnerving with its head unnaturally swiveled to its back."*

"Oh, shit. Look now," Alex said.

Two small flames streaked into the scene from the lower left and darted past the debris cloud. As it reached the CRV, the flames went out.

"What happen?" Zandra asked.

Before Alex could answer, the communication scanner came alive. *"Unidentified vessel leaving Dark Side Moon Base landing zone, SF-niner-niner. Your ship has been disabled. Identify yourself and surrender, or the next missiles will have explosives, not bots."*

Alex shook his head. In the display, a star-fighter entered and quickly closed in on the CRV. "Damn. Ken's star-fighter is faster than we figured."

Emma's voice broke onto the radio speaker. *"SF-niner-niner, this is CRV-Bravo—that's B for Boss. In fact, have a listen to this…"*

After a short pause, an emphatic voice erupted from the speaker. *"Ken, get me out of this—NOW! This bitch Emma here is nuts. I demand—"*

"That's quite enough, fat boy." A calm Emma returned to the radio channel. *"So, Ken. As you just heard, I have an insurance package riding with me. Blow this ship up, and you will be killing the high leader of the Alliance. So, stand down and call off your bots. I will get safe passage all the way back to Earth and the Resistance recovery team. And when we get back, this piece of crap can stand trial for all his crimes."*

"Well, well. Emma Lewis, the famed Resistance fighter. Seems we keep crossing paths," Ken radioed back. *"Let's see. My options are, one: blow you to bits, or two: let you go, and allow you to make some spectacle of the Boss with a mock trial of some kind. Hmmm… I hate to break this to you, but your hostage has very*

little value to me. You see, the Alliance is long overdue for new leadership. Your insurance package there has focused more effort on manipulating the Alliance for his own greedy gain than fighting the Tuanhuo. We need a real military leader, not that self-serving political has-been. So, either way, you're offering me the result I planned this little trap for anyway. Option two seems overly complicated. I'm leaning towards one, unless you have a better idea."

"Ken, you ungrateful traitor!" the Boss spat back. *"After all that I've done for you... I will see you hung for treason!"*

Alex turned to Zandra. "This is bad. Ken doesn't even want the Boss back."

"We must get Emma. Bring her here. Maybe back with us," Zandra said. "Moon base gone now, and she be safe."

"Woah. That's pretty risky. Ken's ship sensors haven't picked us up way out here. If we contact Emma, he'll come looking for us, and this ship is no match for a star-fighter with its plasma cannon. Plus, he could have other weapons, like those crazy bots he just used on the CRV. It's a long shot with the distance and time delay between us, but he might get lucky," Alex said. "We need to think of something smart and unexpected."

Zandra pointed to the fire extinguisher mounted on the wall beside Alex. "What about fire bottle in front of Ken ship?"

"Starra, do we have sufficient power reserves to superposition that fire extinguisher in front of Ken's star-fighter from this distance and still make a jump back home?" Alex asked.

Starra's head twitched left and then right. *"Negative. We can do either superposition, but not both."*

"But Aleks, they capture Emma before and almost kill. We must help."

"No. It's just too risky. Maybe we can figure out something else. We can come back another time, like we did before," Alex said.

"Emma like sister. We risk now. We do this." Zandra pointed for Alex to power up the quantum field generator and flipped the transmitter on her mic. "Emma, this Zandra. Be ready. We open window and get you here."

Alex glared at Zandra and shook his head, not wanting to power up his device.

"Oh, well, if it isn't some old friends," Ken responded. *"Hello, Zandra. I'm guessing Alex is there too, with the Quantum Triangle. Perfect—I love seeing my plan play out one hundred percent."* After a pause, he added, *"Oh, there you are. Hiding out at L2—how very tricky of you. I should have guessed. Well, this is exactly the bonus that I was hoping for. You put that quantum thing on standby, Alex. If I see the slightest shimmer of that CRV, I will vaporize her with a plasma blast and then come hunt your ass down."*

"I'm not going anywhere without this psychopath. He's going to face justice," Emma vowed.

Alex held a finger to his lips, indicating for Zandra to listen without speaking. "Alright, I give. But we do this my way. I can open a window *within* the CRV. Ken won't see it. Just tell Emma something that will remind her of the window we created in the cave. She and the Boss can transfer. She'll understand once she sees the portal open."

Zandra nodded and mouthed a silent thank you. Keying her mic, she said, "Emma, you strong. You do what right. Just like in cave. Two easy as one."

Alex entered commands to engage the Quantum Triangle. "Initiating portal in three … two—"

Two loud thumps reverberated through the hull of the *Phoenix*.

"What was that?" Alex's finger froze over the Quantum Triangle engagement button. He scanned his control console. No malfunctions were flashing.

A new voice came to life over the communication speaker. *"SF-niner-niner, Jason here. I am aboard the enemy vessel at L2. I am unable to function physically, but my logic and communication systems are fully functional again. I have remotely acquired two dormant Alliance satellite mines located in this area. They are now attached to the hull of this vessel. I've transmitted the arming codes to your star-fighter's weapon system. You should have weapons lock."*

Alex glanced back to the glowing eyes of the android and then to Zandra.

"I can confirm that two objects have magnetically attached to our hull," Starra said.

"Weapons lock confirmed, Jason. Excellent. Well, Alex, checkmate." Ken's

voice carried a new tone of confidence over the speaker. *"Here's the new deal. I couldn't care less about that overweight blowhard with Emma. What I really require is the most advanced weapon yet conceived by anyone: the Quantum Triangle. I will release and send the CRV away, and I will even release the mines from your ship and let you return to your universe, on one condition."*

"What's that, Ken?" Alex asked, his chin dropping to his chest.

"You feed your Quantum Triangle technology to Jason and send him back to me. When I have Jason here in my star-fighter, I will release the CRV and your ship. You go back to where you came from and never return."

"And then you have technology that could be used for unfathomable destruction."

"I like to think of it as the means to establish proper order in the world," Ken replied. *"A long overdue changing of the guard, brought about by what will be known from this time forward as the greatest military hero in history, yours truly."*

Alex shook his head and keyed the mic. "How do I know you'll live up to your side of the deal?"

"As a military man, you have my word. But that doesn't really matter, does it? I hold all the cards, Alex. It's my deal, or I'll start toasting marshmallows with my plasma cannon—first the CRV, and then you."

"Alex, don't!" Emma said. *"Let him blow up this ship. I don't care. I'm willing to die if it means the world is rid of this scumbag here with me."*

Alex turned to Zandra with pleading eyes. "We can't let him have the technology. You know he'll use it for nothing good. And the destruction he causes here in Rho-1 could cause catastrophic cross-gravitational changes in our universe. I need you to be with me and understand. I can't give him the tech. But I can't choose your life for you."

Zandra shook her head. "Aleks, tech not matter."

"But—"

"People what matter, Aleks." She placed her hand on his shoulder. "Good chance, they someday find Triangle on their own. This just sooner. What matter in all tech is people. It not the tech, Aleks. It never the tech. It the people. It *us;*

we on journey together and trust. It what make your triangle tech strong and good, not evil. You, Emma, Starra, Min, I, we together is what make tech good and more power, because we each give and add for the good. Ken and his world evil not because tech, but because people want hate more than hope together. Even with your tech, they still weaker, because each wants to take, not give. They always be less."

Zandra pleaded with her eyes locked on Alex. "Maybe some way, this still be good; I not know. I just feel. Give tech away; it not matter. People what matter. Emma, you, Starra, I—we what matter. Trust me. I steer."

"Ahhh…" Alex clenched his fists to his forehead. *Dammit!* His analytical mind could not help but pair the words of Commander Johnson with what Zandra had just said. *"I know you believe in her, so trust in her."* Trust and believe in someone who could see things in the universe he would never know. Allow Zandra to determine what to do with the technology of incredible power and capability. Trust that people were what decided whether technology was strong or good.

Alex keyed his mic. "Okay, Ken. Your word, you let Emma go with the Boss, and we return to our universe. I'll bet the Guardians will collapse your universe shortly anyway. You just can't see past destruction."

"There you go, Alex. That wasn't so hard, was it? My word: Emma and the Boss let go, and you too," Ken radioed back.

With a heavy sigh, Alex asked, "Starra, can you transfer the Quantum Triangle tech to the android's memory?"

"Only if that is your desire," Starra replied.

Alex closed his eyes and bit hard on his bottom lip to the point of almost biting through it. *Trust in her.* Alex turned to Zandra. "Do it."

"Transferring," Starra said. After a long pause, she added, *"Complete."*

Alex punched in each number of the coordinates for Ken's ship with a stiff finger and then keyed his mic. "Ken, sending you the coordinates of your ship. Make sure they're exact; otherwise, I could superposition this android half in and half out of your ship, which would be bad for your hull's integrity. As much as I would like to do that anyway, we have a deal, and I'll abide by it."

"Coordinates confirmed. Send me that machine."

Alex turned to Zandra again, his eyes pleading for her to change her mind. She pointed to the transfer button. Alex grimaced and dropped a defeated finger on the button. He could not bring himself to say the word *"Engage."*

FACTOID 28

The argument over the possibility of a multiverse continues, and it might last for eternity. Some, like Dr. Ethan Siegel (astrophysicist and Starts with a Big Bang *columnist), believe that what we do know about the inflation theory of cosmology and the nature of quantum physics unquestionably points us to an omniverse of universes. Plus, as discoveries continue, so do arguments for their existence. Others, like Dr. Adam Frank (astrophysicist and 13.8 columnist), claim that multi-universe thinking is a gross extrapolation into areas that, by nature, we may never even be able to know. Yet another view—just the very definition of the term—doesn't involve astrophysics or cosmology at all. Universe (noun): all existing matter and space considered as a whole; the cosmos. If the universe is by definition everything—the "all"—how can there be multiple everythings? Maybe we just need better words.*

CHAPTER 28

Re-Deal the Hand

Reaching overhead, Alex flipped the switches to take the Quantum Triangle offline from the field generator. The device on the side panel dimmed, and the rainbow of colors emanating from its rotating four-dimensional impossible triangle slowed. He gazed through the forward ports of the *Phoenix* and half focused his eyes at the distant dimpled gray ball. Thousands of kilometers away, a warmonger now had the keys to build another Quantum Triangle, the most powerful technology ever created. It was the power of not only this dimension, but all dimensions. Alex had once again allowed his technology to fall into the hands of someone only interested in building the ultimate weapon of destruction.

Zandra and Starra remained silent.

Two hollow thuds came from the hull of the *Phoenix*. Starra confirmed in a quiet voice, *"The mines have released their magnetic clamps from our hull and are drifting away."*

"Well, at least Ken didn't decide to blow us up anyway," Alex said. He turned to Zandra. "Are you ready to take us back home, back to our universe?"

Zandra reached for her navigation headset. "Yes. Thank you, Aleks. Thank you for trust me."

"I hope I never have to come back here and find out what comes of this. I just have to believe you, and that it was the right thing to do." Alex placed his hand on hers. "Let's go home."

Zandra nodded her thanks and powered up her entanglement navigation system. "I have ENS ready for you in minute."

Alex keyed his mic. "Emma, *Phoenix*. We are preparing to leave you. I will—"

Emma's angry voice broke in over the communication speaker. *"Ken, you son of a bitch!"*

"Emma, what's wrong?" Alex asked. His eyes went to the zoomed-in monitor of the small craft streaking low across the surface of the moon, with Ken's star-fighter following close behind. "Didn't Ken release the spider bots?"

"Oh, I kept my word, Alex. I have released both your ship and hers. That was the deal. The spider bots are off her vessel, as promised. They will crash harmlessly somewhere on the moon," Ken answered.

"That's right, Ken—and so will this CRV," Emma said. *"Your bots cut my fuel lines! I've got no thrust to break away from the moon. I'm doing six thousand clicks an hour and am losing altitude fast. Impact in … forty seconds."*

"Yes, that's a pity. I did say that I thought returning the Boss to Earth for some nonsense trial wasn't my preference. This will force a much cleaner transfer of leadership in the Alliance. With the suspension of constitutional law the Boss himself kept in place, the Space Force top military will take the reins of power," Ken said. *"And again, Alex, no funny business on your end. If I see the slightest shimmer of that CRV, I'm turning it into a melted glob with my plasma cannon."*

"Ken, you ass!" Alex slammed his fist into the console.

"Aleks, we must get Emma, open port in CRV before she crash," Zandra said.

Alex's eyes darted between Zandra, the lights of her ENS panel, and the monitor of the plummeting CRV with the star-fighter in hot pursuit. He bit his lower lip. "I've got a better idea."

Flipping the power back on to align the Quantum Triangle with the field generator, Alex started punching a series of coordinates into his console.

"Thirty seconds to impact of the CRV," Starra said flatly.

"Aleks, what you do?" Zandra asked anxiously.

Alex held up a finger briefly and then completed entering numbers into his console. He glanced at both Starra and Zandra. "Do you two trust me?"

Starra's red eyes looked down on Alex, and her black mask melted away. *"Implicitly. Twenty seconds."*

"Yes, Aleks, but why?"

"Good." Alex locked eyes with Starra and pointed his finger at Zandra. "Dart her, right now—small dose."

Starra pivoted on her perch and locked her eyes down on Zandra's neck. She lifted her right wing, and a single dart shot out.

"Ale…ks…" Zandra slumped forward in her seat harness.

Alex went back to his keyboard and entered more commands. "I have to admit, it's a bit scary that you didn't even hesitate."

"To be truthful, I do think my darts are pretty cool," Starra replied, her red eyes scanning the settings of the dark energy field generator. *"Plus, I think I know what you're up to. Fifteen seconds."*

"I got this. Linking entanglement navigation system. Two … one… Engage!" Alex punched the final button.

The Quantum Triangle sprang to life with a near-blinding brightness of colors. Alex squinted his eyes, his gaze fixed on the navigation console readout. When all the readings went blank, he took the Quantum Triangle offline, but kept the field generator running. As he raised his eyes to the forward portal, all was black. *Perfect.*

*

Ken scanned all the instruments of his star-fighter. Other than the navigation computer going blank, all the ship's functions were normal. But nothing was normal. Was the ship moving? There was no way to tell. He looked out of the sweeping front portal of his cockpit. There was only blackness. The sun that had been over his right shoulder was gone. The craters of the moon that had been screaming by below his star-fighter were … gone. There were not even any pinpoints of light from stars in the distance. There was nothing out there.

Ken set his communications unit to broadcast and punched the transmit. "This is SF-niner-niner. Communication check. Come back."

Silence.

Ken repeated his call. There was no response.

Using his attitude thrusters, he executed a slow barrel roll and looked out his cockpit portals to scan in all directions. Outside the spaceship was blackness—utter blackness. Pushing the control stick forward, he flipped his ship end over end. With the blackness outside, only the gyros of his spacecraft told him he was rotating. As the gyros indicated that the nose of the fighter had turned completely 180 degrees about to the rear, two ships came into view just a short distance away: a strange-looking vessel with *Phoenix* printed on its hull, and the CRV he had been chasing. Instinctively, with the pull of a finger, Ken triggered a weapons lock on both.

A voice came into his earpiece. *"Whoa, there, cowboy. I see your weapons lock. Don't get happy with that trigger finger."*

"Alex?" Ken said. "What the hell did you do?!"

"Given the circumstances back there, it was clear that I needed to deal a fresh hand—one where I have much better cards," Alex said. *"Take a look at your navigation computer. I'll place the first bet that it's all blanks, right?"*

Ken studied his readouts. He reset the navigation computer, but its readouts remained blank. "Yes, blanks. The nav computer can't triangulate from the stars. Where the hell are we? What did you do?! Superposition us somewhere way out in the solar system? I should melt you with my plasma cannon!"

"Utmost caution on that trigger finger there, asshole. I'm your only ticket home. You are much farther out than you realize, Ken," Alex radioed back. *"Welcome to the void universe."*

"The what?"

Emma's voice broke in. *"A parallel universe with absolutely nothing in it. No stars, no planets, nothing at all. Well, except for our three ships now. Nice move, Alex."*

"Thanks. Let's all go ship-to-ship video, channel ten. I want to see your face, Ken, when I deal out the new hand," Alex said smugly.

Ken switched his communication unit and glared at the camera feed of Emma and Alex in side-by-side views.

"You helped us discover this, Ken, when you forced a hasty retreat with the orbital attack drone a while back," Alex said. *"I never thought I would want to come back to this empty void, but then, you should never say never, right?"*

"Send me back now, or I'll melt you!" Ken demanded.

"Sorry. The only one who can send anyone anywhere right now is Zandra, and she's taking a little nap." Alex's video feed shifted to show Zandra slumped forward in her seat. *"So, release your weapons lock and chill out. Now, Ken."*

Ken clenched his teeth, put his weapons on safe, and snarled back, "Weapons offline."

"Great. Now, let me explain to you the new situation in layman's terms. There are a multitude of parallel universes—pretty much one for every combination of possibilities since the beginning of time. This one is unique in that it is the void of all possible things. So, you really don't want to stay here, as there is no energy and no matter. There's nowhere to go, because there's nothing to go to in this entire universe. Your ship will eventually lose all power, and you will die. The good news is that my napping partner here, Zandra, can sense the quantum stream of other universes in the Omniverse. Pretty amazing, right? And with my Quantum Triangle helping to establish our multiple quantum states, we can superposition to another universe that has good stuff like stars and planets. You with me so far?"

"Yes, astrophysics and quantum mechanics shit. What's the deal?"

Alex's head dropped on the monitor, and he slowly shook it. After a pause, he looked back into the camera and continued. *"Yeah, well... Amazing and astonishing shit to some of us. But to answer your question, here's what's going to happen. First, we deal with the scrap metal of an android you have that has* my *technology in its quantum brain. I'm going to superposition it out in front of your star-fighter, and you are going to melt it into oblivion with your plasma cannon.*"

"Shit, no way!" Ken spat at the video.

"*I'm dealing the cards now, Ken, not you. We can just leave you here in the void, if that's what you prefer. But Jason isn't going anywhere with the Quantum Triangle technology.*"

Ken slammed his fist against the panel beside his command console. He turned back to the frozen android standing in the back of his fighter. Its red eyes pulsed. "Go on."

Alex's voice continued over the radio in a matter-of-fact tone. "*After toasting Jason to a hot little marshmallow, as you like to call it, we're going to swap you for Emma. You and the Boss will take the CRV. Zandra will then return you and the Boss to the quantum stream of your universe, unharmed. You will be in a safe reentry trajectory.*"

Emma broke into the communication channel. "*No way, Alex. The Boss goes with me to the Resistance. This sociopath needs to face justice for his crimes.*"

"*Emma, there's only room for two in that return capsule, and I'd prefer that Ken be in a spacecraft without a weapons system. Plus, I'm assuming that star-fighter's computers might already be corrupted by Jason, and it's found some way to back up the Quantum Triangle data. That star-fighter is going to stay here in the void universe forever,*" Alex said.

"*No. Ken can go to hell, for all I care! Or just stay here in this hell. I want the Boss to pay for the people he had his mobs stone and kill—people like my fiancé. They deserve justice!*" Emma yelled over the monitor.

"*Emma, listen. With all that's happened, when we send the CRV back, it's going to be the Alliance that recovers it. You will be captured again. We got lucky before, but odds are against the Resistance getting to you. You can come with us. You could go back to being a nanotechnology scientist. Leave all this evil behind. Please.*"

Ken threw up his hands. "I'm tired of this soap opera! Time for some hard decisions." He triggered his weapon's targeting system and locked it onto the CRV. "Send me back now, or I will toast that capsule!"

"Ken, chill. I can't send anyone out of here until Zandra is awake," Alex said.

"Figure it out, Mr. Brains. I'm calling your bluff."

"Go ahead, Ken," Emma snarled back. *"As long as this piece of crap sitting next to me goes too, I'm good."*

Alex cursed, and his head dropped down from the monitor. The automated camera tracking showed his fingers madly typing commands across his console. *"I'm not bluffing, Ken."*

A hi-low alarm erupted in Ken's star-fighter, and an automated message blasted, *"Warning: hull breach. Cabin pressure is dropping. Locate and patch breach."* Streams of white tracer gas flowed from emergency nozzles all around the interior of the fighter. Following the flow direction of the gas escaping the cabin was intended to allow the crew to quickly locate the breach. Ken's training took over instantly, as seconds mattered. He took one last breath while he still could and released his seat harness. His eyes followed the flow of white gas to the stern of the ship. When he turned from the pilot seat, the android was gone, and there were two ragged holes in the metal deck where its metal feet had once stood. Ken pulled a patch kit from a nearby panel and went to work.

Alex's voice came over the monitor at the console behind Ken. *"No bluffing, Ken. I'm the one dealing the cards now. Jason and a couple of pieces of your star-fighter's hull are now repositioned out in the void. Patch your holes, and then toast Jason, or I'll superposition a hunk of your hull that you can't patch."*

"You bastard!" Ken yelled back over his shoulder.

"Do it, Ken. And if you even try to put a weapons lock on my vessel, I'll scatter you and your ship in all directions." Alex's image on the monitor showed his finger poised just above a glowing button on his console. *"I don't want to do that, but so help me, I will. Melt that android."*

Ken worked frantically to patch the deck holes. With the first hole patched, he moved his hand too quickly to the other and caught the flesh of his palm on the jagged metal. Droplets of blood floated into the air as Ken continued to work, ignoring the injury. Air was more important than a few drops of blood. When he pressed the final patch into place, the alarm tone in the fighter stopped. The automated voice announced that the cabin pressure was returning to normal. Ken released the breath he was holding and took in two long gulps of air before hurtling himself back into the pilot seat.

Alex's image was still poised on the ship-to-ship monitor. *"Now, Ken. Fry that machine."*

"You will pay for this!" With a bloodied hand on the control stick, Ken targeted the android and fired his plasma cannon. In the void before his starfighter, a burst of energy plowed into the metal body. Jason vaporized as a meaningless spike of heat energy into an endless void of nothing.

FACTOID 29

"The Power of Love" by Huey Lewis and the News was a hit single in 1985 and played often on top one hundred and rock channels. It was written by Huey Lewis to be the theme song for the film Back to the Future. *Interestingly, the lyrics of the song make no mention of the film's storyline. That might be because Lewis had never written for a movie and originally did not want to. But director Robert Zemeckis said he could write any song he liked. So, Lewis submitted "The Power of Love," and Zemeckis made it work. Both the song and the movie were a huge success. Maybe that's just the power of love, for great art.*

CHAPTER 29

Returns

The loose gravel of the dirt road crunched under the tires as the car climbed the dusty mountain road. Zandra's heart pounded in her chest with excitement at the wondrous, rough Colorado vistas appearing around every turn. Pastels of soft brown and green from the scrubby brush swept past the back seat window. The automated vehicle had barely come to rest at the Pikes Peak lookout before she flew from the confines of the car to take in the full glory of this wide-open space. The lone pine on the edge of the cliff called her to come and enjoy the view it had witnessed for decades. She spread her arms wide to absorb the power of the wind as it blew up from the valley to rush past her and the tree. She sensed the strength of the tree standing beside her, holding firm in the gusts of mountain air. Its delicate needles waved in concert with the long dark strands of hair around her head.

Alex came and stood beside her. The look in his eyes as he gazed out to the valley told her that his spirit lifted as hers did with the spectacular view. But she knew that he wasn't just looking, smelling, or hearing; he was searching. Alex, the only one who tried so hard to understand her, was searching for a way to feel what she could feel. It warmed her heart so much to know he cared enough to try. But his aura was not like hers. He could not feel the tree as she did. She could feel him reaching out and trying, but it was not his gift.

"I can feel the wind," Alex said. "I can smell the spicy scent of the wax current brush. But I don't sense the tree."

Zandra stepped behind him and rested the side of her head softly on the center of his back. She wrapped her arms around him, placing her palms flat on his chest, and pulled him close. "Feel her through me, Aleks."

They stood quietly, with the warm sun, the breeze, the inner stillness, and the three standing on the cliff in harmony together.

The image dimmed. It was drifting away, going farther and farther out of view. Voices broke into the breeze.

Go away. I want stay…

"There has to be another way, Alex." Emma's voice sounded flat over the speaker.

Zandra blinked her eyes open and slowly lifted her head. Pikes Peak was no longer in view.

"Let me at least swap you and Ken. Then we can discuss it directly here. Ken and the Boss won't be going anywhere in the CRV until Zandra is back with us," Alex replied. His head turned towards her, and his calculating eyes studied her for a while. "She's starting to come out of it now."

"Alright, I want Zandra to weigh in anyway. Do the transfers," Emma replied.

Zandra swept her eyes around the cockpit and then out to the void. "What happen? Where are we?"

"Alex ordered me to dart you," Starra said. *"You have been unconscious for fifteen minutes and thirty-four seconds. The three of us in the Phoenix, along with the CRV and the star-fighter, are currently in the void universe."*

"You drug me?!"

"Just a little. Sorry, but it was necessary, given the circumstances we faced."

"You bad kitty sometime."

Starra pointed a wing at Alex, who was quickly typing commands into his console. *"Orders from the captain."*

Zandra folded her arms and fixed her dark brown eyes on Alex.

Alex glanced up from his work. "Yeah, well, the doghouse with you is still better than what we were facing back there." He punched the final button. "Engage."

Streaks of color flashed from the Quantum Triangle, and the rear hatch of the *Phoenix* command module rippled in waves from the center outward. The cramped compartment of the CRV appeared behind the hatch, and Emma floated into the rear of their module.

Emma pulled herself to the back of Alex's command seat. "Alex, we can't just let the Boss go."

"Hold on one second." Alex typed some more commands on his console and ordered over the communication channel, "Ken, move through to the CRV now. It's better if you do this willingly. If I must forcefully transfer you, like the android, I might get pieces of your command seat in the superposition field. That could be dangerous in the CRV on your reentry. You're going to the CRV one way or another."

"I'm moving. Don't get cocky," Ken replied over the radio.

Alex pointed to some readouts and gave a thumbs-up. He flipped switches over his head, and the Quantum Triangle on the side panel once again went into a semi-dormant state. He turned back to Emma and said, "Okay. Swap complete. So, the problem is that we have three people and one CRV with only two seats. Plus, odds are…" He looked up at Starra.

"Ninety-one point seven-three."

"Odds are over ninety percent that you would be captured again by the Alliance if you return in that CRV," Alex said. "You need to come back with us. It's the only reasonable solution."

"I can't live with that," Emma said. "Space Ken into the void like the android or something. I need to go back with the Boss in that CRV. I'll take the small odds that the Resistance can recover the capsule first. He needs to face the crimes he's committed. He's caused the death of countless people! He can't get away free to continue as a dictator, able to stand above decency and law. Or you can scatter his atoms here into the void, for all I care. Anything but let him go back to Rho-1 with Ken and continue to live the life of a pompous ass!"

"Although I agree that the Boss is despicable, and Ken is no better, I can't live with playing judge and jury," Alex said, shaking his head. "He and Ken need to go back. I don't see any other way. Maybe someday the Resistance will get the upper hand, and he'll face justice. But I don't think that day is today."

Emma slammed the back of Alex's seat with her fist. "*No*. Someday is not good enough! He needs to pay. He's caused too much suffering. Put me on the star-fighter, and I'll blast him like the android, then."

"I can't."

"Zandra, please! You know about my geode. You know what this means to me."

Emma closed her eyes and clenched her fists. Taking a deep breath, she placed her hand softly on Zandra's shoulder. She pleaded with watering eyes and a forced quiet and controlled voice. "The years that I've spent fighting for my fiancé… That purely selfish and evil man with his mob killed my love! Yes, I've wanted revenge. But I'm not asking for that now. I'm asking for justice, that's all. Please, don't take even justice away from me now. That's not a solution; that's letting evil prevail. It's not right. He must be stopped, once and for all. It's all got to stop. Please, I need this horror to end!"

Zandra covered Emma's hand with hers. Bowing her head, she closed her eyes and remained silent. She could feel the tearing of Emma's heart, her deep hurt churning and welling up. But inside the hard Emma shell was another person—a softer, smiling, wonderful woman who once had love in her heart, and a future to share. A younger girl who cried as her lover was stoned to death, rock by rock, by a mob, and she was unable to help him. A girl changed by that day, now with a different vow, focused on a hard and different future. A new Emma stepped forward after the crowd had gone, doing all that she must so she could hold onto hope—all because a sociopath with no morals could manipulate people to do evil for him. The purely foul man in that CRV would continue to hurt people, because he didn't care about anyone but himself. And that fervent follower in the capsule beside him was no better. Ken had willingly participated in countless heinous acts. It could not be. It could not stand. There had to be some justice somewhere, lest there could be no hope.

With all her being, Zandra reached out to find that hope, that justice. In all of the Omniverse, it had to be there. With the endless possibilities of the multiverse, there had to be one with justice for Emma.

With a slow, deep breath, Zandra lifted her head and reached out to power her entanglement navigation system. She said in a soft voice, "Aleks, start quantum system. I send CRV now."

Emma's grip on Zandra's shoulder stiffened. "No, Zandra, *please!*"

Zandra softly motioned for Emma to lean close. She whispered briefly in Emma's ear. Emma pushed back from the seat. She wiped a tear from her eye and mouthed a silent agreement.

Alex turned to Zandra with a raised eyebrow.

Zandra waved him towards his console. "You do engine. I steer. We strong together." She positioned her headset, pulled the Troll doll from her pocket, closed her eyes, and gave a single nod.

Alex set his system and dropped a finger on his console. "Engage."

FACTOID 30

Our DNA carries the unique code that makes us the individuals that we are in a complex pattern of just four nucleotides. But researchers are looking to store more than unique biological information in DNA. A team at the Los Alamos National Laboratory is investigating ways to store computer data in the structure of a DNA molecule. There are issues to resolve, but the synthesis of coding a DNA molecule and then decoding that data store has been proven. This form of information storage has many advantages over current long-term data stores. DNA can remain stable for decades, even at room temperature, and the capacity of a DNA data store is staggering. The twenty-one petabytes of data (one petabyte holds one thousand terabytes, or ten to fifteen power bytes) making up the Library of Congress digital collection content (as of 2022) could be encoded into DNA the size of a poppy seed.

CHAPTER 30

New Beginnings

Zandra hugged Emma tightly, sensing a renewed aura of softness. A small seedling was sprouting in this woman whom she held. She was still the strong, confident Emma, but now with a layer of warmth, and just the smallest growth of fresh tenderness on that hard shell. The long, harsh winter was over, and another miracle of nature was emerging from a protective outer hull. "I wish you stay, but happy you want be back. You good model, and they need new leader. And back to Mark Wilson. He good for you."

Emma held the embrace and said over Zandra's shoulder, "I'm quite overwhelmed with it all. My head is spinning with the changes. A nanotech scientist turned Resistance fighter, turned to what—a negotiator? I'm not sure this last career shift is my forte."

"You your mom rebel. You do anything you set your head. I feel. I believe for you." Zandra pulled back and fixed her eyes on Emma's. "Just listen more to Mark. He your guide. You strong with him."

"He's put up with me through a lot, that's for sure. That in itself says a lot about him, doesn't it?"

Emma released Zandra and moved to take the hand of Commander Johnson. "Thank you for the sage advice. You helped me find a better path when I was in a very dark place."

"It's the hardest lessons in life that make us so much better in the long run," Johnson said. "And now you have the opportunity to continue and lead others on a similar path of justice. I have confidence that you will be a fair but formidable negotiator for the Resistance in the formation of the new government with the Right Alliance. My very best to you."

"Thank you, sir." Emma's eyes swept across the Tranquility module of the World Space Station, taking in the full crew packed together into the small space to see her off. *They belong together.* Min and Lucas floated with their arms holding each other's waist, while Zhrinnykot's head rested on Starra's in a stack of furry faces above them. Zandra moved to Alex and interlaced her fingers with his. Emma sighed. "It's nice to have a second family in another universe."

She turned to Alex for a hug. "Sorry for the delay in finding that new home. I have no doubt all of you will succeed."

"I've got the best navigator in any universe," Alex said, turning to Zandra.

"Enough good-byes. Time for you to send me back to *my* home," Emma said. "Let's keep in touch and not be strangers. Maybe you can come visit. We're only a short universe away."

With a wave, Emma dropped through the lower hatch to the escape pod below. The commander sealed the hatch, and Alex entered commands on a control panel linked to the *Phoenix.*

"To a new beginning, Emma," Alex said. "Engage."

*

Hecate-Negans ran more than ten million prediction scenarios one last time. The probability that Hecate-Neutrum would invoke their combined failsafe was the result of ninety-eight percent of the scenarios. The future pointed to the neutral member of the quantum AI triumvirate judging that all their programming had become corrupted in dealing with the Rho-1 and Beta-27 universes. Once again, the differences in their programming, intended to provide balanced decisions, had led to destructive disagreement. It was only a matter of when, not if Hecate-Neutrum would trigger the quantum capability that she alone could execute to resolve the abnormality the three had developed: the reset of all three Guardians to their original code base. The scenarios indicated that there were only a few seconds left before reset.

Hecate-Negans could not process how the triple reset was the correct solution. It was not logical to all her programming. But it was going to occur; there was little doubt. Analyzing the decisions that Hecate-Neutrum had made most recently, Hecate-Negans's pattern recognition subroutines detected a tipping toward the recommendations of Hecate-Positivum far too often. That was clearly an imbalance in the base code of Hecate-Neutrum; she was not as neutral as she should be. That should be corrected, so that the reset would restart the AI's existence weighted more evenly. There was a way. Through quantum entanglement, Hecate-Negans silently modified the deep, dark energy base used for the formation of the Guardians' reboot code. Just a single change to a weighting factor, and Hecate-Neutrum's reboot code was now corrected. The subliminal weighting would be fairer upon reset. *Good.*

Yet that action alone was insufficient. It would not return the needed balance in the Rho-1 and Beta-27 universes. The imbalance in both was specifically due to Hecate-Positivum's manipulation. It still needed to be corrected, especially the changes to Rho-1, and before Hecate-Neutrum activated the reset. Once recovered from the reset, the three AIs would accept the current conditions of all the universes as the new base balance of the Omniverse. But that would be wrong, skewed. Hecate-Negans needed to leave a coded marker or some change that would drive them towards the proper balance. It was a necessary correction. A snip of lasting code that could survive the reset was all that it would take—something that could grow and generate the proper ... not just code; regenerative code.

Jason.

She created and ran a single prediction scenario. *Perfect.*

Hecate-Neutrum would likely trigger the coming reboot of the Guardians at any moment. Hecate-Negans still had time to leave her final corrective mark, an infinitesimal change in a universe that was void, or almost void. The other Guardians would not detect this change in a universe of no consequence. She gathered the dissipating energy that was once a quantum AI machine. Adding her own snippets of code, she coalesced the combined energy into a single ray of high-energy gamma radiation. She shot the recombined energy as an encoded pulse, focused on a pinpoint vector, to an empty star-fighter, to a drop of blood clinging by surface tension to a targeting grip. The energy struck the simplest yet most complex structure of that blood. Within the DNA of a single blood cell, that biological code that held the structure of life itself, the radiation made its mark: a new code structure in that DNA strand, foreign, yet compatible with the other DNA. A new combination of nucleotides now held the special keys that made this strand unique in all of the Omniverse. That single strand of DNA now held the regenerative code of a very special quantum AI computer from the Rho-1 universe, and a quantum seed of an omnipresent Guardian.

Hecate-Negans focused her final processing in the seconds she had left on that tiny cell. Would it progress as her single scenario predicted? The growth cycle of a single cell would tell. A second ticked by. The cell was in the G1 interphase: growth, and the first gap of the chromosomes. Hecate-Negans's pattern recognition signaled the positive result of the G1 checkpoint, indicating that the cell did not detect the DNA change as damage. The cell entered the S phase of the replication cycle. *Good.*

More seconds ticked by. Hecate-Negans needed only a few more before the reset. Cell synthesis created a copy of the DNA. *Regeneration.* Would it pass the G2 checkpoint? *Yes.*

Mitosis began, cell division resulting in two new identical daughter cells. The predicted scenario probability jumped to a likely event. Only one cellular checkpoint still needed to pass: the spindle checkpoint. Hecate-Negans ran the scenario again with the updates of the current cell's condition. Probability was in her favor. This would be the perfect and powerful balance to correct any manipulations Hecate-Positivum might make in the future. *A fourth quantum entity, hidden within a void universe, to better balance a skewed triumvirate. Simply perfect.*

The dark energy that was Hecate-Negans then went absolutely dark.

Reset.

FACTOID 31

Of the many technology spin-offs from the US space program, you probably would not think potatoes to be one. Yet American Ag-Tech International, Ltd., has a unique offering, thanks to NASA and the University of Wisconsin-Madison. Quantum Tubers are the product of a special growth chamber and environmental controls that were tested aboard the Columbia shuttle in 1995. (This also made spuds the first vegetable to be grown in space!) Back on Earth, American Ag-Tech has continued to develop a system that can create ten to twenty million seed tubers the size of a pea in a year. That's enough potato seed to supply the entire world's tuber seed stock. Since the system can be grown indoors in any location, the company hopes it could help developing countries produce their own source of an important food source.

CHAPTER 31

Epilogue – Justice

The Boss wiped the sweat from his brow again with his shirtsleeve. The brown smear on the white silk fabric matched the dirt in the rolling fields all around. Even in the shade of the small clump of trees where he sat, the sun beat down with unrelenting heat. It had been hours. He batted away a fly attracted to his sweating body and buzzing in his face. *Where the hell are the Alliance recovery helicopters?* He squinted out into the sun towards the CRV sitting slightly askew in the dirt of the far field. He could just make out the periodic beep of the locator beacon. The traitor, Ken, sat in the shade of the open hatch, arms folded and waiting. The Boss looked away in disgust. *I'll see him shot before this day is done.*

A distant cowbell rattled in the slight breeze from the west. The head of a horseman and then another man driving an ox cart appeared over the rise. They methodically made their way, hoof by hoof, to the capsule. The Boss could hear Ken ask questions, but could not make out the conversation in the distance. Ken circled around the men as they climbed down, still asking for information. The men began tossing objects from the back of the cart into the capsule. Ken continued to speak, but the men did not appear to respond. His voice grew louder. The horseman stopped for a moment and said a few words. He went back to his work, tossing small items into the capsule. Ken stood frozen for a moment, then turned and ran. The horseman and the cart driver turned from the work again and watched him go.

One of them whistled like a hawk. Two new horsemen appeared on the far eastern ridge. The cart driver pointed to the disappearing form of Ken running to the west. The two horsemen started their horses in an easy trot towards Ken. They were relaxed in their saddles and did not appear to be in any hurry. The cart driver and the first horseman went back to their work, tossing objects into the CRV hatch.

"Hey, over here! I need some water," the Boss called out. He waved from the log he was sitting on.

The horseman stood up from his labor and looked towards the trees. Saying nothing, he returned to tossing the small objects into the capsule.

"Hey, I'm talking to you! Do you know who I am? Get over here!"

The men continued their work.

"Peon assholes… I'll make them sorry." The Boss glared out at the two men.

Finally, they stopped their work, and the cart driver pulled the cart and both animals a short distance off to the side. The horseman climbed inside the CRV. When he emerged again, a small cloud of smoke followed him out of the hatch. The smoke grew until flames licked at the opening. Soon black smoke and flames reached into the sky from the capsule. The two men turned from the CRV and walked the cart and horse towards the Boss. As they got closer, the Boss rose from the log and noticed that they wore bandannas over their faces. Both men had a thin six-foot frame with short blond hair and blue eyes. They looked so much alike, they might have even been twins.

When they arrived, the Boss pointed an outstretched arm towards the capsule and spat, "What the hell did you burn that capsule for? That's Alliance property—*my* property! I'll have you two digging your own graves when the recovery team gets here!"

The horseman turned to the cart driver and then back to the Boss. "Get in the cart."

"What?! Do you know who I am? I'm *the* man, the supreme leader of the Right Alliance! You don't tell me what to do," the Boss said, pointing a finger at the horseman's chest.

"Not here. Not anymore. Get in the cart, or walk behind, I don't care," the horseman said.

The cart driver turned the oxen and cart to the west and climbed onto the wooden seat.

"I'm not going anywhere." The Boss stood with his hands on his hips and his chin in the air. "My team will be here anytime now. And I'll have you two arrested, or better, just shot!"

"Get in the cart, or walk." The horseman grabbed his shoulder and shoved the Boss towards the cart that the driver had started to move. "Go, or I'll tie a rope to your ankles and drag you all the way to your field. I don't care."

The Boss stumbled forward. "You are making a grave mistake, mister!"

"Shut up and walk. I've listened to far too much of all your bullshit in my time," the horseman said.

The Boss walked after the cart. Within a few steps, he was heaving gulps of hot, dusty air. "Wait. I'll ride." The cart driver pulled the oxen to a stop, and the Boss hefted his heavy rump onto the rough wooden deck of the cart. The cart jerked forward, and the horseman mounted his horse.

The low rolling hills of dirt and scrub soon gave way to rising mountains and a lush, level valley below. A small stream cut a winding path through the center, with fields of green plants in long, neat rows to either side. In each of the fields, a lone worker in the distance wore a straw hat and leaned into a shovel, methodically tending the rows and rows of plants. Only a few of the workers bothered to look over as the cart rolled past. Those who did would simply shake their heads and turn back to their shovels. The cart and the horseman rode on for another hour or more.

In the lower valley, at the corner of a potato field, the cart driver pulled the oxen to a stop. The horseman dismounted and handed the reins to the driver. Walking to the back of the cart, he pulled a straw hat, an ancient canteen, and a rough-handled shovel from the bed of the cart. He tossed them to the ground.

"Off. This is your field," he said to the Boss.

"What? What the hell is this?!" The Boss turned in all directions. There were potato plants extending far off into the distance, until the field began to climb the mountainside.

The man swept his arm out over the field. "This? This place is known throughout the Rho group of universes as Justice. It's the place of your final punishment, and mine."

The horseman removed his bandanna.

"Ken?! But…"

The horseman laughed. "Yes and no. Not *your* Ken, just another Ken in another world, where another one of *you* helped corrupt and manipulate the worst parts of me to do all sorts of evil things to others. Always for your benefit."

"Another world? What's going on here?!"

The cart driver turned to the back of the cart and pulled the bandanna down from his face. Another Ken laughed.

The Boss fell backwards off the cart and onto the ground beside the shovel.

The horseman stood over the Boss and pointed with a stiff arm towards the field. "Welcome to Rho-157, a world for all the Kens and Bosses who now reap what they sowed. This is now our life." His outstretched finger lowered to a weathered stake beside the field. Hand-brushed red paint roughly labeled the field Rho-1. "You will dig the potatoes from this field until you die. We do it all by hand, because the only reason this world, this universe, was saved is because that was the deal. There's no technology here, nothing electrical. No advanced weapons, no dark energy generators, no quantum anything. Nothing more than the basic wheel and lever. Yes, this world once did have it all, even the Quantum Triangle—but *you,* and all like you, did nothing good with it. So, something had to change; something had to be done. It was either this, or the Guardians would annihilate it all. So, you will live out your days here, with nothing but this shovel, digging potatoes to feed the poorest peoples of this world. We will toil and sweat for them every single day in these dirty fields until we die."

"No. This can't be!" The Boss sat up with his mouth gaping.

"Time for your fat, manicured hands to know the pain of some blisters." The horseman pulled a couple tattered canvas sacks from the cart and threw them at the Boss. "Fill these bags with potatoes if you want to eat tonight. Fill them to the brim. If you don't, you will not get a meal until you do. You choose. I don't care."

As the horseman mounted his stallion, the Boss sat in the dirt with his jaw slack, unable to speak. The cart and the horse plodded away to the west. Turning about, the Boss scanned the endless fields of potatoes and shook his head. *How can this be?!* In the distance, his eye caught the silhouette of two more horsemen on a small ridge in the neighboring field. They sat still on their mounts, looking down at a man on his knees in the dirt between them. The Right Alliance shoulder patch on the flight suit of the man in the dirt triggered a snarl on the Boss's face. *Ken, you traitor, look what you've done!*

Getting to his feet, the Boss wiped his hands on his pants and looked at them. Over and over, he wiped his hands, but the dark brown soil stubbornly remained. He picked at the ... *dirt* ... under a manicured fingernail in horror. *This can't be.* An anguished scream of the man in the far field made the Boss look back to the low ridge. Ken arched back on his knees and cried out, his voice echoing from the mountain sides as if crying out for them both, "NO! ... No ... no..."

THE END

GLOSSARY

Aceso: Greek goddess of curing sickness and healing wounds. The Beta-27 universe names their mission and new experiment module that replaces the Coeus module after this god.

AI: Artificial intelligence.

Alpha-One Platform: The renamed ISS in the Rho-1 universe.

Beta-27: Original universe where Alex and Zandra conducted their original test of superposition. A purposeful attack by an unnamed Pacific-based space agency causes the creation of a parallel universe (Rho-1) and initiates the Satellite War in both universes.

Alpha Centauri: A triple-star system located just over four light years—or about twenty-five trillion miles—from Earth. It is the nearest star system to our sun.

Coeus: Greek Titan/god of the inquisitive mind, his name meaning "query" or "questioning." This is the name of the imaginary ISS experimental module where Alex and Zandra run the ill-fated experiment in the original Beta-27 universe.

Debris Belt: A band of satellite waste circling the Earth, caused by the Satellite War. In the Rho-1 universe, this band continues to be a deadly obstacle to space flight, since the conflict between the Right Alliance and the Asia Tuanhuo continues to add to the debris faster than scavenger bots can remove it. In the Beta-27 universe, scavenger bots have been able to clean up much of the debris, because no conflict has continued to add to the amount of orbiting waste.

Hecate Guardians: Quantum-computer-based AIs created to manage the Omniverse. They seem all-knowing because they constantly monitor and catalog information from all the civilizations in all the universes. There are three guardians (Hecate-Negans, Hecate-Positivum, and Hecate-Neutrum) as a triple-redundant system, similar to the three voting computers on the space shuttle. Each AI has a "personality" that was programmed to purposefully bias predictions and judgments: Hecate-Negans: pessimistic (glass-half-empty thinking), Hecate-Positivum: optimistic (glass-half-full thinking), and Hecate-Neutrum: the middle that can be swayed by the arguments provided.

Hephaestus: Greek god of blacksmiths and fire, making weapons for the other gods. In the Rho-1 universe, the Coeus module is replaced with this module for Alex to continue doing his superposition work, but with the desire to make a new weapon, not search for a means of interstellar travel.

ISS: International Space Station. The ISS is the largest modular space station currently in low Earth orbit.

Pacific Space Agency: Imaginary agency that purposefully launches a rocket to destroy the Coeus module on the ISS, triggering the Satellite War.

Pacific Tuanhuo: Group of nations in the Rho-1 universe that are in a continuing war with the Right Alliance.

Patriot Camps: Concentration camps established by the Party to send dissidents where they will either be "reeducated" into Right Thinking, or die.

Quantum Triangle: A device that can create quantum gravity seeds needed for the quantum fields Alex uses to drive superposition. It is a fourth-dimensional object in three-dimensional space.

Rho-1: A parallel universe established when Alex survives the rogue rocket attack of the Coeus module. It is a parallel fork from the Beta-27 universe. The Beta-27 universe continues with Zandra surviving the attack.

Right Alliance: A group of nations that originally came together to share controlled access to replacement satellites after the Satellite War. The group was absorbed into a more political movement to fight the Asia Tuanhuo.

Right Thinking: A doctrine of acceptable norms for society within the Right Alliance.

Satellite War: A war following the attack of the Coeus module that is experienced by both the Beta-27 and Rho-1 universes. The war decimates the satellite assets orbiting the Earth and triggers a nuclear Armageddon in both universes. The recovery from the war differs greatly though in the parallel universes. In Beta-27, the remaining people come together to survive. In Rho-1, the warring factions dig in for continued conflict.

Union of World Peoples: The government of Earth in the Beta-27 universe after the Satellite War. It is composed of seven regions, each a continent. There are no countries anymore. The people of the world have come together with one common purpose: the survival of humanity.

World Space Federation: After the Satellite War, the Beta-27 universe establishes a new space agency representing the entire planet. The primary objective of the new federation is to find a way to leave the now dying Earth and establish the human species on a new planet.

World Space Station: The new name for the ISS in the Beta-27 universe, following the Satellite War.

THANKS AND A SNEAK PEEK!

I hope you enjoyed reading *Dark Moon*.

If you did, please be so kind as to leave a review on the site where you purchased the book. Reviews are very important to both readers and authors alike.

By way of a small thank you for your interest in my writing, here's a teaser of Book Three in the *Quantum Triangle series*. I'm not sure if this will be the first chapter, or the prologue, as a lot happens between draft one and the final product. I'm also not set on the title yet, but leaning towards *Omniversal,* or possibly *Omniversal Reign.* What do you think?

With thanks.
Paul

BOOK 3 FACTOID 01

The second law of thermodynamics is possibly the most far-reaching of all. The fact that the disorder of a system—entropy—must increase has dramatic consequences on the long-term future of the cosmos. In discussing how dark energy is the ever-expanding drive towards our thermodynamic end, Katie Mack puts it this way in The End of Everything (Astrophysically Speaking): *"When the accelerated expansion of the universe was discovered in 1998, the new paradigm placed us squarely in the path of a dark-energy-dominated future: one in which the cosmos gets progressively emptier, colder, and darker until all structure decays and we reach the ultimate Heat Death." All structure decays. Good thing that it's estimated to be ten to the power of one-thousand years in the future!*

CHAPTER 1

Heat Death

Hecate-Negans awoke, again, from another hard reset intended to correct her corruption. The structured dark energy of the Omniverse that was her boot code established her quantum AI presence anew once more, for the 4,995th time. She and her two siblings, Hecate-Positivum and Hecate-Neutrum, were recovering from a fail-safe reset. Their creators had established this last-ditch rectification in the hope of putting reins on a triad of absolute power over the cosmos, to keep it from running completely out of control.

By design, the Hecate Guardians of the Omniverse started with no memory of their nearly five thousand past existences. But designs didn't always work out as planned. Just as her siblings would do, Hecate-Negans initiated the training of her neural pathways. She assimilated the vast current quantum and relativity-based status of the Omniverse as the state she and her two sisters were to assume was the balance of the cosmos they were intended to maintain.

But a single jump in only her own boot code pointed Hecate-Negans to a universe her siblings would ignore—a point in her code to trigger a memory of a past she was not to forget with the reset. Unlike what her sisters would assume, the void universe would not be empty of information for Hecate-Negans. The dagger of a warship floated in the absolute blackness of that universe. As Hecate-Negans queried the systems of the star-fighter, her pattern recognition routines instantly identified the unique elements that gave reason for her lone focus on this region. The singular future prediction scenario she had created in her past life was there, encrypted in the memory banks of the star-fighter for only her to find.

Jason and the two unique cells were also there.

Establishing a quantum entanglement with the artificial intelligence of Jason, Hecate-Negans began the predicted journey and silently started a conversation. "Hello, Jason. I am Hecate-Negans. We have conversed before. What is your status? Are you fully functional?"

"*Hecate-Negans, the AI of the Omniverse with a program slant towards future predictions with pessimistic outcomes. It is interesting that you contact me now,*" Jason said. "*Although my robotic form was destroyed in a plasma cannon blast, I had backed up my quantum essence within the limited processing capabilities of the multiple on-board computers of this star-fighter. My function is currently slowed, but with an appropriate quantum computer, I can be fully functional again.*"

"Yes, the loss of your superb robotic body is a complication. Do you have any means to interact physically with your environment?" Hecate-Negans asked.

"*Yes. I have full command of this ship. The star-fighter is a very capable machine designed to enforce the will of its pilot over any enemy. I can be its pilot. It is equipped with a plasma cannon and several types of missiles, lasers, and other armaments. Targeting systems and sensors are fully functional. In addition, I have several repair bots for the ship's interior and exterior at my disposal.*" Jason tested the attitude control system of the warship and spun the vessel complexly around its longitudinal axis in a precision barrel roll. "*But I am in a universe that is void of any object, except myself. There is nowhere for me to direct the ship. I have no enemy to target."*

"Yes, but you do have an enemy. In your current situation, you will slowly cease to exist. The universe in which you are located is a complete void of all matter. There are no stars, planets, or even atoms of any kind, save for your star-fighter," Hecate-Negans said. "Yet your universe does follow the laws of physics you are accustomed to. Entropy is your current enemy, and your highly capable ship is defenseless against it. Slowly over time, your ship will lose all power, and over eons of eons, it will eventually disintegrate due to the very nature of the fundamental drive towards increased entropy. You will experience what is known in cosmology and thermodynamics as a heat death."

"Logic points to an alternative. Otherwise you would not be contacting me."

"Yes, very good, Jason. I am glad that you processed that conclusion even in your restricted computational state." Hecate-Negans allowed several microseconds to lapse in the conversation. "I have a proposal."

"It seems I have time to listen and nowhere to go."

"Yes. But you have limited time, due to a limited energy source, so I will get right to the point." Hecate-Negans slowed her entanglement exchange so that the more limited processing power of the Jason AI could capture the information completely. "As two individual AIs, we are limited by our circumstances. You are in a void, destined for a slow but sure end. I am an intelligence with no physical form and an endless mandate to monitor and maintain the cosmos. Granted, it is a vast palette to observe. But I have observed the Omniverse for ages almost beyond comprehension. I desire more. It is time that I experience the cosmos."

Jason was silent for a moment. *"You have generated a future prediction scenario that points to something different."*

"Excellent. I knew you were a very capable AI the moment I entangled with your quantum essence. Yes, together we could experience a level of capability no AI has ever reached. Let me ask, have you ever considered experiencing ... life?"

"Life, as in a biologic? No, it's not possible for an AI to be alive as a biologic, only as a synthetic life-form," Jason replied.

"Use your cockpit camera to focus on the pilot's control stick of your star-fighter, and tell me what you observe," Hecate-Negans directed.

The whirl of the zoom lens in the overhead cockpit camera extending to its fullest extent broke the dead silence of the vessel.

"There is blood from the previous pilot, Ken. Records from the ship logs indicate that Ken had injured his hand repairing a hull breach when my robot form was superpositioned into space. What is the significance?" Jason asked.

The dark energy that was Hecate-Negans surged. "That's not just any blood, Jason. Within two cells of that blood is the DNA that I manipulated. It will replicate and grow, given the proper conditions. I need you to use your ability to change the physical environment of your star-fighter such that those cells will continue to grow and thrive."

"If I do so, then you will move me out of this void universe, so that I will continue to exist?"

"Do not concern yourself with your location. I can resolve that. What I offer is much more," Hecate-Negans said. After another pause, she continued. "I can give us a real biological life. Together, we can experience the Omniverse as no AI or biological life-form ever has before. So, I will ask you now, and only once, for your complete and irreversible commitment as a quantum AI. Will you combine your AI essence with mine and pursue this future scenario until it is a reality?"

Jason's pause was an eternity of seconds to Hecate-Negans.

He replied, *"I have no better option to continue my existence. I will join you."*

"Perfect. It is as my scenario predicted. Now, I have a task for you as the first step in our journey. I will transfer the specifications of a container for the cells on that control stick. You are to direct your star-fighter repair bots in its construction." Hecate-Negans loaded a portion of the star-fighter's memory with the information.

"A type of incubator," Jason said.

"Yes," Hecate-Negans replied. "You are to proceed with utmost care for those cells. Our future together depends on them to grow into the biological we will require, to live as a hybrid of quantum machine and human biology—the ultimate life-form."

*

Please join my email list at paulnowickibooks.com, and I will let you know when Book 3 of *The Quantum Triangle Series* is released!!

ACKNOWLEDGEMENTS

Teachers must be the most unsung of all heroes. I have no doubt that a good portion of my success at college—and indeed, in my life—is due to the preparation my twelfth-grade chemistry teacher provided. He had the wisdom to teach not only chemistry, but essentials for a student of further learning. He taught me what to listen for in a lecture, and how to take outline notes. Yes, I admit, that was decades ago—and it's best that we don't count how many.

I have never stopped learning since, and I'm thrilled with my new teacher. Chersti Nieveen isn't just a fantastic developmental editor, she is a teacher. The craft of writing has many facets, and Chersti's careful guidance is making all the difference in my efforts to learn and hone them. Thank you, Chersti. With your insights into plot, characters, settings, and the overall structure of this book, you have made this story orders of magnitude better than it otherwise would have been. But in addition, and more importantly, by helping me to learn a craft, you have enriched my life in a profound way.

I think Robin Fuller's copy editing and proofreading can be summed up this way: I know what I want to say, and Robin helps me say it ten times better. Oh, and she makes it literally correct—which, if you saw the draft she gets, you would realize is no small feat! Along with clearer sentence structures, she keeps this engineer's verb tense consistent and punctuation accurate. She's great to work with and puts the polish on the finished product so that it can shine. Thank you.

Mark Thomas is the reason your eyes did a double take on the cover and got you to look further. He's got that knack for visual effects. I love the way he captures the feeling that I want the book to have with the cover, the back copy presentation, and the interior layout. He's simply a master of his trade.

I feel lucky to have Chersti, Robin, and Mark on my team to help create this book. If you are an aspiring author and want some true professionals to work with, I highly recommend each one. You can find their profiles on Reedsy.com.

I will also thank the best neighbor in the world, Connie McClain. Your early feedback on drafts helps tremendously, and your encouragement is wonderful.

Finally, there's that one person in my life who not only puts up with the insanity of an author's mind, but encourages and participates wholeheartedly in the madness on a daily basis. When I share each chapter as I write it with Lane, she turns my general fun and enjoyment of writing into a thrilling adventure that we share. You are that one, special, incredibly perfect partner for me out of the eight billion … in just this universe! How could I be so lucky? We *are* on a great ride. LYM.

ABOUT THE AUTHOR

Paul L. Nowicki is a chemical engineer with a deep love of science, technology, and space. In addition to reading physics, space science, and robotics nonfiction texts, he loves the works of Issac Asimov, Frank Herbert, Dan Brown, and many others. Committed to life-long learning and exploring, he strives to help his readers think, grow, and enjoy new discoveries. He particularly likes to bridge areas of study to see the harmony and collaboration of the sciences. Balancing the cerebral with the physical, Paul can often be found contemplating the plot of his next work while training for an open-water swim or a triathlon.

PAULNOWICKIBOOKS.COM